TALES OF THE EMERALD TRIANGLE

Memoirs of a Marijuana Grower

KEVIN STEWART

10 Falls Press

Dedicated to the humble hemp plant.
You could save the world if we let you.

And to the men and women who worked to return you from exile.

The obscure we see eventually.
The completely obvious, it seems, takes longer.

—Edward R. Murrow

PART I

FOLLOWING A DREAM

Prologue

Ihave never considered myself a criminal. An outlaw yes, but in my mind, I was a freedom fighter. I was a marijuana grower, and that meant little more to me than I was a rebel, fighting for a cause I believed in. In every other aspect of my life, I have been a law-abiding citizen. I've worked, paid taxes, raised a family, and before my involvement with pot growing, my biggest run-in with the law had been a speeding ticket. Until an hour ago, I had never even carried a gun. Given a few minutes to think about it, I don't think I would have picked up this one. With time to think, Garrett and I probably would have let the bastards we were chasing escape with our pot. But the situation had escalated so quickly, and we felt we were past the point of no return. It had been only an hour since he had pulled me over, but a lot can happen in an hour.

Garrett was really agitated, and that wasn't his style. I knew something was up even before I pulled over to the side of the road. He was waving wildly from his truck as he skidded to a stop behind me.

"I hope he isn't pissed off," I said to my girlfriend, Debbie. "I didn't see him behind me until a minute ago."

Debbie was the first to notice him and had been watching his histrionics. "Something's wrong. I'll bet he got busted."

I jumped out of my truck and hurried back to see what was up. At this time of year, a pot grower always fears the worst.

Garrett shut off his engine. He stuck his head out the window and in a controlled panic started telling me the situation. "Big John called me fifteen minutes ago. We're being robbed!"

"What the fuck do you mean, being robbed? By who?" I shouldn't even have been going to my farm that day. I was taking the year off and Garrett was running the place in my absence. By risking the land, I was getting thirty percent of his crop, and if things went wrong, I'd be the one left holding the bag.

"Two truckloads of bandits crashed the gate dressed like a CAMP raiding party," Garrett explained, shaking his head.

"How do you know they're not from CAMP?"

"Big John got a good look at them and heard them laughing and talking trash. It's not bullshit; you know Johnny." His voice trailed off. Clearly, he was thinking about what to do next.

Garrett's mobile phone rang, and he picked it up. "Yeah?" He listened for a minute and then looked at me.

"It's John again. They're still there. He's hiding by the property line." I heard Garrett tell John we'd be right there. It was Garrett's show, but it was my head on the chopping block, so I demanded to know the backstory before we took off.

I found out that two weeks earlier, Big John found a sandwich bag and an empty bottle on a trail near the patch. He told Garrett about it, but they didn't tell me. Garrett didn't think it was important, but Big John felt otherwise. In his mind, it was a bad sign—either cops or rip-offs—but he was working for Garrett, and Garrett felt that anybody planning to rip the place off or raid it wouldn't be so sloppy as to leave such obvious evidence behind. He figured it was a hiker, a hunter, or a woodsman. Just because someone had been on the property didn't necessarily mean they'd scoped out the patch.

As it turned out, they weren't cops or rip-offs, they were rip-offs pretending to be cops. Harvest was beginning and the timing couldn't have been worse. Dressed like cops, carrying automatic rifles, and driving official-looking vehicles, they had busted through the gate at ten or so that morning.

Garrett was in town shopping for provisions when the shit came down. Big John heard them roaring up the drive, grabbed his mobile phone and a few cold beers, and fled out the back door of my cabin where he'd been waiting for Garrett to return. Hiding in the bushes, he watched the raid unfold. Four roughnecks wearing camouflage military uniforms and carrying Uzis kicked in the front door and ransacked the place. One of them stayed behind to secure the area and the rest piled back into their trucks and sped off in the direction of the patch. Big John moved deeper into the woods and called Garrett.

This all came down minutes before Garrett saw me on the road. We were pulled over near a friend's driveway, so I dropped Debbie off and told her to head up to their place. I didn't want her in harm's way. We hauled ass to the property, about twenty minutes away. On the way I used my mobile to alert as many locals as I could to the situation, but nobody was home.

Garrett had a gun with him. It was just a 9mm pistol—not much in the way of arms when the enemy is packing Uzis—but it would get their attention.

Reaching my driveway, Garrett blew by the smashed gate with me on his tail. We planned to use the old ranch truck he was driving to block the road and cut off their escape route. The first half-mile crossed an open meadow on my neighbor's land, but at my property line the terrain changed, becoming steep and heavily wooded. I knew if we left the truck on the road, rip-offs wouldn't be able to get around it.

We had just parked the truck on a blind curve when Big John showed up and said all was quiet. I pulled a four-way lug wrench out of Big Blue, my burly Ford F-250 4X4 pickup truck, and took the wheel lugs off two of the ranch truck's tires. Rolling the truck back and forth a few times caused the tires to fall off, effectively blocking the road. We stationed ourselves about twenty yards above to wait, behind a large fallen tree. If Big John was wrong, and they turned out to be cops we were big-time fucked. He assured us they weren't because if they were, there'd be cops crawling all over the place by now and we'd be getting flown.

Minutes after taking our position, we heard the thundering sound of vehicles barreling down the road toward us. They were hauling ass and owing to the curve, didn't see our trucks until it was too late. The first guy slammed into the ranch truck, with enough force to drive it into the front end of mine. Big Blue wasn't hurt, but the ranch truck was jobbed.

From the looks of the rip-offs' windshield, the passenger had busted it out with his head. Knocked semiconscious, he tumbled out, stumbling, and scrambled back up the road. The driver hopped out and fled in the same direction in time to stop their second truck from crashing into the wreckage. In the minute it took us to get to the carnage, they picked up their sorry-ass partners and quickly backed up the road. They were out of sight by the time we got to the trucks.

They left a gun behind, a Mini Mac-10, on the floorboard of the truck. Certainly not the caliber of an Uzi, but at that point, we'd take what we could get.

"Eureka!" Garrett said triumphantly, holding the Mini Mac. "Check this thing out."

We could hear the rip-offs driving across the hillside above us. Garrett handed me his 9mm. There was another way off the property, an old skidder trail put in by loggers and by the sound of their truck, they'd found it. The road was about seventy-five yards above us and continued onto the neighbor's land. The roads then came together at the bottom of the driveway, and we ran like hell to get there before they did.

The bandits barely got to the crossing before we did, and aiming at their truck, we managed to get some shots off. I emptied what few rounds I had into the engine compartment, nailing the radiator, and Garrett shot at the tires, hitting one. We didn't stop them but knew they wouldn't get far on a flat.

I ran back up the hill to get my truck. I lit Big Blue and roared back down the driveway. They had a good head start, but the flat tire and leaking radiator left a distinct trail on the gravel road making it easy to follow them. We could tell they'd turned left at the end of the driveway and were heading east. In less than a mile we saw their dust rooster tailing behind them and caught up to them in no time. But they weren't going down without a fight.

Garrett cried, "Look out, he's gonna shoot!"

That was all Big John needed to hear and he ducked under the dashboard. One of the rip-offs was riding in the back of their truck, sitting on a tarp-covered pile of marijuana. Our marijuana. He squeezed off a few rounds when we got close, so I backed off. We kept our distance on the straightaway, but when their truck hit a series of sharp curves, I pulled in closer. Garrett kept the guy in the back of the truck pinned down by popping off a few rounds. The guy riding shotgun was trying to shoot at us too, but that's a lot harder to do than it looks in the movies, especially on a bumpy dirt road with one flat tire.

With their engine overheating and spewing steam, the driver was doing a hell of a job keeping the truck on the road. But, going as fast as he was, he couldn't deal with the combo of a flat tire, the shooting, and the curves. When the tire finally popped off the rim, he lost all control of the truck and ended up in a ditch.

They jumped out of the truck with their guns blazing. Since I'd emptied the 9, we only had the Mini-Mac and without knowing how many rounds were left, I backed Big Blue out of range as fast as I could. We didn't have a plan but had to do something. I put Big Blue in park and started to get out of the truck.

"Give me the gun. When I wave at you, drive forward like we're charging," I said.

Garrett didn't like that plan, so I barked, "Then you go."

"Go where?" he asked, his voice betraying his effort to appear calm.

"Up there," I said pointing, "behind that rock. Wave when you have a clear shot."

He sat in silence for a moment. I could tell he was wondering how he'd found himself in this mess. That same thought had passed through my mind more than once in the last half-hour.

As Garrett put his hand on the door handle, I said, "Shoot over their heads, we don't want to kill anybody."

He gave me a "what the hell" shrug and said, "Those cocksuckers aren't getting my pot," then jumped out and scampered up the embankment.

Garrett Nash was a Nam Vet and as he committed to the plan of action, the soldier within him took over. Getting down on all fours, he quickly crawled to the position I had seen from the road, then carefully looked over the rock and assessed the scene for a minute. Looking back at me he shrugged, silently mouthing the words, "I don't see them."

By then Big John was hiding in the bushes next to the road and didn't see where they were either. "Maybe they ran?" he said as he inched his way into position to get a better look.

They had either fled on foot or were hiding out somewhere waiting for us to reclaim our plants. I pulled Big Blue around the corner to get a closer look. Garrett was stationed above me, not knowing what to do next.

"Stay put and cover me," I said loud enough for all to hear. "I'm going to get the pot." I wanted the rip-offs to think John had a gun too.

I drove Big Blue slowly towards the truck, keeping an eye on their rear window, having a hunch that one of them was hiding there. I didn't see the would-be sniper who had climbed a small madrone tree above the road, but before he could draw a bead on me, the branch he was on snapped. He fell about 15 feet and landed on his face. Mountain justice, as they say.

As the other bandits emerged from their ambush spots, Garrett aimed over their heads and squeezed off a few rounds, and they turned tail and booked it out of there.

When the shooting started, I backed quickly out of range and stopped Big Blue below where Garrett had taken cover. He jumped into the back of the truck, while Big John got in front with me. The rip-offs were high tailing it down the road, but instead of chasing them we set about retrieving our crop before anybody else came along.

It was hard work transferring the load. The plants were wet, sticky, and tangled up together but we stayed with it until all the plants were in my truck. We should have been worried, but we were too busy saving the crop. Time passes quickly in situations like this, and in about ten minutes we were loaded and ready to roll. But we weren't home free. We were still a couple miles east of my driveway and had to get back there without being seen.

I drove like a madman with Garrett riding on top of the load to keep the tarp from flying off. In less than five minutes we reached my property without incident. But as I turned onto my driveway and headed up the hill, I could see the flashing cherry tops of an approaching sheriff's car. All the shooting must have alarmed one of the neighbors enough to call the cops. I could get away by driving off the back of my property, but there were still two wrecked trucks in my driveway and one of them was still loaded with pot.

We went in on the skidder trail, backtracking the route taken by the thieves, and when we were roughly above the wrecked trucks, I stopped. Garrett jumped out and headed toward them. I told Big John to get behind the wheel of Big Blue and drive off the backside of the property, then took off into the underbrush following Garrett.

When I caught up with him, Garrett was in his truck rummaging through a grocery bag. He grabbed a twelve-pack and threw six of them away to make it look as though they had already been downed. I watched him chug a couple as he walked, then pour another one over the front of his shirt. He didn't have much time to compose himself before the sheriff's car skidded to a stop at the foot of my driveway. Hiding in a thicket of whitethorn above the road I had a pretty good view of the show.

There were a few rounds left in the clip, and aiming up the hill, Garrett shot them off. The rounds alerted the cop that he'd found the right place. I heard the engine shut off, and a car door open then close. Garrett started singing, "I can't get no-o, satisfaction, I can't get no-o, girlie action, but I've…"

"Hello," The sheriff called out.

Garrett waited a minute, like he'd been surprised, and in his best imitation of a drunk answered, "Huh?"

"It's the sheriff. Please put down your weapon."

"What?" he shouted, trying to sound confused. "Hooz there?"

"I'm the sheriff," came the gruff reply, sounding a little testy. "Put the gun down now."

"OK, OK," he said loudly, slurring his speech, "Iss out of bullets, anyhow!"

Garrett dropped the gun on the side of the road and backed away from it. Holding the nearly empty twelve pack of beer, he wobbled a bit as the sheriff approached. The cop had his gun drawn but sizing the situation up, lowered his piece. Garrett set the remaining beer down.

Putting his best drunk act, Garrett raised his arms into the air.

"Is that your only gun?" the deputy demanded.

Garrett paused a moment, as if he had to think about it. "Yep," he slurred, waving nonchalantly in the general direction of the Mac. "Iss the only one I got."

"Is this your land? Do you have identification?"

"Oh yes, I live here." Acting subtly more sober. "It's my place, and I have ID." His hands were still up and he gestured at his back pocket by tilting his head.

The cop looked almost bored as he quickly ran his hands over Garrett in a cursory frisk. He backed up and told him he could put his hands down. "OK, lemme see some ID."

Garrett pulled his wallet out of his pocket and produced his driver's license.

Once the cop was convinced that Garrett was who he claimed to be, he relaxed a bit more and put his weapon in its holster. He said, "You know you gave your neighbor quite a scare with your shooting." He gave Garrett one of those down the nose, dorm-mother looks and said, "How many beers have you had?"

"Jus' a couple." Garrett shrugged sheepishly.

He looked at the near empty twelve pack and shook his head.

"Just a couple? I've been in the sheriff's department for over twenty years," he said in an admonitory voice, "and every time I've asked a drunk how much he's had, he tells me two beers!"

Garrett half smiled in a Huck Finn manner and said, "It might have been three."

The cop choked back a chuckle, and holding Garrett's driver's license like it was a dirty diaper, gave it back to him. "Don't let me see you on the highway today."

"No sir," he agreed in a slightly brown-nose tone, "I'm not going anywhere."

"See that you don't." He turned and started back down the drive. He walked maybe twenty feet, then turned and asked, "What happened to your gate? It looks smashed in."

The question caught Garrett off guard. "Gate?" he froze. "Oh yeah, the gate. I don't know, I found it like that." He tossed in, "Maybe the neighbor knows."

The sheriff stood motionless for a moment, as if he didn't believe any of this, but he just shook his head to one side and grinned. "Good-day, sir."

I watched from under the bushes as he disappeared around the bend. From where I was hiding, I saw Garrett's legs start shaking so badly he could barely stand. Suddenly he fell to his knees and vomited, the stress of the past hour finally catching up with him. Down the driveway, I heard the sheriff laughing. Garrett looked up and started laughing too.

The scene was surreal. After coming close to death and delivering an Oscar-worthy final performance in front of the sheriff, there was my buddy, on all fours, laughing hysterically over a pool of his own barf.

I couldn't help but think to myself, "I gotta find a new line of work."

Chapter 1

Morning Dew

The story has to start somewhere. The morning dew on my shoes was from Golden Gate Park, San Francisco, California. Like thousands of others, in what's become known as the "Psychedelic Sixties," I had heard the sirens' song and migrated west in hopes of finding God. If that didn't happen, at least I figured I would meet some people I could relate to and enjoy the time I spent looking. I wasn't exactly sure why I was on planet Earth anyway, and I couldn't imagine a more beautiful place to be while I worked it out.

They say you can't make an omelet without breaking a few eggs. The omelet of future thought might well have come from the heads that cracked in this period. For many, the door marked "What's next?" wasn't opened by meditation or prayer, but rather by the inhalation of marijuana smoke. Whether this was a step forward or backward is open to debate. But by and large, the people who lived through the experience will tell you that it was a positive one.

In the 1920s and 1930s, pot smoking was not a mainstream activity. Centered around the Jazz scene, a user would drive to Harlem, where the dealer would pop the top off a tobacco can and place marijuana from the can onto the lid. As much as the lid would hold cost maybe a few dollars and that's where the term lid of pot came from. In the sixties, you could still get a lid for five or ten dollars, while real connoisseur pot like Acapulco Gold, Oaxacan, or the best I ever smoked, Panama Red, cost the astronomical sum of twenty dollars an ounce. Sinsemilla (seedless marijuana) hadn't arrived on the scene yet, so sometimes as much as half the weight was seeds.

Before long, those seeds were finding their way into gardens and planter boxes. My first pot garden was an indoor job, around 1969. The house I was living in was a large rundown Victorian inhabited by a motley crew of your basic San Francisco hippies. My room was a small cubbyhole in the attic that opened to a large storage area. I started my first garden back there in a space about the size of a pickup truck bed, framed with one by two-foot boards, and lined with vinyl I scrounged from a waterbed reject heap. For lighting, I acquired some industrial light fixtures that a local factory was discarding. The only things I had to pay for were the Gro-Lux® bulbs and the potting soil. I also had a few plants growing on the back porch and several more scattered among the coleus and split-leaf philodendrons, where they shared the few sunny spots our second-floor apartment offered. In all, between twenty and thirty plants were growing around the house. In short order, they became the focus of my horticultural hobby. Each plant had its own personality and was happy to be living among the assorted houseplants. It was hard to imagine, absurd really, that these little plants were wanted fugitives, routinely hunted down, and when found, summarily executed by the most powerful political entity on earth, the U.S. government.

It didn't make any more sense to us then than it does now. We naively believed that sooner or later our government would wake up to the fact that it was not going to have its way on the issue of pot prohibition. We figured it would eventually capitulate and put its energy into something that mattered, like the environmental nightmare we had inherited from several generations of industrial pollution, the population that was spiraling exponentially out of control, or the proliferation of nuclear weapons amongst terrorist states. In the sixties, the general population didn't understand what was happening to the ozone layer, the rainforest, or what the long-term effects of chemical medicines would have on our immune systems. We would ultimately pay dearly for our neglect. Concerning the real problems facing mankind, our government could only afford to pay lip service. When it came to marijuana eradication, and hassling, arresting, and jailing of marijuana users, they were willing to spend real money.

In those naive days, we had no way of knowing the enormous sums of cash that would eventually be involved. We didn't have a clue as to the real reasons hemp had been outlawed in the first place or the power and prestige of the industries that gained the most from its continued prohibition. Back then it was all about getting high, having a good time, and not getting busted.

To tell you the truth, in those early days I got about as close to growing good smoking dope as the Warren Commission got to figuring out what really happened in Dallas. The reasons were varied, but it ultimately came down to overestimating my green thumb and underestimating, by volumes, the information and patience needed to produce decent pot. In other words, I naively thought you could get high smoking the leaves, so before they ever flowered the plants died from acute defoliation.

In those days there existed maybe a dozen books about growing pot, and as a body of knowledge, they seemed self-contradictory. Some instructed you to give the plants a lot of water, some give them very little. Light and soil conditions reflected what had worked for each particular author, and the reader came away with the feeling that damn near anything you did would result in a bountiful harvest.

Other than the experiment, and the enjoyment I received from the hobby, I really learned nothing of importance about cannabis production back then. I profited even less. In fact, I never even harvested any buds. In mid-summer, some friends of mine needed help moving to Texas, and I thought it would be cool to spend the summer kickin' it in the Southwest. Unfortunately, I picked a shit bird named Mitch Something-or-other to watch my flat, and shortly after I left town, he pulled up the rest of my plants and sold all my belongings at a garage sale. It turned out the guy was a junkie, and he was probably geezin' some smack he bought with the money from selling all my stuff.

I phoned him from Austin. "Hey Mitch" I said, "It's Duncan. How's it going?"

"Duncan?" He sounded half-asleep. "Duncan Easley? Oh wow man, I never thought I'd hear from you again. I thought you were, like, moving to Arizona."

So, I basically got fucked out of my stuff. But in those days, it was all about being a Brother, and it wasn't hip to get overly attached to your material possessions. I let it ride.

During my last year in San Francisco, I met a woman who had that certain glow about her. Carrie was a keeper.

She had a child-like innocence about her, but she was also strong and adventurous. Forever smiling, she was tall and slender, and still slightly awkward. A small-town tomboy transforming into a big-city woman. We met just in time. I was a mid-west acid casualty standing on the edge of oblivion, one step away from giving up on the material world altogether. Carrie had an inner beauty stemming from a quality of caring and an inability to focus on things negatively. She grabbed the kite string and brought me back to earth, just enough. She was a bit of a Pollyanna, but in the heady days of Flower Power nobody seemed to notice.

It was a time when people were trying hard to look below the surface and not judge each other by what our incomes were. If that hadn't been the case, she probably wouldn't have looked twice at me. For all outward appearances, I had no future, precious little present, and what past I had been able to accumulate by age twenty, was "purple hazy."

Inflation was raging and the cost of living, or in my case, the cost of hanging out, was quickly outpacing my earning ability. I figured the time had come to move up the coast. I moved out of The City much the way I had arrived in Berkeley a few years earlier, without a pot to piss in. No job, no assets, no home, but I had a lover, a VW van that I'd purchased for a hundred and twenty-five bucks, and a fractured kaleidoscope of a dream.

Things were working out. Carrie was beautiful, and willing to try to save me from myself. I was lucky. In time, we got married and lived in Monte Rio, a small river hamlet about an hour and a half northwest of the Golden Gate. Monte Rio boasted a biker bar, health food store, gas station, post office, and seemingly more street people per capita than anywhere else in the United States. It was also paradoxically, the summer camp for the Bohemia Club, a private, highly exclusive, elite, men only, all-white club that included some of the richest, most powerful men in the world. Sometimes, the Secret Service would clear the street people from the bridge when a hotshot in a limousine passed, but otherwise the place was sleepy.

We lived in a modest boarding house called the Skyfish Lodge, located on the Russian River. It had been a brothel during around the turn of the century, the Russian River's heyday, and nobody was sure if it ever stopped being one. Strangers would knock on our door at two in the morning asking odd questions like, "Is Pookie home?" My son was born there, on a mattress on the floor of our apartment with the Moody Blues playing in the background. As my young family bloomed, my life was transforming. When the only goals were paying rent and having a stash of greenbud, I could hang out doing odd jobs, but fatherhood brought with it certain responsibilities. The love that I had for my boy made accepting those responsibilities easy. Life was cool.

I didn't try growing pot in Monte Rio. Living in the middle of town, it didn't seem like such a safe bet. But I was able to keep myself supplied with the herb by running errands for dealers and peddling a bag here and there.

Our neighbors, two openly gay men, had a few plants between their back door and the river. As the summer passed, Carrie and I watched them grow from our back porch. One day two sheriff's deputies arrived. In a mean-spirited display that became a hallmark of law enforcement's effort to control the spread of marijuana, they not only uprooted the pot plants, but also systematically destroyed the rest of our neighbor's garden. The image of those two fat-assed, donut-eating, attack dogs of the system stomping on the poor innocent vegetables left an indelible stain in my memory. It illustrated to me the petty-minded nature of law enforcement as it pertained to pot.

Other than that, those were the happiest days of my life. In September we found a nicer place several miles out of town, somewhere between Monte Rio and Cazadero. A woman known for her abilities in the garden had occupied our new home before we did, and spring brought many surprises as the property exploded in a celebration of new life. The soil in our backyard was rich bottom land and as deep as you could possibly care to dig. Carrie picked up gardening where the woman before her had left off. Her efforts produced an amazing array of fine looking and tasting veggies which seemed to appear by magic out of the ground. Sadly, we lacked either the foresight or the nerve to plant marijuana that year.

In the winter of 1975, the first pounds of really kick-ass homegrown appeared on the scene from Kansas. Those pounds consisted of the first true club-bud Indica that I had ever seen, and they were laden with seeds. Big, fat, dark and healthy, the seeds just begged to be planted. In the spring of '76, after celebrating the arrival of our second child, a lovely little girl, we found the nerve and planted our first backyard crop.

The hauling in of amendments and digging was my department, with a little help from my friend Chet, also known as Cruiser. The planting and tending work belonged to Carrie, and she delivered the goods. The plants came up with the largest fan leaves I'd ever seen. (Fan leaves are the ones that you see symbolizing marijuana.

In the book "Drugs in History," the author says that the fan leaf logo has been found on a smoking-pipe carbon dated at around ten thousand years old.)

The big hurdle early on was to avoid confusing the sexes of the plants. To an untrained eye, the pollen sacs that appear on the male plants look like immature clusters of seeds at first. If someone hadn't come along at the right time and showed us which was which, we might have pulled up our bud producing females, and we wouldn't have been the first or last to do so. The other challenge for a couple of poor hippies, besides getting caught, was not picking at the plants for something to smoke before they were ready. In those days every third person on the river was dealing, so it was easy to find tasty nugs. We found enough around that summer to keep us toasted until we harvested in the middle of September. Although we didn't get enough to sell, the half-pound or so we managed to clean kept us in A-bud stash for quite a while.

We loved the place but couldn't afford to buy the home we'd been renting, and during the winter it was sold. I needed to support my family and Carrie's dad offered me a job in Montana. I must have been in a state of complete mental constipation, because I took it. For a while, it seemed that would be my last experience growing marijuana.

Montana is an anachronism, more suited for living in the past than embracing the future. We were West Coast Hippies, and not embraced by the locals. Despite that, Montana had its charms. It's a rugged land full of rugged folks who found among themselves a wonderful sense of community, however provincial, in a beautiful yet desolate part of our country.

The tie that seemed to bind them was their love for Montana and their disdain for everywhere else. They loathed California and Californians, on whom they blamed most of society's ills. My job was working construction with a crew of redneck good ol' boys. Everything they believed about the rest of the world had been condensed into the unofficial state motto, "Gut shoot'm at the border."

Their attitude toward Californians was best summed up by a popular bumper sticker that showed the smiling yellow-faced "Have a nice day" character, except theirs read, "Have a nice trip back to California."

It took me less than two weeks to decide that I had made a big mistake by moving there. The economy was in such bad shape, coupled with the fact that the working stiffs in Montana were practically indentured servants, that it took us almost a year before we could afford to move away. Even then we only had the gas money to make it as far as Portland, Oregon. We ended up doing a year there.

It's hard not to like Portland, but I was never happy there. The closer I was to Northern California the more I missed it.

About this time, the pot growing that had slowly come of age in the seventies kicked into high, and I mean High gear. I knew several growers who, in my absence, had gone from those few plants on the back porch to plantations making hundreds of thousands of dollars a year. One guy I knew made over a million dollars in cash every year! The guys I knew who were making bank had, for the most part, had been working stiffs and the money hit them like a tidal wave. A lot of guys just couldn't handle it. I knew a grower who wrapped fifty thousand dollars in duct tape and used it for a football. I knew of two different growers who lost forty grand each by getting coked up and forgetting where they hid their money. One of them rented a backhoe and dug up his whole forty-acre property and never found it.

One of my buddies, Tex, became involved with a very successful operation. It was comprised of a group of friends who were not only hard working and clever but were college-educated in agriculture and still had contacts in the university system. They were bright enough to find out the inside skinny on what the plants needed, and when they needed it. Tex was working for fifteen percent of the crop and averaging two-hundred and fifty grand a year. It wasn't too long before he went into business for himself and that was when my phone rang.

Carrie was the one who answered that fateful call. I can remember the smile on her face as she said, "Tex, how are you? Are you in Portland?" She held the phone against her body and said, "Duncan, it's Tex," but I was already on my way across the kitchen.

He had named himself Tex. In the marijuana subculture, you were supposed to let your "handle" evolve. I personally thought it was bad form to give yourself a nickname, but I didn't know of any rules about that, and even if there were, when you make a quarter mil you can pretty much call yourself anything you want. In fact, Tex was a Jewish kid from the east coast, and he looked about as much like a guy named Tex as the Pillsbury doughboy.

"Hey Tex, what's going on?"

"Things are going good, Duncan. How 'bout yourself?"

"Oh, pretty good. Working a lot."

"Do you remember what we talked about before Christmas?"

I had gone to Redding to visit him before the holidays, and Tex had laid a couple of nice bags on me as well as an opportunity to consider. "Yes, I do."

"Are you ready to be a farmer?"

The question conjured up sweet memories from my childhood. I had secretly wanted to be a farmer in one way or another since I was seven years old. Not a typical dream for someone who basically grew up a "corporate brat." My father had started working at General Motors after World War II. He was transferred around a lot on his climb up the executive ladder, and for the most part we lived among an affluent crowd, playing golf and tossing T-bones on the grill over the weekends. This was in the fifties, and as a travelling rep Wisconsin was my dad's territory. He was headquartered in Milwaukie, but in a stroke of luck he found a beautiful farm for us, and as a kid I was lucky to spend two years living in dairy country. It was 1957, and I was six years old.

My boyhood friend was the twenty-year-old son of an old farm couple up the road, the Millers. Orville was a true farmer. His Ma and Pa lived there as well, but they were semi-retired, and Orville did most of the work on the farm. Playing farmer with Orville taught me many things, but mostly it taught me the satisfaction of a hard day's work. I would show up in the morning after breakfast and do chores for Orville all day long. My specialty was mucking out the dairy stalls and shoveling the manure to the front of the barn. Because I was too small to load it into the spreader, Orville still had to do that. But I know I saved him a lot of time, and he appreciated me coming around. When I had the stalls clean and new straw put down, Orville would let me climb into the silo and pitch down silage for the cows. City folks don't understand this, but on a hot summer day the silo is the coolest place you can find on a farm.

In the summer of 1958 Orville got a new bailer. Shiny and red, it was the coolest thing I'd ever seen, although I was only seven and hadn't seen many cool things yet. When the hay had dried in windrows and was ready for bailing, Orville hooked the bailer up to his old Farmall tractor then attached an antique flatbed wagon to the back of the bailer. I can still see myself as a farm boy all those years ago, armed with a pair of grappling hooks and riding to the fields of mowed hay on a wagon pulled by Orville's big red tractor. I was standing tall for seven years old.

By then Orville was used to me hanging out with him and he knew I could do a few chores. But on this hot summer day, even he must have been a little impressed. I bucked hay-bales all day long and those fuckers weighed more than I did. In his silent American hero style, he didn't let on how impressed he was, but I know one thing, at the end of that day he backed a monster load of hay into the barn, and I had stacked every bale!

Next to the barn was a grain silo made of corrugated steel on a concrete slab. I sat down on the edge of that slab and looked westward over the rolling hills of rural Wisconsin. That may have been the first time in my life that I sat and watched the sun go down, and as I watched the sky turn fifteen shades of crimson and gold, I tasted euphoria. Years later, that day still stands out in my mind.

My farm life ended not long after that, when my family moved to the city of Milwaukee. But those two idyllic years in the dairy country left me with a deep love for the agrarian life.

Farming is not a glamour job, and I doubt that I ever openly professed my feelings for farming, but on Derby Day 1982 I became a farmer again. Ironically, I also became an outlaw working for Tex.

Tex and I fantasized about growing pot several years earlier when we had become friends on the Russian River, but nothing had ever come of it. He got his break while I was in Montana, and from time-to-time Carrie and I would get a package in the mail containing "Kind." Kind, or as the Jamaicans say "Kine," is A+ quality pot. As 1981 drew to a close, Tex invited us to spend the Christmas holidays with him at his place. That's when we first talked about me coming in with him. He thought it would be a year before he could start his own operation, but a month or two later a piece of property unexpectedly fell into his lap. Tex was hot to go.

He wanted me to think it over, but I said yes immediately. Most of my friends were already on board the Green Bud Express and I felt like I was missing the train.

Tex let me know we were getting a late start, and I might not make much money that year. I told him it wasn't important how much money I made since wealth had never been a big motivator for me. To Tex, I was talking blasphemy. With him it was *only* about money, so with a measure of disbelief mixed with contempt he asked me why I would do it if the money wasn't important. Without thinking I said, "Because it's a revolutionary act," and I meant it.

Pot had a bad rap back then. But as a young hippie, it had helped me cope with an angst-ridden adolescence and I knew in my heart that it could help the world to chill out. So, it wasn't the money that motivated me, it was the potential of the herb to create a kinder, gentler existence that drove me to risk it all and become a grower.

I was working in Portland at a dead-end construction job in an industry that held no satisfaction for me, and the idea of being a pot farmer was a dream come true. I was moving back to California. I was getting a chance to do something that I loved to do, and I would be paid for doing it.

While we were on the phone together Tex told me to sleep on it. I knew I wouldn't have to, but I promised Carrie that I would consult the I Ching, an ancient book of Chinese wisdom known also as The Book of Changes. I can't remember the exact hexagram I threw but one of the lines translated to, "Chance of great success, but beware, when dealing with weeds they can grow quickly out of your control." If a warning buzzer was going off in my mind, I never heard it.

Five short weeks later Tex unlocked the gate to a one-thousand-acre piece of property, got back in his truck, and disappeared into a cloud of dust. My new partner Ethan pulled through driving his International Harvester school bus and I brought up the rear in the truck I had recently purchased with Tex's money.

On the first of May 1982, I got out of my truck, closed the gate, and considered what lay before me. One thousand acres of deep green forested hills, spring-fed streams, open meadows, and a future beyond my wildest dreams.

Looking back through the mists of time, I see now how that singular act separated me from my past, changing the course of my life. I'd chosen to be an outlaw and there was no going back.

Chapter 2

Serenity Park

May. In the world of growing pot that's a late start. It would have been a late start if we were going back to an established farm, but as it was, we were at ground zero, and didn't even have a road into our parcel. We did have five hundred babies, or starts, growing at Tex's farm so we had that going for us. But those plants were only two weeks old, barely what we called "Uppins," a two-inch tall stem with two round dicot leaves and the tiny first pair of fan leaves.

I'd spent a week at Tex's farm in the middle of April getting some of the basics taken care of.

After Tex's call, I gave my employer two weeks' notice and spread the story around the family that I was moving back to California to get back into the landscaping business. What affairs I had were quickly put in order and one drizzly morning I hopped on a Greyhound bus for California. Tex met me at the depot in Redding. The two of us waited in a nearby bar for Ethan, who was to be my partner for the summer. His bus was due in about an hour. For all but the harvest period, this farm would be a three-man affair, consisting of the owner, commonly referred to as "The Goomba," and two helpers, referred to as "tenders."

By the time Tex and I returned to the depot, Ethan was standing by the side of the bus waiting for his luggage.

"That's him." said Tex spotting Ethan through the glass as we walked through the lobby. We walked out to greet him, and amid the noise of idling diesel engines and the incense they produced, I met my partner for the summer.

"They let you on this bus?" Tex asked jokingly.

Ethan turned around quickly; his long brown hair held in place under a well-worn Smokey the Bear hat. "Tex!" He grabbed Tex and gave him a big hug.

"Ethan, this is Duncan. Duncan, Ethan. If you guys want to tell each other your last names that's your business." Tex was just being funny, but the concern for anonymity underscored the nature of the business we were getting into.

"I don't give a fuck," I said and held out my hand, "I'm Duncan Easley."

"Ethan Daley," he said with a wide smile, "Glad to meet ya."

Ethan was a big, likable, easy-going guy. With a few years of college under his belt, he was engaging and articulate. But he was from the hills of Virginia and when he wasn't feeling overly confident, he would revert to his "aw shucks" persona, pretending he was an ignorant hillbilly. He was a hell of a worker though but had trouble getting himself going. He wasn't fast but he was steady, and he brought an important tidbit of knowledge to our operation.

Ethan's family had been in the tobacco farming business since before the Revolutionary War. He claimed their family collection of memorabilia contained a charter signed by King George II, granting their family title to grow tobacco in colonial Virginia. That fact didn't resonate with us at first but at harvest time we applied many of the principal concepts he had learned from his family about drying and curing tobacco to drying and curing marijuana. The results were fantastic. Over the years I've grown some great tasting herb thanks in large part to Ethan's knowledge of tobacco curing.

We had about an hour's drive to get to Tex's farm. On the way, he regaled us with tales from the "Emerald Triangle," as our marijuana growing part of the world was becoming known. It was named by the pilots searching overhead for the little "Emeralds" on the forest floor. We had nicknames for those pilots, but I'll go into that later. As Tex told us story after story about growing, my mind drifted to a classic '40s movie I had seen for the first time only a few weeks earlier. Tex parked in front of his cabin and Ethan and I grabbed our shit.

"Tex's stories remind me of a movie." I said, "Have either of you guys seen Humphrey Bogart in "The Treasure of the Sierra Madre?"

We were walking up the path toward Tex's cabin. Ethan's face formed a look of surprised amazement and for the first time I noticed his uncanny resemblance to Mad Magazine's Alfred E. Newman.

"Yeah," he said, "Last night!" We all laughed, but also felt an unsettling quiver in our hearts, remembering that the movie ended with one of the guys dying and the others losing their hard-earned gold.

Tex unlocked the cabin, and we went inside.

"Hey Duncan, how's about rolling us a fatty?" Tex had always appreciated the way I rolled although, with him being a Sagittarius, I could never get them done quickly enough.

Like most of the seventy million Americans who at one time or another smoked pot, I started when I was in high school. Why do you think they call it *high* school? The first summer after graduating I was laboring on a construction job and one of the crew rolled his own cigarettes. I had never seen anyone roll a cigarette before and he must have noticed that I was interested because he decided to give me a demonstration of the finer points that I've been able to put into practice over the years. When I was on my game and the pot was dried right, I could twist up hooters that looked like they came from a pack of Camels. Tex quit complaining and we all got good and baked on his trademark Kind.

"Why do they call it Kind?" Ethan asked.

Tex passed the joint to him and exhaled a cloud of blue-gray smoke, "Because it's the kind everybody wants."

"Would you look at this shit Ethan!" I said as I held the rolling tray up to the light so we both could appreciate the buds we were smoking. They were about the size of cucumbers. It was the seed stock of the strain we were planting, and the tray was littered with hundreds of fat seeds. I later learned not to plant only one strain of seeds because you can never be one hundred percent sure that you haven't bred a desirable quality out of, or an undesirable quality into your seed strain. Sometimes the most valuable traits get lost between generations and you end up spending your summer tending a crop of "No-high." That year we planted almost entirely one strain of seeds. Looking back that was one of the biggest risks we took. Hell, Ethan and I didn't know anything then and we figured Tex must have all that stuff worked out.

The land Tex was buying in Mendocino County was still in escrow and the deal wouldn't close for two more weeks, so we had no choice but to set up our cold frames and plant our starts at Tex's farm.

The plan was to spend the next day buying materials for the cold frames and the different components of the planting soil mix. I naively assumed the job would take a few hours of shopping, and a couple more to bang the frames together. If we didn't hit any snags the whole project would be done by dinnertime. Innocence and ignorance. I had been in and around the marijuana underground for over ten years by then, and I still hadn't a clue as to the amount of work involved, tomorrow I'd get a crash course. I went to sleep that night as just another working stiff but woke up the next morning feeling like a soldier in an army without ranks, fighting a battle for the noblest cause of all, freedom.

Oh yeah, and while money wasn't a real motivator for me, I was in line for a shit-pot full of the stuff.

So much for timelines. The sneak around nature of this business was such that time allotted to a particular job had no comparison in the real world. First and foremost were the limits on the number of helpers you can employ. Real-world jobs of this magnitude would typically have more than two workers. It's a farming job, but it's also a building job and a grand game of hide and seek. No one can shop for you. You can't have anything delivered, and you can't "sub" out bits and pieces of the project. Besides being the farmer you're the heavy equipment operator, the builder, the plumber, the electrician, the mechanic, and the maintenance crew. You are also the one who shops for groceries, washes the clothes, and cooks the food. Living in the woods for the summer was wonderful but lacked modern conveniences, and the fact that you were covering your trail as you went meant that just the time it took you to blow your nose was quadrupled.

We planned to start small, and a two hundred and fifty plant patch was small to Tex. In those days we used sixteen-ounce Styrofoam cups for our seedlings. Only the female marijuana plant can get you high, but a pot plant can be either male or female. The percentages typically ran about fifty/fifty, so to get 250 females we had to start 500 seedlings and needed 500 Styrofoam cups to get going. Try buying 500 cups from your local 7-11. We also needed enough potting soil, sand, and steer manure in a 3-2-1 ratio, along with some rabbit poop and various other soil amendments, vermiculite, and a pinch of blood meal to fill all those cups. A 4'x8' cold frame could hold about 125 cups so we needed enough plywood, 1'x2' lumber, screen, Visqueen, hinges, and hardware to build four of them. They had to be constructed in such a way as to allow the plants to be bathed in light during the day, but mouse-proof at night. One mouse could wipe us out early on, so besides having the frames for protection, using peanut butter as bait, we'd need to place traps around the perimeter and inside next to the cups.

At first, I had a problem with killing mice. Why should some poor mouse have to die for me to make a living? But my guilt subsided considerably after a few of our starts got whacked. By late afternoon on our first day the truck was filled to the gunwales with materials, and I was more than ready for the drive back into the hills. I thought the whole job would take us the better part of a day to finish, but we still had more shopping to do. We needed a watering can, hoses, a foliar feeder, camping supplies, and groceries. In the end, the project took us three days and change to complete.

Mixing soil and filling a cup isn't much work, but anything repeated five hundred times starts to look like a whole lot of work. Most of this was done on our hands and knees a half-mile up a trail where the entire load had to be hauled in on our backs. The male plants didn't really figure into our number. Out of two hundred and fifty males we saved a dozen or so for pollen and shit-canned the rest. The female plants, referred to as the "girls," were the focus of our efforts and in the end, we would plant them all.

With the cold frames built and our cups filled with gently tamped-down soil, we were ready for the seeds. A lot has been written about the correct way of putting a seed into the ground. Seeds are shaped like tiny footballs with one end looking rather pointy and the other more rounded. Tex thought the taproot emerged from the pointy end. It's a common mistake to believe that the taproot should be pointed down, since in the end that's exactly where it goes. However, before it can begin its journey into the earth, a seed must find where it is in relation to ground level. The emerging taproot rises to the sun-warmed soil but just before it emerges into the sunshine it turns downward. This allows the sprout with its two baby dicot leaves to break the surface of the ground. If you point the tap root down to begin with it must turn and go up before it turns to go down again, sometimes causing the root to loop over itself or form into a "J." As the plant tries to grow the root can choke off its nutrition and result in a stunted plant.

We soon learned that if the seeds weren't planted too deep, Mother Nature stepped in to work it out, but we started a few extra just in case. It was hard to believe that in a few months, these tiny plants would stand eight to ten feet tall.

Tex had a few tricks and more than a few opinions about growing pot. Even if they weren't as important or as correct as he thought, Ethan and I knew that we didn't know shit about what we were doing and we were more than happy to follow his direction. Tex made a point of saying we must wiggle our finger into the soil when we poke the hole for the seed, so the soil wouldn't be compacted. I never became a big believer in that. It sounded like superstitious minutia, but we wiggled our fingers up to the first knuckle 500 times, dropped the seeds in with the pointy side up, and watered them in.

We planned to split the next day. Tex was going to take care of the watering while Ethan and I headed home to spend the next two weeks getting ready to go camping for six or seven months. I was bustin' out a fatty when Tex walked through the door with a little black fanny pack.

Without ceremony, he unzipped the bag and produced four bundles of cash. Wrapped in rubber bands, each bundle consisted of five individually wrapped "long ones." A long one in pot grower terms was $1,000 and just Tex tossed $20,000 at me like it was his share of the rent money. I would head back to Portland, buy a truck, and return with both it and a cashier's check for the downpayment on the land. Ethan would head home to Santa Cruz and meet back up with us in his converted school bus.

The Greyhound bus left Redding around midnight and with the $20,000 and some traveling stash, so did I. In case you've never done it, trying to put twenty grand into your pocket is about as easy as putting a loaf of bread up your nose. The cash had to go into a daypack that went up on the overhead rack. I was able to detach from the fear of losing it to a degree but not totally. In the end, nothing happened other than my attention was focused on an inanimate object for a longer time than I could remember, and the reality of my situation was shown to me in living color.

I returned to California with a used Ford F-250 and a cashier's check for $14,000. Tex and I met up in Redding and drove to Garberville where Tex's boss Jefe, pronounced "Heffay," Spanish for a walking boss or foreman, owned a palatial home.

Ethan showed up the next morning in his bus and the easy part was over. We drove caravan style to the farm that would soon be known as Serenity Park, about an hour south of Garberville.

Once inside the ranch gate we made it about five minutes before we had our first big argument. But compared to arguments that would come later, this one was mild.

Our caravan consisted of two pickup trucks loaded with tools and equipment, Ethan in his school bus, and me bringing up the rear pulling an old dilapidated 1940s house trailer.

My truck was a five-year-old Ford F-250 that had once been used in a mining operation in Idaho, so it was beefed up but well-worn. The linkage to the transfer case was loose and I was having trouble getting the four-wheel drive into the low range. As loaded down as it was, the truck stalled out at the first serious grade.

Tex barked, "What the fuck is going on?" He had parked at the top of the grade and wasn't too happy about having to walk back down.

"I don't know Tex. The thing doesn't want to climb the hill." I looked out the cab window at him. He was one of these guys who could get really pissed-off in a hurry. He had frizzy, gray-blonde hair and wore glasses that looked like Coke bottle bottoms. When he got pissed his arms would gesticulate wildly and his voice would rise an octave. Imagine Woody Allen going to a costume party dressed as Jimi Hendrix and raging at a cab driver. It was hard to take him seriously.

"What kind of piece of shit did you waste my money on?"

While I was listening to Tex go off, I fiddled with the shifter and felt the thing finally slip into low. "Gee Lou, I'm doing the best I can," I said grinning, stealing a line from the movie Chinatown. The truck lurched forward. In low range it pulled the grade with ease.

"Who's Lou?" Tex yelled as I left him in the dust.

With Tex it was best to keep it light.

Tex was still tending for his old Goomba so he didn't have much time or energy to work with us. But he was the one who picked out the patch site. The days of growing marijuana out in the open had passed, which was a shame. Standing in direct sunshine the damn things could grow to an enormous size. I'd heard growers running small ops claim they grew plants that yielded five pounds of bud. Large-scale growers were getting a pound or better on average. Tex's other operation would manicure about 600 pounds of "A" buds from 400 plants. But times were changing, and the size and weight of the plants would be the first to suffer. It's said that the first casualty of war is truth, but the first casualty of CAMP, the newly formed Campaign Against Marijuana Planting, was plant size. Pot plants do best in full sunlight and growing them under trees reduced their size by at least 50 percent.

The addition of aerial surveillance meant moving the plants into the woods. A patch had to be hidden but still needed light, so more than ever site selection required the utmost care.

Hundreds, if not thousands of species of plant life grow in the forests of Northern California. Besides the famous Redwood and Douglas fir trees, there are many coniferous trees, twenty or more pine varieties, yew trees, scotch broom, blue spruce, Monterey cypress, and assorted cedars. There are also numerous broadleaf trees; some deciduous, some evergreen. In the oak family alone, there might be 60 varieties growing in the region. There's also madrone which drops its leaves in July and August but doesn't completely defoliate. The list goes on and on, and includes the shrubbery:

manzanita, whitethorn, poison oak, and many different ferns and types of ground cover. None of these plants alone would do the job of concealing a pot garden but with the right mix, it became much harder to spot one from the air.

Exposure to the sun's light was critical. Without it the plants wouldn't grow very large and when it came time to produce "juice," forget it. Cannabis hemp gets its name from a class of psychoactive alkaloids known as cannabinoids, the most well-known being THC but it's not the only one. These alkaloids are produced within aromatic oils, or juice as we called it, that primarily protect the plant from sunlight. So, the less sunlight the plants receive, the less protection they need and the less oil they produce. In this situation a grower would be left with leafier buds containing low resin-pot known in the trade as bunk, no-hi, or schwee, and basically worth very little on the open market.

So, herein lay the dilemma. On the one hand, we had to protect our patch from the prying eyes of the aerial surveillance boys, otherwise known as "Shit Birds," but we still needed the sun to shine on the plants. It was going to be tough, but not impossible.

The first question to ask about a potential growing site is "Which direction does the hillside face?" South is ideal but eastern and western-facing sites also work. A lot of growers grew on the north side in the belief that the cops know that southern exposure is preferred. But I've never tasted any kick-ass pot that was grown in low-light conditions.

Once a grower decides on exposure, they have to consider the cover. Most of what grows is green but there are various shades to consider. Pot tends to be among the darker shades of green so it's best to pick sites that contain that color. Manzanita is a shrub that can grow to 15 or 20 feet and is the shade of green most like pot. A grower likes to have some of it available, but the preference is a blend of plant colors and heights.

These are all things that Tex understood and factored into his final decision. I was still clueless and soaking up as much information as I could about what it took to grow pot on such a large scale.

It took the better part of a whole day to find a spot that Tex considered suitable. Once accomplished, Tex marked the perimeter with surveyor's tape and gave us a general idea of the work he wanted done. He then left us with a bag of money to buy the remaining mountain of materials needed to get the patch going.

Some years later I read a story about how a few of the locals were upset because pot growers, "Just toss a few seeds out the backdoor and come back in the fall and collect $50,000." That's like saying we won World War II by throwing a few bullets over the ocean and then had a victory parade.

Each of our 250 plants needed to go into a hole between 6 and 8 feet in diameter when planting time came. Remember, these weren't row crops, they had to be spread out among the existing flora in a natural, helter-skelter fashion. It took us about a week to clear almost half an acre of poison oak and underbrush and to remove about half the trees. It was hard but straightforward work. The challenge was thinning the remaining trees so that light could pass through them. Neither Ethan nor I had ever been a tree climber and many of the oaks, madrones, and firs were sixty feet tall or taller. Removing fifty percent of the foliage required high climbing and we didn't even have a climbing line. The equipment Tex had supplied us with consisted of a belt designed to climb telephone poles, a pair of boot hooks from the Civil War, and my own chain saw that was about as big as the tree I was trying to cut down. That would have been hard enough but, I also had to carry a handsaw, a pole pruner, and a pouch with three cans of spray paint. For camouflage purposes, every cut we made on the trees had to be painted with green, black, or brown spray paint. We didn't want the trees to look like they had just been worked on.

Another problem was the fact that a road was under construction on the ranch that Tex's piece of land was a parcel of, and we didn't want to make any noise that would give us away when the road crew was around. We'd arrive at the patch at seven in the morning and do as much noisy work with power tools as we could until the road crew arrived. Then, we did chores that could be accomplished quietly until they broke for lunch, at which time we would jam like hell on the chain saw or roto tiller until they came back. We would usually take about a two-hour break from one to three in the afternoon and then work until dark. Our most productive hours were in the evening after the road crew left.

Once the general area was cleared, we put a six-foot high chicken wire fence around it. That would discourage the deer, but we also needed to secure the fence to small logs at the bottom to keep the rabbits out. Clearing the patch and erecting the fence took the better part of a week and then we were ready to prep the holes.

One of the most important elements in site selection is the soil. We're not talking Missouri River bottomland here; we're talking steep terrain and funky rock formations. Much of what you find in the California hills consists of Franciscan red shale deposits, lacking many of the nutrients needed to grow pot, and high in magnesium which isn't desirable. Fortunately for us, many old oak trees in our area had been providing the basic ingredients to build fertile soil for hundreds, if not thousands of years, and being a fairly level spot of ground, the erosion was minimal. The moment our tiller started turning, it dropped into the soft earth, burying the tines completely and churning up some very lush topsoil.

Once the holes had been busted in, it was time for the soil amendments. The first thing we needed to address was soil pH. The soil pH for a plant is analogous to the 9 essential amino acids in human nutrition. It doesn't matter if all the ingredients are there or not, the plant only absorbs them if the pH is right for that plant. Over the years, I found slightly acid to neutral soil with pH between 6 to 6.5 to be about right. Our pH was OK to begin with but the manure and other nitrogen amendments we planned to add risked taking the pH lower toward the acid, or "sour" end of the spectrum, so we needed to add two and a half pounds of oyster shells per hole to "sweeten" it up. Besides the 625 lbs. of oyster shells, we hauled in 250 bags of steer manure weighing 40 lbs. each and 125 bags of composted fishery waste weighing about the same. We also carried in 1,250 lbs. of Jersey Greensand for trace elements and 1,250 lbs. of crushed rock phosphate to help with budding when the time came.

To keep the soil loose, we mixed in a half-ton of cocoa bean hulls and, to make sure the girls never got hungry, we added 1,250 lbs. of time-release plant food and 250 lbs. of blood meal to the soil. The steer manure alone was some heavy shit, literally, but adding everything up we're talking hauling in over ten fucking tons of amendments!

Contemplating the task at hand, my mind wandered to how we could use some labor-saving devices and I suggested a couple of ideas to Tex. His immortal words still ring out across the years, "Put the shit on your shoulder and walk."

By the last week of May, we had the place looking like a pot patch and ready to plant.

Chapter 3

Water

Water was the key. It wasn't an issue for Ethan and me yet because Tex was growing our starts at his place near Redding at the northern end of the Sacramento Valley, but we'd soon find out how vital water was to growing a healthy crop.

By this time of year, the valley heat flowed up to the mountains at its north end like a freight train from Hell. It could be 100 degrees at eight o'clock in the morning at Tex's place and our starts flourished in the heat under his care. In a mere six weeks, they were some beautiful bouncing babies! With the patch ready, I drove over to Tex's place to get them. Our pickup had a camper shell on it and I'm glad it did. With 500 pot starts packed into Allied Van Lines boxes and loaded in the truck, the stakes were high. I was also happy the truck had two tanks for gas and made the trip back to the patch without stopping and without incident.

The arrival of the starts raised the ante in two regards. For the past month, we had been hauling shit and cutting trees in preparation for the planting, but only needed drinking water, and however suspicious what we were doing looked, it wasn't against the law. That changed once the babies were on the property. We were now officially lawbreakers, a fact that we were able to put out of our minds after a few days. But, for the first time, we were confronted with what decides a pot grower's fate—water. It didn't take much water to keep the babies alive in the cups but once they were in the ground that would change in a hurry. The plants would need water and plenty of it.

Water in California is a precious commodity. It's also elusive. In the springtime, there's water everywhere but most of it is run-off. You need to see your spring or well in action during August and September to know if it's the real deal, and even at that, it can vary from year to year.

There were two springs on our parcel, one above us and one below. The lower one looked a little stronger, but due to its location, we'd have to catch the water and pump it to a holding tank above the patch. The one above us was farther away but could fill the tank by gravity, an ideal situation if it could be managed.

The terrain between the spring and the patch tank was nasty: a combination of chaparral, ceanothus, and Bryce brush made for a trio of rugged survivors choking a land that nothing with a choice in the matter would inhabit. Their branches can interlock in such a way and grow so thick and low to the ground that it's impossible to walk through or under them and they're not sturdy enough to climb over.

With that combination of briars, thorns, and aromatic oils, any contact with them left our skin sensitive, scratched, sweat-soaked, and itchy. The sun baked our brains, and the dust clogged our noses. We forced ourselves to find a way to unravel a three-hundred-foot roll of black plastic pipe as a water line. Connect ten of those suckers and we were looking at laying three thousand feet of water line! Getting the pipe laid took us two of the hottest, hardest days I've ever worked.

Unfortunately, we still didn't have water. The pipe ran downhill for over half a mile, but there were some ravines and low areas to cross on the way. It took another day of fucking around with airlocks and back pressure valves to get the water running correctly. It turned out that we needed air bleeds at the high spots so that the back pressure didn't keep the water from flowing. As soon as we figured out that little puzzle and poked the last air vent into the line, the water ran like a faucet. It was high-five time and tomorrow we could finally plant. We ate dinner and I slept like a log.

Our water tank held twelve hundred gallons. We didn't know how long it would take to fill but after watching the water flow into the tank the previous day, we were pretty sure that by morning it would be nearly full. Since the babies weren't in the ground yet we only needed about a hundred gallons a day to begin with. We planned to start planting later that day and knew that the next day we'd need some serious water.

Instead of a full tank, what we got was serious heartache. Not only were there less than fifty gallons of water in the tank, but the line wasn't running. It wasn't even dripping. We couldn't imagine what had happened but knew we had to hike back up the hill and start all over again.

Starting over, however, wasn't an option. In straightening a curve, the road crew had plowed through the spring, basically eliminating it under the blade of a Caterpillar tractor. The black plastic pipe we had so carefully hidden was rolled up and stuffed under a bush. We were fucked. Not only were we short one spring and our days of hard labor wasted, but we also felt that our invisibility had been compromised and our month of sneaking around had been all for naught. We had water but it would take a few more days of work and a few thousand dollars' worth of equipment to get it up and running. And that was only half of our worries. I knew I had to talk to the crew working the road and try to find out if they were the type of folks who would rat us out. Luckily, they weren't. They came to our camp and apologized for wasting our spring, and even offered to help us develop another source. They were great guys, and to show them that there were no hard feelings, I bought a half-rack of cold beers for them.

With our peace of mind restored in terms of the road crew, we were still behind the eight ball as far as water was concerned. It was hot and our babies were thirsty. The need for water was critical and time was running out, and the last thing we needed was to have our plants wilt and die. Feeling as though the Sword of Damocles was hanging over our heads, we set about developing the lower spring.

Another problem loomed but we didn't know enough about plants yet to be freaked out. If we didn't get the plants into the ground soon, they would become root-bound in the cups. Through the years I learned that having plants outgrow their starting medium is one of the worst things a grower can do. I don't know the scientific reason for it, but my observations lead me to conclude that it causes the plant to call "time out," time that a pot grower doesn't have to get them started again. In the end, you wind up with smaller, less vigorous plants and a lower overall yield.

The key was water. We could rescue some of the pipe without too much trouble but that was all we had to show for four wasted days. To develop the lower spring we needed another tank, a pump, fittings, clamps, and assorted minutia too numerous to mention. It all went on a list and at dawn the next day I left camp to do the shopping. It took all morning and half the afternoon but by three o'clock I was back. If all went well, the tank would be in place and collecting water by dark, and in the morning, we'd be running the pump.

That's if all went well. Unfortunately, things weren't fated to go well that afternoon. The truck's axle broke in two before I was halfway up the hill, and the rest of the day was spent in a forced march hauling a truckload of irrigation equipment, a motorized pump, and a 1,200-gallon fiberglass water tank up a very long and steep dirt road. The last load fell off our sweaty backs well after dark. Exhausted, we headed out back to camp.

The hike back included a long, steep uphill grade. At the top of it, Ethan slumped to the ground for a rest and looked up at me.

"This is the hardest easy money I've ever earned," he moaned.

I sat on a log with my head in my hands and replied, "If you ever find one part of this business that's easy, let me know."

We reached camp, had a snack, and crashed for the night. I slept like a baby but in the few moments before I drifted off, I wondered if we'd ever have any water. Then I remembered a bit of advice from the I-Ching, "Perseverance furthers, no blame."

We persevered but Tex showed up the next day with the blame. It had been a week since I had retrieved the starts and he expected to find them in the ground by then. When he instead found us installing the new holding tank, he exploded.

You could never tell about this guy. There was something inherently unstable about his personality. He could go from being Santa Claus to being The Grinch in a heartbeat, and there was no way to predict how he was going to react. Tex was one of those guys who felt his life was ruined by having the wrong teacher in third grade. He was forever bringing up stories from his childhood to justify his abhorrent adult behavior. He used the people around him as whipping boys but because we were old friends, I wasn't about to take any shit from him. Furthermore, I was more than able to pay in kind. Over the years, we had some epic arguments, but for a while, at least we remained friends and accomplished all we did by arguing was wasting time.

Tex didn't have a problem with being unreasonable. I guess he felt that it was a privilege of his rank. His motto was, "I don't need excuses, just get the fucking work done." At one point he exclaimed, "I don't need you to think, I need you to work!" as if you could somehow do one without the other. Another one of his famous lines was, "I know everything there is to know about growing pot, and I know everything there is to know about people, just do the work and everything will be fine."

I couldn't believe that anyone would say anything so stupid. The statement oozed hubris. I hadn't hung out with Tex since he came into big money, and it sure seemed to have given him an inflated opinion of himself.

"I know time is critical, and if we came up short, it wasn't for lack of effort," was about all I could manage in terms of a reply.

Tex was a Sagittarius which meant he couldn't stay put too long. He'd let his arrows fly then he was off to do "paperwork."

With Tex gone Ethan and I could get back to doing the real work and by the day's end we had the tank and pump installed. Now, transplanting and getting the babies into the ground could move forward.

My paternal grandfather was a wonderful man. He lived until I was well into adulthood and although he lived far away, we formed a golden bond. I think we saw a lot of ourselves in each other. Somehow our lives and philosophies were in tune. Grampa was born around the turn of the century and although he was technically old enough to fight in World War I and young enough to fight in WWII, he chose to do neither. Instead, he read the Nation Magazine and grew his Victory Garden to support the cause.

Grampa had ways of finding out information that were way ahead of his time. In the Forties, he knew that tobacco smoking caused cancer and quit. He saw through the general bullshit better than anybody I knew. Whereas my dad enlisted in the Navy when Pearl Harbor was bombed, my grandfather remained a pacifist. Though I bear many resemblances to my father, I was my grandfather's boy at heart. I adopted his pacifist attitude and hoped that I acquired his knack with plants as well. He was known for his green thumb and now was when I needed one.

But first, a little background on the marijuana plant. It's considered a "day-short" annual, meaning that the plant produces flowers and seeds as the days are getting shorter. Additionally, a marijuana seed can produce either a male or female plant, and it's usually about a 50/50 split. A pot grower is only interested in the females since they're the ones that flower into buds, which is what gets smoked.

In nature, it's not clear what sex a plant is until the days get shorter. So, the trick pot growers developed was to shorten the days while the babies were still in cold frames. The idea was to force the plant to declare its sex early by darkening the cold frames for a few days. When the plant was a couple of months old, typically the middle or end of April, the grower would cover the cold frames with several layers of black plastic. The frames were covered at roughly five in the afternoon and then uncovered at about eight the next morning, effectively shortening the daylight hours and tricking the plants into declaring their sex early. That way a grower didn't have a lot of extra boys around all summer to feed and water.

In our case, because roughly half the starts were destined to be boys and we had started too late to force the babies to declare their sex in the cold frames, we had to plant twice as many plants as we needed to guarantee the number of girls we wanted.

The identification process was tedious and extremely hard on the eyes, but Tex did the sexing for us that year. The sex organs appeared in the plants' crotches and the boys, strangely enough, had sex organs that were shaped like balls. On the other hand, the girls' organs appeared in a sheath that wasn't as bulbous as the boys' genitals. The sheaths also stood a little taller and a little thinner than the boys' sex organs, but at this early stage of growth, one could still guess wrong.

As the plants grew and the sex organs developed further, the boys' balls become obvious and hung off the plants. We called them "dingle balls." From the sheath of the female organs appeared two translucent, slightly furry, and very sticky pistils that rose up like the antennae of a butterfly, tapering off to somewhat of a point. Those sticky little antennae were what Tex was looking for. If he found them in two consecutive crotches it was one hundred percent guaranteed to be a girl. Just finding one sex organ left us with a one or two percent chance that the plant was a boy or even a hermaphrodite, or herme for short, meaning a plant of both sexes.

I relate this process in detail for those of you who are interested in the ABCs of pot growing, and to give some insight into the problem we faced. With our late start, we didn't have time to darken them for four days and then wait around for four or five more weeks for them to declare their sex before planting them. The seasoned growers I knew aimed to have their plants in the ground by Mother's Day, around mid-May. We were already into June and still hadn't planted a single one.

We prepared 250 beds thinking that was roughly about how many female plants we'd end up with. But we had 500 starts and since we hadn't determined their sex, planting two to a hole was our only option.

We were thinking that half the beds would end up with one boy and one girl, about 25 percent would have two boys, and 25 percent two girls. All the boys would be pulled out and some of the double girls would get transplanted into empty beds.

That was the plan. The math worked out in terms of probability like this; normally, from what we were told, plants sex out at a little better than 50/50, maybe 52/48 or 53/47 in favor of females. Hence our decision to plant two into a hole. So, statistically half of the beds, one hundred and twenty-five, should end up with one boy and one girl. When that's the case you simply pull the boy out. Of the remaining 125 beds, 75 should be two girls and 75 should be two boys. By pulling all the double boys, we would open up 75 beds into which to transplant the extra females.

It wasn't the best plan but with our late start we didn't have a choice and were then faced with two problems. First, the babies got planted more to the side of the bed instead of the middle, so the roots had farther to travel to get the nutrients they needed. The second problem was that plants don't like to be transplanted when they get that big, so we were putting a quarter of our crop at risk of shock and maybe stunting.

But, ready or not, we were out of time and those babies needed to get in the ground.

We had our challenges but fortunately, in our favor, Tex never cut any corners when it came to feeding the babies. From the time our starts had four sets of branches, they'd been getting two types of nutrition; a water-soluble, high-nitrogen plant food, and a sea kelp-based product that acted as an enhancer.

The reason for the high nitrogen fertilizer was to grow the biggest plants possible. During the early part of the growth cycle, we typically used a water-soluble commercial fertilizer with a 28-14-14 or a 32-10-10 NPK number. Those numbers indicated a fertilizer that was high in nitrogen, which is what the plants needed to grow large. Later in the season, when the buds appeared, we shifted to a high phosphorous plant food, maybe 5-52-5, to encourage the best flower growth.

Our girls were spoiled. As babies all the plants got watered every day and fed on a four-day rotation starting with fertilizer, a day of a clear water rinse, then a day of sea kelp, then another day of clear rinse. We also foliar-fed them with the sea kelp product every evening before leaving the patch. It was an expensive and time-consuming process, but we saw it was working. Our starts were growing fast and looked beautiful, but we needed to get them out of their cups.

Time to transplant. That meant hand digging two holes into each bed. This was a real pain in the ass; back and shoulders really. We were talking 500 holes!

The beds were already prepped, and the digging was fairly easy; there was just a lot of it. Ethan and I worked it out that I'd dig and do the planting, and he would haul the babies in from the cold frames and keep me supplied with water for the transplanting. It was early June, and the plants were starting to explode out of their cups. Pot plants tend to do that. Farmers and plant enthusiasts alike should be able to appreciate how fast these suckers can grow.

Tex came over to tell us how he wanted the plants put in the ground. We were in the patch when he showed up and I commented on how fast they were growing.

Ethan chimed in with some of his farm wisdom. "The corn farmers have a saying, 'Knee high by the Fourth of July."

Tex scoffed. "Knee high on the Fourth of July and a pot grower can cut his wrists."

Ethan looked worried "Ours won't be much taller than that will they, Tex?"

We only had a few weeks to go until July, and our starts were only a foot or so tall.

"I wish I could take you guys over to Redding and show you my patch," Tex said, then changed his mind. "No, it would be too depressing for you guys." He held his hand over his head indicating that his plants would be six feet tall by the Fourth of July.

Tex gave us his instructions for planting, which were basically, "Get them in the ground." I'd been a landscaper and much of what he told us I knew was bullshit. Before leaving he gave us a lecture on the perils of working in the heat. The summer had turned into one of the hottest on record, and he left us with a bottle of salt tablets.

In a perfect world, I wouldn't transplant in the heat of the day. I'd get as much done in the cool morning and evening hours and find some other chores to do during the afternoon. But because of how late in the season it was, I planted from the moment I got to the patch in the morning until I ran out of light. Ethan did everything else, like the hauling and watering. By the middle of the afternoon on the first day of planting, we were dragging our asses but staying with it the best we could. The temperature was around 110 degrees, and being a big guy, Ethan was really starting to fade.

We were taking a break when he asked me, "Where did you put the salt tabs?"

I dug around in my daypack for a minute and found them. I was starting to read the instructions, when he snatched the bottle from my hand.

"I want the fuckers now!" he said. He must have been feeling bad already because normally he wasn't so assertive. "Five to eight," I heard him say as he read the label. "I'm a big guy; I can do ten!"

And with that, he quickly dumped ten salt tablets into his hand and swallowed them in two gulps of water from one of our canteens.

The heat seemed to have slowed my mind as well. What did I know about salt tablets? But the sight of somebody taking all those pills at once concerned me enough to get the bottle back from him and read the label for myself. It read, "1 or 2 tablets every 4 to 6 hours, not to exceed 5 to 8 in a twenty-four-hour period, depending on weight." Ethan had just eaten 10! At that point there wasn't much I could do, so I got back to planting.

Tex wanted the babies planted quickly but I could tell they'd been in the cups too long; the roots were all bunched together, and I decided to soak them first in a pail of water with vitamin B-1 added to gently untangle their roots. Experience in the landscaping business had proved to me that this extra step mattered.

Roots don't like light, so I kept the plants in the shade of my body while transplanting them. I'd heard that some growers pulled the lowest pair of leaves off the little round dicots and buried the plant almost up to its first set of branches, but my preference was to leave the root knuckle, where the plant and the ground meet, exposed to the air on its top. I tried not to damage the roots when I filled the holes in with soil. Then I lightly compressed the soil and thoroughly watered the plants in.

Plants tip toward the sun in a way that exposes as much of their green leaves to the light as possible. This is caused by a light sensitive plant hormone called auxin, so I guess a quick word on auxin is in order. Auxin aids growth. It runs toward the light source and is the reason plants bend to follow the sun. Our baby pot plants were leaning to the sun in their cups so when I transplanted them, I turned them away from the sun. This forced the auxin to run to the other side of the plant immediately after it was planted, theoretically stimulating the plant's growth.

It took several minutes to plant the way I did. I knew a guy who took hours on each plant, but most growers just popped them out of the cups and threw them right into the ground. I had gotten a few more planted when Ethan returned with a tray of starts, moaning as he approached.

"I don't feel so good," he said weakly. His contorted face was literally squirting sweat like a watering can. "I need water," he gasped, and I handed him my canteen. He sucked it all down without stopping, then asked for more. His face was dripping like a faucet, but I didn't have any more water to give him.

"What do you think will happen if I drink the tank water?" he asked.

"I don't want to make that call," I told him. "It's an old tank Tex has had for a while and who knows how many lizards died in it?" In fact, we had already added plant food and B-1 to the water, so I didn't know what to tell him. But it didn't matter what I thought. Ethan's thirst was making him irrational and he started drinking water straight from the hose. I joked with him that I was afraid he was going to drain the tank and I would have to stop planting and go pump water, but my real concern was that the guy would have a heart attack. What would I tell the coroner?

Ethan was in so much stomach pain that he couldn't stand up straight, and one look at him would tell you his engine was about to blow. He took the afternoon off while I kept working.

I knocked off at dusk and walking back to the camp remembered Ethan's salt overdose. Happily, the worst had passed; Ethan was fast asleep and the noise of his snoring for once sounded good.

The planting procedure was repeated 500 times over the next seven or eight days. But finally, around the 15th of June, we were in.

Our spring proved to be a good one and we could pump more than enough water, at least in the early going. The problem was that it took so long to water all the plants by hand that there wasn't time for all the other chores that we needed to do. Work was piling up and the water system wouldn't be completed until the end of July. Some jobs were barely completed and others not at all. We just didn't have the manpower.

Twp of the most time-consuming jobs that summer were mulching and thinning the canopy. Ethan did most of the collecting and spreading of mulch while I took charge of the tree work. In the end we didn't get all the work done, but we completed the essentials. With only two workers on a job that size, that was the best we could do.

We settled into our summer routine. Getting up when the sky turned gray, we were in the field by seven-thirty. We worked from then until twilight, with a two- or three-hour break during the heat of the day. We did our watering in the morning because I'd heard somewhere that plants take in their nutrients with the rising temperature. The afternoons were spent doing the rest of the chores. Removing light blocking foliage consumed most of my hours.

By the first of August we were beginning to see our efforts pay off. The plants were exploding and as tall as us. The patch was host to twice as many plants than we had room for, and it was increasingly difficult for us to move around. They were beginning to show their sex so we figured that problem would take care of itself before they got too big.

Tex showed up one morning with a hank of bright yellow yarn. Each female plant would be given a necklace of gold, and the boys would be pulled. Marking them that way meant we wouldn't have to re-check plants that had already been sexed.

I'll never forget the excitement of that day. Ethan and I didn't have a clue what Tex was seeing, but he kept saying, "Here's another one." We were stunned, our crop was over 75% female! We ended up with 386 girls. We didn't get the added elbow room we had expected, but decided we could live with that problem.

These were not 386 plants of various sizes. They were all big. They looked like soldiers in the Russian army: tall, wide, and robust. Because of the care and nutrients we supplied, the plants grew like jocks on steroids. For the next stage of growth, each plant had to be what we growers called "tied" for support.

Marijuana in its natural state has enough structural integrity to support itself, but our plants were hardly in their natural state. The soil preparation alone would have produced some oversized plants, but we were watering them and feeding them one form of plant food or another every other day, plus, up until late July they had been foliar fed every night. The plants grew so fast that from day to day we could actually see the difference. They were taller and their branches were longer, and when the buds appeared they would be fatter and heavier than anything the plants could have dreamed of in their natural state.

When the buds appeared in early August, we shifted over to a high-phosphorous plant food with NPK numbers 10-52-10 and rotated with the kelp mix as before. The branches and buds were exploding. Without being tied, the plants would have fallen over or worse, the branches would have broken off.

The plants needed support. By the middle of August the average height of each plant would be eight feet, with the stalks at the base being roughly as big around as a man's wrist. By harvest time some would be as big around as a man's forearm. Each plant and its branches had to be supported by strings that hung from wires that crisscrossed the patch. The process of getting plants "tied" was the most tedious, time-consuming chore that we faced. We had 386 plants and each of them needed a spider web of sisal twine spun around it for support, and we were some of the slowest goddamn spiders you ever saw. So, we tied, and tied, and tied, and needed help to keep up. So, because Tex knew everything there was to know about growing pot, and everything there was to know about people, we soon had the help we needed.

That's how we got our first harvest helper, Rolly.

Chapter 4

Send in the Clowns

Rolly was an old friend of Tex's. He was some kind of an Eastern guru wannabe. In a cosmic brother sense, he possessed many admirable qualities. Unfortunately, none of them had anything to do with manual labor in general or farming in particular. The guy was a human lava lamp. "Not a great worker" would be a world-class understatement, but he was a likable enough guy. He kept Ethan company while he worked, and I guess that counted for something.

In defense of anyone stuck with the job of tying, it's a pot grower's purgatory. Done in the hottest part of the summer, the plants are sticky, and the goo finds its way onto your skin making it itch like hell. If you've grown runts, you usually skip this part of the job. We didn't have that luxury. Our plants were big and getting bigger every day. We couldn't afford to skip this chore; one big rain and they would all be lying down in the mud.

As the summer passed, we managed our living arrangements quite nicely using the school bus for the kitchen and Ethan's sleeping quarters, while I slept in the small trailer. Harvest would change that in a hurry. We planned to have a cook, one packager, four or five pickers, and maybe an extra helper. There would be nine or ten of us living there for a couple of months, so we needed places for everybody to sleep. We also needed a place where the pickers could work and a large, very large, shed for drying the plants.

The job of building the various structures needed for harvest fell to me. Around the first of September, Tex dipped into his bag of losers and hired another one of his buddies, Jacques Canard, to help me. We figured Tex must have had an in at the local home for the blown. Where else did he come up with these guys? This training wheel Bozo acted like he had descended from European royalty, and maybe he had, but if he wanted to peddle his aristocratic bullshit, he'd come to the wrong place. We were running out of time and had some major work to do.

"Mon dieu, patron, theece eez impossible," was his standard exclamation. "Ah cannot do eet" was his knee-jerk reply no matter how simple a chore was. He was as close to being a jellyfish as anyone I have ever met. I guess he hadn't heard, but we fought a war and tossed off our Kings and Queens in exchange for democracy. In fairness to Jacques, much of modern America seems to have embraced the trappings of an aristocracy so he might have been confused.

I put him to work building noise-making booby traps. They would go off with a loud bang but weren't going to hurt anyone.

We made our booby traps out of rat traps. Each one had been modified to hold a twelve-gauge shotgun shell with the pellets and packing removed. These were then screwed to trees ten or twelve feet above the ground so nobody would accidentally have one explode in their face. We ran fish line, strung about chest high, through a series of metal eye bolts for the trip wires. That kept Jacques busy for a while, but what we really needed was a dryer and that meant a week's worth of hard physical labor.

The drying shed was an indispensable tool in high-grade marijuana production. Even in those rare years when the weather cooperated and stayed hot and dry, fog could roll in overnight and ruin the flavor and smoking characteristics of our summer's work.

This is where Ethan came in handy because of his tobacco grower background. Keeping a pot plant's wonderful taste and aromatic quality really comes down to how it's dried and cured. It's all about inner cellular integrity, and I'm sure an entire doctoral thesis could be written on the subject. Ethan's rule of thumb was simple; keep the moisture going slowly in one direction—out. It was OK if the pot dried and became wet again from moisture that was still in the stalk. If, however, the pot dried out and then took on moisture from the air, for some reason it would taste bitter.

To ensure control over the ambient temperature and humidity around our crop as it dried, we needed to have a room big enough to hold it all. If we'd only had a few plants, we could easily have dried them in the back of a VW bus heated by a couple of Coleman lanterns, not unheard of in those days. But the crop we were sitting on was huge and required a bit more space.

The dryer we constructed was awesome; a forty-foot long by twenty-foot-high airplane hangar-sized building made of plastic pipe. Patterned after a WWII-era Quonset hut, the shed was constructed mostly of 1-1/4" pvc schedule 40, heavy gauge, plastic pipe and covered by a custom made 40-foot by 40-foot green/brown canvas tarp. I don't know whose idea it was, but it was the standard drying shed design of the time. It was big, warm, and dry. The post from the ground to the ridgepole was 17 feet high in the front and, owing to the slope of the hill, twenty-five feet high in back. The ridgepole was 40 feet long, supported by poles made from five sizable fir trees and set in concrete like fence posts. The ends were clear plastic sheeting to allow for natural light, with another clear sheet 20 feet down the ridgepole that divided the shed into two halves.

The building had two levels, but the upstairs was little more than a catwalk. Each level had several rows of re-bar running the length of the shed, from which we would hang our plants to dry. It was also outfitted with two 400,000 BTU orchard heaters that sucked about twenty gallons of propane a day when it was rainy and cold, and kept the building heated between 80 and 90 degrees around the clock. The clear plastic front and back were lightly painted to reduce the shine without stopping the light. Since the building was located under thick trees we didn't put a camo net on it, but we did hang branches on it to 'phlage it somewhat.

Tex showed up at the farm on September twenty first and I had just returned from a few days off with my family. It had been raining at the farm for three days and he was pissed.

"Where in the fucking hell have you been? It's raining, you should'a been here!"

"It wasn't raining in the city, Tex. It's not even raining in Ukiah, so lighten up." I had been in San Francisco with Carrie and my kids.

"You didn't have a TV in your hotel room?" Tex was the captain, and he refused to lose arguments on his ship.

"I haven't seen Carrie all summer and the weather was the last thing I wanted to look at." Why was I arguing with him? It was a no-win situation, he was the Goomba.

He started back up. "These buds were so tight last week. Look at them now!"

The three days of rain caused a growth spurt and plants showed signs of what's called "helicoptering," a growth spurt that pushes the stem out of top of the bud, causing a few baby fan leaves to grow out of that new stem looking like helicopter rotors.

It was really a lame argument anyhow, because Ethan and I were pilgrims, a pot grower term for a Rookie, and there was no way in hell that we would have cut the crop down without Tex giving the order. Now that Tex was there, all we had to do was to get Rolly to wake up and Prince Jacques to get his head out of his ass, and we would be ready for harvest.

As I said, we had one big fucking drying shed. It was so big that we thought we could get our whole crop inside. But in fact, the shed only held eighty plants. It wasn't the building's fault; the plants were just too damn big and there were too many of them.

Over the years I've been involved in harvesting plants that you could easily cut down with hand snips and carry four or five in each hand. Plants that small would yield maybe an ounce or two of manicured buds per plant. Our plants were so big they needed to be cut down with pruning saws, and some of them required two of us to hump them from the patch to the dryer. The only plants we had under eight feet tall were a couple of "Rudys," or Cannabis ruderalis, a Russian strain. Handling the rest of them was like carrying tall, wet, gooey, Christmas trees.

But the pot we had grown was kick-ass and worth the effort. The resin was so thick that after an hour we had to scrape it off our watch faces with razor blades to just tell the time. It was well after dark by the time we called it a day and our clothes were so covered with dark sticky resin that we looked like auto mechanics after a tough day in the pits.

We had cut down and hung three hundred and fifty plants on lines. Because we were only able to get the first eighty or so into the shed, the two hundred and seventy others went on ropes strung between the trees.

Six months ago, I'd been making five hundred dollars a week pounding nails. I went to sleep in the dryer that night with a half a million dollars' worth of pot hanging on a rope. Not bad for a pilgrim in his first year out.

Drying a crop this large took weeks of work and the curing process was critical to our success. The key was not drying the pot too fast, too warm, or getting it too dry before we could manicure it, and not leaving it too damp when bagged. It really boiled down to patience, vigilance, and like Ethan had professed, allowing the moisture to flow in one direction. We had to be sure that the dry pot wasn't allowed to become moist from ambient humidity. Buds go through a period where they're too dry to keep in the air all day and must be sealed in plastic overnight. The moisture that remained in the stem flowed into the flower and the next day we dried the bud some more. We had to be vigilant during this phase. If the buds got too dry, they would crumble into dust. And if the buds had to be remoistened by spraying water into the bag, the resulting smoke could become harsh and funky smelling.

When the plants started drying out they had to be bucked up into smaller branches and stored in what we called "Body bags." Large trash bags were common, but we used extra large, heavy gauge bags used in the construction industry to get rid of asbestos. Because many of our plants required more than one bag, at one time we had over four hundred bags in the dryer that had to be opened and checked for moisture every day for a week. The bags were tied shut with sisal twine, and after a week our hands were ravaged with rope burns.

When the pot was dry enough to manicure, we moved the body bags to a storeroom under the platform that the pickers' tent was on.

The only consideration left was how to stash our booty. Tex showed up one day with a U-Haul truck full of the biggest plastic barrels I'd ever seen and each could hold over thirty pounds of manicured pot. I rented a backhoe and spent a long afternoon digging holes in the woods. Each hole was as far off the road as I could get with the machine, and big enough to hold several barrels. With that task accomplished, Ethan and I were finished with the work we had to do. Now we had a place to store the weighed and packaged pounds until they were sold. From then until the clean-up started, we could relax a little and watch the harvest crew do their work.

The harvest crew that year was an eclectic group: Ex-hippies, 'Nam vets, assorted hangers-on, friends of Tex, and Rolly's sister Robin, a union activist.

Robin Slatsky. Fresh from a five-year stint with Caesar Chavez and the United Farm Workers, she was genetically engineered to bust balls. She had that kill-or-be-killed New York City subway survivor mentality and viewed the world as a battlefield on which to fight worker oppression. In general, I found myself agreeing with her opinions regarding management/worker relations, but a pot farm hardly fits the standard business model. Back then it was a criminal activity and hardly within the purview of OSHA. When dealing with zealots however, all bets were off, and her hardline mindset caused my internal baloney meter to go soaring into the red zone. In very short order I found myself squaring off against her militancy.

The context of the early skirmishes hasn't survived in my memory bank clearly enough to retrieve, but they were about such earthshaking issues as how many times a year you should wash your dog, and what kind of soap you should use. I'm not kidding. Really lame shit that left me shaking my head. Robin liked to argue and brought considerable intellect and a deep feeling of missionary zeal to the table, no matter how mundane the subject was.

We were farmers after all, and it wasn't long before her real passion and expertise—the plight of the farm worker—became the cause du jour as she attempted to foment a worker rebellion among our pickers.

Her criticism was based not so much on the working conditions or the pay, but more the notion that the grower was reaping obscenely high rewards, and somehow, we owed some of the obscenity to whole crew. At that time green bud was selling for $1,600 a pound. Our first year's production cost came to $300 a pound including the $100 a pound we paid the pickers for manicuring. Our net was $1,300 a unit, split seventy percent to Tex and fifteen percent each to Ethan and me. In other words, Ethan and I were working for $195 a pound and we'd been hard at it all summer. I don't know what her idea of fair was, but I'm betting that Santa Claus doesn't treat his seasonal Elf help better than we treated our pickers.

Although technically they were seasonal farm workers, at Serenity Park they weren't exactly laboring under the hot sun in fields of zucchini. A day in the life of our crew started with breakfast being made to order. Our cook was an experienced restaurant line chef who would have two kinds of coffee and fresh baked sweet rolls on the table by the time the workers moseyed in. Eggs and potatoes, sausage or bacon for the meat eaters, pancakes, hot or cold cereal, and a big fatty rolled for the wake-and-bakers. Since there was no time clock the pickers could start whenever they wanted. Some did an hour of meditation or yoga, others sat around and smoked pot and shot the shit. No pressure. But since it was piecework at $100 per pound, they usually got going quickly.

In those days the buyers controlled the market, and the pot had to be manicured to perfection. Each bud, no matter how big or small, had to have all the fan leaves trimmed off so only pure bud remained. Once a picker was up to speed two or three pounds a day was considered pretty good. That was $200 to $300 a day cash, no deductions of any kind. To sweeten the deal, the pickers got to order and drink whatever brand of beer, wine, or hard alcohol they wanted, and how much they drank was up to them. They could smoke all the pot they wanted and occasionally someone had a little cocaine to toot. They were also allowed to keep all the hashish that accumulated on their scissors and hands. It was common for a picker to amass two or three ounces of finger hash before the end of harvest to keep or sell.

Lunch was a smorgasbord and dinner was usually a feast, with the pickers choosing their favorite meals. Cost was of no concern, and it wasn't uncommon for us to polish off a couple of bottles of French champagne after dinner.

I have a sneaking hunch that more than a few people reading this would jump at the chance to have these conditions where they work, but apparently this wasn't enough for Robin.

While Robin understood the legal component to the debate, not being a marijuana enthusiast, she didn't grasp the bigger picture. I tried to assure her that the scope of the issues around cannabis and hemp were real but didn't expect her to understand.

Robin was unaware that only about fifteen percent of the strains of hemp are cannabis hemp; the kind that gets a user high. The other eighty-five percent are purely commercial raw material and possibly the most utilitarian plants that grow on earth. While Robin was familiar with Maslow's pyramid of basic human needs—food, shelter, and clothing—she wasn't able to grasp that hemp could supply all three of these and put a good buzz on your head at the same time.

The debates with Robin were fought in a series of small skirmishes, but she really had a bone in her nose about pot. She never grasped the basic hypocrisy in biting the hand that fed her. Pot was paying her wages, so no matter what her feelings on the subject were, she should have kept her opinions to herself. One day she tried to stage a work stoppage. I believe she thought that we wouldn't fire her out fear of being ratted out. But whatever her thoughts were, by the time I had her bedding rolled up and tossed into the back of the truck, she figured her bluff had been called and she backed down. We let her finish the season but as far as I know she never worked in the business again.

Harvest dragged on. Personalities clashed, and the mood was uptight. Naming the place Serenity Park was a joke the pickers made up, but Tex didn't get it and the name stuck. It was like calling a 300-pound guy Tiny.

We knew we had a bountiful crop, and in our wildest dreams hadn't figured on netting three hundred and thirteen pounds for all our hard work. We had a mountain of pot to trim with only four pickers; three of whom were pilgrims. The crew put in long days but it wasn't enough to finish the job so when the pickers at Tex's place finished cleaning his crop, we sent a hundred body bags over for them to finish for us.

Tex treated the whole crew to a short holiday at Squaw Valley and barely got folks home in time for Thanksgiving. Ethan and I spent the last week in November cleaning up the mess and burning the waste. On December third, the season finally ended. Driving a used Audi I'd picked up with my earnings, I headed up Interstate 5 and returned to Portland dripping money and holding a stash of pot befitting royalty. Despite all I'd gained, however, I was a physical and emotional basket case. There had been a gradual welling up of anxiety throughout the year that I'd been too busy to notice. It was time to decompress.

Chapter 5

Lumpy Gravy Train

The sudden windfall of cash and stash was a surreal mix of euphoria and frustration. Landing back in the real world with a boatload of cash, as opposed to more standard forms of remuneration, had advantages and disadvantages that were hard to foresee.

On the plus side, cash is as liquid as it can get. On the minus side, there was a limit on how many greenbacks I could flash around without becoming a target. There might have been tax advantages on the face of it but over the long haul, in terms of having a life and investing in the future, the flood of cash and the lifestyle that accompanied it was as much of an impediment as a blessing. It was something like winning a lottery, just because you're not poor anymore doesn't necessarily mean you're rich.

Another issue was motivation. I think it was the famous jockey Eddie Arcaro who said, "It's more difficult getting up early in the morning when you're wearing silk pajamas"." A pot grower coming off a good year can stop being a worker bee and wear any kind of pajamas he wants. It's easy for him to believe that he can dip into the honey jar at will. Compared to the adrenaline rush and potential jackpot for growing marijuana, the workaday existence of the great

American middle-class begins to appear like a lifetime of drudgery. Let's face it, once you've dropped out and done well there's not much incentive to drop back in.

Then there was the problem of safety and portability. Cash was bulky. It had to be hidden and could be lost or stolen. I knew a guy who checked out of his room in a Hwy. 101 motel forgetting that he had hidden a bag of cash behind the curtains. He and his wife were twenty miles away when they remembered it. By the time they got back to the place about a half an hour later, they found the room door open, and the housemaid in the room making the bed. He calmly walked past her, retrieved his bag of money and left. He had come about as close as you can come to losing fifty grand.

I also had a good friend who had just sold $26,000 worth of pot and was going home with the money when he got pulled over by the state patrol. The cop smelled pot smoke and found some roaches in my friend's ashtray. In the process of searching the car, the cop found the twenty-six grand. Luckily, that was in the eighties before the confiscation laws went into effect. Had they been in effect, that money would have been confiscated, reported as $10,000, and my friend would have to prove to the IRS that the rest of it was his. Back then the cops hadn't figured out how easy it was to dip their bread into the gravy, and my friend was able to talk his way out of it. It turned out that the cop thought he was on his way to *buy* pot and was content to catch him driving back with the bud.

There was a story that landed in the news about a father and son who were cutting down a Christmas tree near Ukiah and found $10,000 that some grower must have hidden in the woods.

And knew a guy who buried his whole stash of pot in barrels and then it rained heavily, and they all popped out of the ground and rolled down a mountainside. Much to his horror, he spotted them in a neighbor's field the next day. That was a close one.

Over the years I've gathered a few near miss stories of my own. I once buried $7,500 in a shallow hole near my tent and an animal dug it up and carried it away. It took me damn near three days of hiking around to find it. There were some teeth holes, but otherwise it was no worse for wear. Another time I buried some money in a Tupperware container. An animal dug that up too, ate the plastic, and left the money in a pile in the middle of the woods. Had somebody been hiking on that trail, they would have found a cool twenty grand.

Cash can mold, burn, or just burn a hole in your pocket. It has a certain energy, and depending on how you deal with it, it can be a positive or negative experience. But I don't want to snivel about it. We should all have that problem to work out, but many growers found that having a huge amount of cash around was not all it was cracked up to be.

Another downside of the business was the duplicity that became a necessary part of the lifestyle. Tex told me going in that the worst part of being a grower was lying to your friends and family. He could say that because he'd never been busted, but aside from that he was probably right. A grower had to always have a line of bullshit at the ready. You never knew when some salesclerk or your mom was going to ask you where you worked. You've been selling insurance for ten years and now you're collecting pinecones and mistletoe for a living?

Sitting in a coffee shop one day, I overheard two little old ladies talking about their grandchildren. One woman asked the other, "What's your grandson Tommy doing for a living these days? I never see him around town anymore."

"He's up in the hills running seismic cable," was the innocent reply. Yeah right. I got yer seismic cable right here, Granny.

How much or how little bullshit you ended up concocting depended on who your friends were, how close you were to your family, and more importantly, where their heads were concerning marijuana. My friends were counter-culture folk, and many of them were also growers. With them there was no need to be duplicitous. However, my own family was pretty straight so, for a variety of reasons, they weren't privy to the dirty low-down of my employment.

In the end I chose to follow the advice of an ancient sage: "Never tell an unnecessary lie."

My parents and I had never been too close anyway. The Depression and WWII had indoctrinated them in their most formative years. The trauma of Pearl Harbor galvanized and militarized their entire generation to such a degree that I didn't see how a person could keep from being swept away by it. Add to that, our country never mustered off a wartime footing when it was over, and the military-industrial complex was born.

My father went to work in the private sector after the war, but the company he worked for could have easily been the Pentagon. Having regimented his life to such a degree it was only natural that the approach he took to raising a family was that of a platoon sergeant. He wasn't as bad as some, but we lived in a "My way or the highway" home environment. If I hadn't been born so hardheaded, sanctimonious, and rebellious, I might have shut up and fallen in line. But by the time I was 13, the ugly die had been cast. Bit by bit it turned physical, and before long we were engaged in full-scale guerrilla warfare. What was happening between my dad and me was a common sixties era phenomenon. Kids were specializing in embarrassing their parents and I took the concept to new heights. In short, I was a frustrated rascal and ended up running away a lot to avoid his fits of rage. I left home for good at sixteen, with blood running out of both my ears.

A few days later, after my dad had cooled off a bit, I got word though the grapevine that he wanted to see me. He pulled his Cadillac up to the curb in front of the local movie theater, and I got in. We talked for a minute or two, I can't remember the conversation, but he gave me fifty bucks and told me not to come back. He needn't have worried since by then I'd heard the siren's song—I was already drawn to the West Coast.

As the years passed and I began raising a family of my own, our positions towards each other softened and we grew closer. But because of the geographic distance and all the bad blood between us, it took decades to achieve any sort of reasonable relationship. Ironically, just a day or two after Tex phoned me in Portland with the job offer, my dad called. He had been working at the same corporation for thirty years and was about to retire. He must have had a few drinks. He was slurring his words and waxing sentimental. We small-talked for a while and at one point he got pretty emotional and said, "You know, you were a tough kid to raise, but in the end, I realize you were always honest with me, and that's what's really important." The next thing out of his mouth was "So, what's new?"

I said, "Dad, I'm moving to back California to get into the landscaping business."

Tex had only one reason for being in the marijuana trade—money. His motto was, "The more the merrier, the quicker the better." He had a history of childhood deprivation that left him hungry for the good life. My reasons were more complicated, with money being only part of it. I was an old-school hippie, of the large-dose LSD variety, esoterically seeking a larger Truth. Not many people got that far out, even most of the counter-culture folks from that time. For me, it was about opening the doors of perception and freeing the mind.

For Tex, it was about opening the doors to the bank. We never did see eye to eye, but as friends we respected each other's point of view. I knew that Tex had grown up the son of struggling immigrant Polish Jews, who raised him and his sisters in a sixty-five-dollar a month, cold water walk-up flat in the Bronx. Compared to Tex, my upper-middle class childhood was unbridled luxury. I certainly couldn't condemn a man for wanting a lifestyle that I took for granted, and Tex had enough hippie in him to see that my cosmic ramblings on freedom and self-determination contained a bit of truth, at least when viewed through the right kaleidoscope. The fact that we argued endlessly really didn't matter because in the end our desire for success was the same regardless of our motivation. I remember once asking Tex, "How much money can one man make in a lifetime?" and he replied, "I'll let you know."

If I hadn't already believed he was ambitious, Tex's second year plan went a long way toward convincing me. It called for three new gardens with 750 new holes and three more tenders. We were going to grow a thousand plants. Sounded like fun and in theory seemed doable. We were quadrupling our workload and only a little more than doubling our manpower. But we had an early start and figured that the extra time would more than make up for the extra work.

Tex wanted Ethan to move to Redding and tend his place. Tex had bought out his partners and thought Ethan and Rolly could handle the patch. It was already established and quite upscale compared to Serenity Park. Tex let me hire an old buddy of mine from the Russian River, Treeman Dan, a hardworking guy I knew I could rely on. With seven hundred and fifty new holes going in, we were going to need a lot of tree work done and that's what Dan did for a living, hence his nickname.

Tex re-hired Jacques as a tender along with two of Jacques' buddies from LA. Tex couldn't have picked three less qualified people if he had rolled them out of a psych ward in wheelchairs.

I already knew from the previous year that Jacques was your basic European nobleman wannabe without two francs to rub together. He hadn't done a day's work in his life and was in no hurry to start now.

His buddy Lowes Petty was a diagnosable sociopath. He fancied himself an artist but was really just a loudmouth bully who could draw. Lowes had so many addictions that he was usually comatose by lunchtime. He was a dangerous combination of big and mean. The guy weighed in at over 200 pounds and was a good head taller than me. No gentle giant, this guy blustered his way through life snarling at people and scaring babies. In retrospect, it was probably lucky that he nodded out as much as he did.

The third guy, Richie Moonbeam, was as close to unconscious as you could get without being legally declared dead. I think his last acid trip took him to Toon Town and he never quite came back.

While Jacques and Lowes had some obvious developmental problems, Moonbeam was seriously fucked up. He had seen Star Wars about 900 times. We figured he stopped brushing his teeth so he could look like the Wookie, Chewbacca.

The only thing the three of them seemed able to do was argue. They could argue about anything, at any time. Their morning argument became a fixture of camp life as they fought to decide who was going to do what. The problem undoubtably stemmed from Tex's management style. He considered himself the boss even though he was never there. He felt that the tenders should all be equals, and that we would somehow manage our affairs through some sort of administrative osmosis. So Treeman Dan and I worked together, and we let the Three Stooges, as we referred to them behind their backs, have at each other. They were in such mental limbo that reaching any form of accord between them was virtually impossible. I'd have been better off trying to teach three monkeys to sing Italian opera.

Being on the same 1,000 acres with these guys was bad enough, but being cooped up in a trailer with them on rainy days was pure hell. And, as if the gods were making a game out of placing obstacles in our way, it rained 55 of the first 60 days we were there, easily being the wettest spring in all the years that I had lived in Northern California.

So much for male bonding. With the rain pouring endlessly we lost the extra time that was to offset our lack of manpower, and quickly found ourselves seriously behind the eight ball. The task at hand would have stretched us to the limit had we been able to get along and had good weather, but as it turned out, we hated each other, and the weather sucked.

We needed over two thousand starts to get one thousand girls. Just the task of poking drain holes in two thousand cups took us the better part of a morning to accomplish. We needed yards of potting soil mix to fill the cups and several new cold frames to hold them. It took us over a week to get the nursery going.

Also, somewhere between thirty and forty tons of material had to be hauled into the forest. The seven-hundred and fifty new plants required three new patches, with weeks of tree work and brush clearing to be done. To get our thousand holes we needed to add seven-hundred and fifty new ones. And because the new patches were going in so far from the original, a completely new water system had to be built. The new system needed to be roughly three times bigger than the one we built the year before. Beyond that, all the holes needed the soil amendments added and tilled in. Our only hope was to work together, and that was nearly impossible. The fact that Tex had hired guys who didn't know how to work in the first place just exacerbated the problem. The fact that nobody got along with anybody else was the real fly in the ointment.

The work was never finished and what was done was slipshod and marginal. Looking back at that year, Tex had just bitten off more than the Stooges, Treeman Dan, and I could chew.

From the start, our plants developed poorly. Because of the interminable rain, the dark skies, and the cold days and nights, the babies languished in their cups. Showing very little interest in developing, what growing they did manage was stretching to find some sunlight, leaving the plants spindly or leggy. Our cold frames were slapped together and far from mouse-proof. Since Tex had handled the starts the year before, we were all just pilgrims when it came to handling the nursery.

When the starts were uppins, we noticed some of them losing their foliage. One morning, a few of our cups just had little stalks in them. It looked like we were growing toothpicks. Mice. By the time we realized what was going on and got the overdue mousetraps into the frames to fix the problem, we had lost over a hundred babies.

We slogged through whatever spring work we could accomplish in the wet weather but couldn't start tilling the soil until it was sufficiently dry. As a result, our starts became rootbound long before we were ready to plant. Not necessarily a fatal condition, but a situation a grower prefers to avoid.

Remembering all the arguments that went on, I have trouble believing we finished any work at all. Miraculously, given our nursery losses, by the early summer we had over nine hundred girls in the ground. We still had a mountain of work to do, and it wasn't getting any easier to get along with Moe, Larry, and Curly. At some point we split the camp in half. The LA guys went to a new campsite and tended the two patches on the south side of the road. Treeman Dan and I stayed at the old camp and tended the two patches on the north side. The situation was so acrimonious that the new guys even refused to come and ask my advice when they came up against a problem, so, as a result, a lot of their time was spent doing unnecessary work.

"Lowes, what the fuck is this?" I found Lowes putting in a tomato garden in a clearing behind our camp.

He looked at me with his typical contempt and snarled, "It's a tomato garden, what the fuck does it look like?"

"From here it looks like a tomato garden," I said sarcastically, "but from the air it's going to look like a pot patch. Besides, we're running out of water. How are you going to keep them alive?"

"I'll think of something." The guy was a real jerk.

"You're going to pull them out and 'phlage this mess or your dumb ass is on its way back to La La Land".

I could say whatever I wanted to, but there was no way I could make him actually *do* anything. When he realized that Tex would jump in his shit would worse than I did, he backed down and tore out the tomatoes.

Add to that, Richie Moonbeam was doing their tree work and had spent days thinning the trees just to the north of the patch where it had no effect whatsoever on the amount of light available to the plants.

Under a flag of truce, the warring factions had a quick meeting and decided that Richie should do something other than tree work. Lowes decided Richie should work with him installing the irrigation system.

What seemed like a good idea at the time set the table for another disaster. The two of them screwed it up so badly that it's a wonder any of the plants on the new side survived. The new patch was located on a steep and rugged hillside, and anyone with a basic understanding of gravity and the nature of water pressure should have been able design a system in their sleep.

The lines needed to run horizontally across the hillside so the water pressure would be about even from hole to hole. Their big fuck up was installing the water system so the lines ran up and down the hill, rather than across the hillside. The effect of this was that the water pressure was too high on one end of the line and there was no pressure at all on the other. The plants at the bottom of the patch were being drowned, while the plants at the top got no water at all and were in real danger of dying of thirst. When Tex finally realized what was going on, he blew a fuse and put me in charge of straightening things out.

Eventually, we found ourselves growing pot in a more or less commercial fashion. But dealing with the clowns continued to result in one land mine after another. Any chore that required real labor was typically put aside while the boys found something easy to do.

Instead of being the predicted pain in the ass, Jacques Canard, aka the "Royal Flush" with his all his shortcomings, ended up providing us with some much-needed comic relief. His reasons for not working became legendary. When it was Jacques' turn to rake leaves to use as mulch he informed us, "Hah yam a partneer, hand hah do not mulsh." That became our battle cry for the year.

Beyond all the petty squabbles and turf wars, we were finding out how much sunshine mattered to the girls. The Campaign Against Marijuana Planting (CAMP) was in its second year, and the aerial surveillance had increased noticeably. Unfortunately, keeping the plants hidden from the snoops kept the plants out of the sunshine as well. Instead of the big, uniform crop we had the year before, we found our plants struggling just to get going. In the end, some made it and some didn't. To add injury to insult, almost a hundred of our plants turned into hermaphrodites and had to be pulled out before they pollinated themselves and the rest of the crop.

Whatever was going on genetically that year, it wasn't good. By the end of August, we were down to fewer than 850 girls and many, maybe a couple of hundred of them, were real runts.

I once read something in the Pot Growers Bible by Ed Rosenthal, that explained how we got so many females the year before. What I think happened was that someone screwed up two years earlier combining two incompatible strains. When this happens, a phenomenon called "hybrid vigor" occurs resulting in plants that display all the positive traits of both strains. We got lucky that first year, but because we lost the pure breeding strain, we were now seeing some strange plants.

As September rolled around, we were still hoping to get five or six hundred pounds of decent bud and would need a much bigger crew than we had the first year. We hired a builder from Monterey who added a couple of rooms onto the side of the school bus. By the end of harvest the crew grew to almost twenty.

This led to some classic scenes. We sent the cook and two pickers to Safeway with six hundred dollars, and they brought back two dollars in change. They pulled four shopping carts up to the check stand; one full of alcohol and another full of Hagen Daz ice cream and Mystic Mint cookies. The other two were filled with top shelf items such as steaks and fresh salmon, the best shit they had and lots of it. Their haul was so outrageous that when the manager saw what they were buying he came out of the office, bagged their groceries, and helped them load it all into the truck.

Harvest that year was a two-month long party. We had thirteen pickers and a few of them were quite good-looking women. It's amazing the transformation that takes place when women come on the scene. By the end of the summer, the crew had become crusty creatures of the woods but the day the first pickers arrived, it was back to clean clothes, close shaves, and a more civil way of behaving.

For all the extra manpower, grief, and work, we ended up with only eighty-three more pounds of pot than the year before. Not exactly chicken feed, but the fact that the pie was being cut six ways instead of three meant my share was about $30,000 less. Working for Tex meant taking a fair amount of abuse and, coupled with having to deal with the Stooges, it became clear that it was time to get my own place. To his credit, Tex acknowledged the fact that he had hired losers and was stuck with them, but he offered to lend me twenty grand to buy land and get my own place started if I wanted out. I couldn't say yes fast enough.

That's how I became a Goomba myself, deepening my roots in the profession I loved and getting in a whole lot deeper than I ever expected.

PART II

THE NEXT LEVEL

Chapter 6

Honey Bear

Buying property with the express intent of growing pot is racked with peril. For starters, depending on the size of your down payment for the land and the amount of equipment you need to buy, the first year could easily cost fifty thousand dollars. The first year at Serenity Park we spent sixty grand, but Tex had the money to spend. Serenity was a big piece of property and we didn't even have a pickup truck when we started. I planned to grow on a much smaller scale, two hundred and fifty plants at the most, but even then, I was looking at a minimum investment of thirty long ones to get up and running. That was a hefty ante. At least I didn't have to buy a truck, since the money I made at Serenity Park had provided me with a big, burly, blue Ford F-250 4x4 pickup that soon became known as Big Blue.

There were several question marks going in, and I wouldn't know the answers to most of them until harvest. Was the place a "hot spot"? CAMP—the Campaign Against Marijuana Planting— seemed to go where the fishing was good. Would my neighbors be asshole rednecks? Was my land a favorite spot for hunters? Were any of my neighbors planning a timber harvest? If that happened, the woods would be crawling with woodchucks from the Bureau of Land Management. Was the terrain suitable? Was there enough cover? The patch, the living scene, the parking scene, the drying and picking sheds all had to be hidden from the aerial snoops. Beyond all that, would the water be sufficient? Without water, I wouldn't be a pot grower, just a smelly, dirty guy crawling around on a hillside.

Speaking of water, the problem with water in Northern California was that it's seasonal and could vary from year to year. During a typical winter water was everywhere. Wells were full, springs were gushing, and streams were running. In the spring, when the plants were small and didn't need much water, there was typically plenty to go around. By the end of July when the plants were huge and needed a lot of water, sources were starting to dry up. Ultimately, it's what your water supply looked like in August that was important.

Bottom line, I was looking for land over the winter and had to take the seller's word for how great their water supply was. Caveat emptor and I'll leave it at that.

The phone rang on a Sunday morning. It was Terry the realtor. I was wrestling with the kids in the rec room and it took me a minute to answer.

"I didn't wake you up, did I?" he said.

"Who's this?"

"Terry Sharpe. I've got a place for you to look at."

"Oh. Hi Terry. The kids are making so much noise I couldn't hear you." I turned to Carrie. "Honey, see if you can quiet the kids down a little."

"C'mon you guys, let's go make breakfast." Carrie got the dog and pony show headed for the kitchen.

"Ok, what do you have?"

"Eighty acres near Willits. My partner has walked it and says it's real pretty."

"How much?"

"I got it written down here somewhere." A few seconds passed and I could hear Terry shuffling papers on his desk. "Sorry, I've been looking at so many places in the last couple of days it's hard to keep 'em all straight. Here it is. They're asking sixty."

"When can I see it?" I asked.

"I'll be in Willits this afternoon. I won't have time to walk the land with you, but I'll take you to the property line and show you where the flags start. John says it's well marked."

I didn't want to hurt Terry's feelings, but the last thing I wanted to do was have him with me while I walked the land. A pot grower had different concerns than the average land buyer. "Sounds great Terry. Where do you want to meet?"

"There's a little diner on Commercial Street. I can't remember the name but it's right off 101."

I knew the place. The locals called it "The Greasy Spoon." I asked him for a few more details, but he didn't know much about the place. The real estate blurb said it had water. We agreed to meet at noon and I hung up the phone.

I walked into the kitchen to get another cup of coffee. "Has Terry found something?" Carrie asked.

"Yeah, eighty acres." I was pulling on my hiking boots. "And it sounds like it's right behind Serenity Park."

Recalling my misadventures with the Three Stooges, she said "Oh great," her voice dripping with sarcasm, "Now you get to be near your friends."

"It's OK. It's good to know who your neighbors are. Might be close as the crow flies, but it's a long way around if you're driving."

I had a better idea where we were going than Terry did as I followed him east from Willits on the road past Serenity Park. We drove over a ridge between two large hills and then down into a beautiful rolling meadow. I knew the road well but followed Terry back and forth a few times while he figured out the landmarks that his partner had given him. He finally decided the parcel was up a long dirt road heading north. We followed the road until we came to an unlocked gate that fit the description he'd been given.

That's how I found Honey Bear.

The road was washed out about halfway up the hill, but other than that I saw I could easily move right in and get to work. I met the owner who assured me that the place had seven springs and that water would be the least of my problems. Knowing the cost of roadwork, I knocked eight grand off the asking price and the owner accepted. I thought I'd name the place Seven Springs, but the first day I was on the land I saw a medium-sized black bear trying to get honey from a beehive in a large oak tree, and the name Honey Bear stuck.

It turned out that the seven springs were only a figment of the old owner's imagination. By the first of June, they had all dried up and I was stuck between a rock and a hard, very dry place. It was too late to drill a well. By the time I could get one in and operational, my girls would be dead. The only quick option was to find a way to haul water with Big Blue. Luckily, I wasn't the first person in the history of the world to need to haul water in his pickup truck, and some clever manufacturer was making collapsible water tanks just for that purpose. I bought the 500-gallon size and a 5,000 gallon an hour transfer pump and was back in business.

The search for water became the central problem as the summer wore on and the hills became increasingly parched. The nightly search was time-consuming and dangerous. My crew and I didn't know if we were snaking other growers out of their water, if we were fucking with ranchers whose cows depended on it, or if we'd be discovered by some busybody asshole who would rat us out. We ended up visiting several different waterholes on a rotating basis.

At least once a night, but usually twice, I would head out around midnight and scout a place to pirate some water. I'd four-wheel down a streambed to a water hole and begin the drill. My tender would hop out with the pump and connect the in-line, toss it into the water, then I'd fill a five-gallon bucket with water and prime the pump. We'd then start up the pump and about six minutes later the bag would be holding a little over five hundred gallons of water. Those first few minutes were always nerve-wracking. The pump didn't make much noise but in the moonlit silence of the California backwoods it sounded like a diesel truck. Nevertheless, the bottom line in this business was you did what you had to do.

Meanwhile, Serenity Park had turned into a real clown show. Tex never believed my accounts of the Three Stooges and was sure that it had to do with personality clashes between me and the boys and everything would be fine when I was away from the scene. Well, it turned out that they were even bigger hoseheads to Tex than they were to me. They didn't understand Tex's low threshold for taking shit from people and after the first couple of meetings at the start of the year, he was so disgusted with them that he fired their dumb asses and sold the place to one of his associates. I would have paid money to see the looks on their faces as those oafs were shown the gate.

The guy Tex sold Serenity to was the biggest operator of pot farms that I had ever heard about. R.O. Mosby was doing to the pot business what McDonalds had done to the hamburger business. R.O. had over ten farms and was rumored to have yearly sales of over two million dollars, yet, to look at the guy, you'd think he was a down-on-his-luck Hollywood character actor. He was large and rough around the edges, but the feature that a person was most likely to remember him by was his blue glass eye. His one real eye was brown and the combination of the two was pretty unsettling. He had a habit of staring at the person he was talking to with the glass eye while looking away with his good eye. I never knew why he had a blue glass eye, but he definitely kept people on edge. Another enigma about R.O. was that nobody knew what the initials "R.O." stood for. But he hauled tons of green bud around and according to Tex, ran the tightest ship in the industry.

I remember the first time I heard about him. Tex mentioned his name in passing the first year we grew together. His exact words were, "I know a guy named R.O. Mosby and he's the sweetest guy you'll ever meet, but if you double-cross him, he'll take you into the woods and blow you away." With Tex you never knew if he was talking literally or figuratively, or if he was just puffing shit up. In this case, I was pretty sure that he was exaggerating, but the story and the name R.O. Mosby stayed with me, nonetheless. It was obvious to me that he was Tex's role model.

R.O. was from Atlanta, Georgia and had connections to many of the old hillbilly families in the rural south. He hired a pretty rough crew that looked like they were straight out of the movie, Deliverance. His walking boss, Vernon Sheffield, was a real character. Unlike R.O., he had monochrome brown eyes that looked like the end of a double-barreled shotgun. They appeared to be set just a smidge too close together and his eye sockets looked like they were about twice as big as they needed to be. His eyebrows were nearly hairless and that added to the illusion of size. His eyeballs looked big too, and you could always see the whites of his eyes completely surrounding his irises. Due to his bizarre and unsettling features, we nicknamed the guy "Bunny Eyes." The three roughnecks he brought with him to do the tending we called Billy Joe, Billy Bob, and Billy Wayne. They became known as "The Billys," but sometimes we called them the "Killer Bees." It was a bit of a put-down, but they seemed to take it in the good humor that it was meant, and even started referring to Vernon as Bunny Eyes.

We were all in the same business and we knew that from time to time we'd have to help each other out. Serenity Park wasn't the only farm on the hill anymore. Two others had started in the second year, and a fourth was starting this third spring. There was a lot of horseplay and good-natured banter between the various farms, and even the occasional card game.

R.O. had a larger-than-life reputation, so I just assumed he would run a first-class operation. But I soon learned that in this business, never assume anything.

The four guys R.O. hired didn't seem to be getting their books from the main branch of the library. Taken together, I doubt that their IQs broke 200, but they possessed a Southern graciousness and charm that was disarming. Whenever you met one of them on the road, he'd put a cold beer in your hand and want to chew your ear off. We figured that being farm boys and having R.O.'s unlimited resources and experience to help them along, Serenity Park would be Fat City by harvest time.

Serenity Park had an old ranch house by the main gate that we used as a collective security post and a place to hang out and drink beer. The acreage by the gate wasn't used for growing pot, and there was a radio warning system in place, so if the storm troopers ever invaded, the folks up the hill could be alerted and would have a few minutes to clear out.

Friends of mine, Kurt and Jenny Gergen, rented the house and lived there with their young son, Casey. Through them I kept apprised of the goings on with the rest of the ranch. Unfortunately, Casey was going through some serious medical problems. The poor guy was born a preemie and having a hard time breathing. He was finally diagnosed with something called tracheomalacia and by the end of the summer was admitted to the pediatric hospital at the University of California in San Francisco. Kurt and Jenny asked if I would stay in the house at night while they were gone in exchange for using their water, an offer I immediately accepted. It wasn't too far a drive from my place and the water was limitless. I could fill the truck up with their garden hose and make as many runs as I wanted. To me it looked like a godsend. Two loads a day was a thousand gallons, about right for my needs.

During that period I got to know R.O. pretty well. It was apparent that his crew was making the Stooges look good, a nearly impossible feat. The stories coming off the hill that year had mostly to do with the antics of The Billy Club.

The guys were backwoods slobs who lived in a world of filth. Dirty dishes, clothes, and general crappus piled up everywhere. They never took their trash out, and by June the cool little scene we had built in the woods was so strewn with garbage that I finally stopped going by to visit. The Billys liked their scene this way because it drew the bears in and they considered the ranch their private game preserve. They were shooting bears without game tags, poaching deer with bows and arrows, and fishing in a creek where salmon spawned. Basically, real unconscious redneck shit. They turned one ranch pond into a swim club, complete with lounge chairs and a blue and white umbrella. When they weren't hunting or fishing, they were racing Four Trax Honda ATVs around the ranch.

On those rare occasions when they did work, they drove their ATVs right up to the patches so that after a while a blind man without a cane could find their gardens. Considering that work was their last priority, the fact that their crop turned out looking like a bonsai garden shouldn't have been too surprising, but the biggest fuck-up was the one that left me wondering about R.O. as much as it made me wonder about his help. At some point he should have known his crew was out to lunch. They wore their ignorance like a badge of honor but by the time R.O. figured out he'd been royally hosed it was too late to do anything about it.

In a nutshell, the chuckleheads hadn't sexed their starts. To virtually guarantee a disappointing result they hadn't planted two to a hole either. R.O. thought he had a one-thousand plant operation going on but once he realized the plants hadn't been sexed, it turned into a five hundred plant op—ouch. That's like leaving the gate open and having a herd of deer come in and eat half your crop. The Billys had told R.O. that they knew something about growing marijuana, but in my book, it was the Goomba who had the responsibility to make sure he's not being bullshitted.

By pure chance I was at the ranch gatehouse on the day R.O. found out that half his crop was likely to be male. I thought he was going to have a heart attack. I'd been in the kitchen getting a beer when I noticed him in the driveway. He was in such a raging state that when I first saw him, I knew something big had come down. He was hunched over, exploding sweat and slapping himself on the thighs. His face was puffy and red. For a minute I thought he was choking and I ran out thinking I would have to give him a Heimlich squeeze. He straightened up and looked at me as if he didn't know who I was. Unsure of what to do, I offered him my beer. He held it for a minute with a quizzical look on his face, and then threw it with such vengeance against the porch steps that it exploded into powder-size fragments of glass and foam.

"Those ignorant crackers!" he spit the words out dripping with bile. "Those backwoods motherfuckin' piles of dog shit." Extremely scatological stuff. I didn't know what to say, R.O. was clearly freaking out.

"They didn't sex the fucking starts!" When he started talking about the plants, it became clear to me that this was the first time all summer that he'd seen the gardens. I thought he was going to break down and cry. "The crop is half male and the plants aren't anywhere near waist high!"

I was afraid to say anything, so I just nodded sympathetically while R.O. raged on. I thought a guy with all he had going on could have shrugged his shoulders and written the year off, but he wasn't wired that way. I could see right away that he was at war with his help and trouble loomed. He got back into his truck and sped up the hill. I shrugged it off. I was busy with my own problems and as the summer passed, his situation simmered beyond my view.

My plants never fully recovered from the weeks of water stress in early June, but they were well formed, even if they were a little on the small side. The strain was kick-ass, the plants had good sun, and they were putting on some tasty looking buds. Finally, I could think positively. It was my first year with my own property and I figured that by next spring I'd have a pond built, a well drilled, or both, and I'd be in a good position for the following season.

The way I saw it I was working in my chosen field, doing work that I loved to do on an absolutely beautiful piece of property, so if the money was good rather than great it didn't bother me much.

It surprised and saddened me that more of the guys I was working around didn't see it that way. Ever since pot farming had become such a big money scene, there was an accompanying element of gold fever. The hippie in me wondered what had happened. Weren't we all supposed to be brothers, working for our Mother Earth to bring magic and medicine to the people of the world? What a Pollyanna pipe dream pile of horseshit that was. The truth was, most growers were in it only for the money.

As harvest started, the rumors filtering down from Serenity Park indicated that the year was a total waste as far as R.O. Mosby's crop was concerned. As well as being totally incompetent as growers, The Billys were also drunk and fighting most of the time. I was hearing stories along the lines of how Billy Bob was going to kill Billy Joe for stealing the last of his meth, and that the last meeting with R.O. broke up when Billy Wayne chased Bunny Eyes down the driveway with a shotgun. Bunny had called Wayne's girlfriend a whore, the irony being that she was that really was a whore. She worked in a whorehouse in Nevada and only came to see him once a month when she was having her period. You'd think that the kind of guy who had a whore for a girlfriend would have thicker skin, but he loved her. Enough said.

Also, R.O. told me he was dealing with some heavy shit in his life, and only some of it pertained to growing pot. Beyond the ten farms that he owned, he had an extensive real estate portfolio and was in the middle of a lawsuit with Bank of America. Basically, his financial empire was coming apart at the seams and he was stressing out big time.

It was early October. Harvest had arrived and because my crop was so small, my year was nearly over. I didn't need the water anymore, but I was still using the gatehouse from time to time. Kurt and Jenny were still in San Francisco taking care of their son, so a few of us took turns spending the night at their house. At harvest time security became a very big deal so every night someone was at house, watching the gate and manning the CB radio in case the shit

hit the fan. My crew was small and my tenders had a pretty good handle on things, so I could come and go from my farm freely.

I was at the gatehouse late one night polishing off a six pack and watching The Shining on the VCR when R.O. showed up again. He asked me how I was doing I said, "Things could be better Lloyd, things could be a whole lot better."

I could tell by his blank stare that he didn't get my comment, so I added, "It's a line out of the movie I'm watching."

R.O. just waved it off with a distant look on his face. Something was up.

It was almost midnight but I was wide awake and happy to have some company. "You want a cold one R.O.?" I started rummaging through the fridge.

"OK, but it'll have to be a quick."

He flopped down on the sofa. I could tell he didn't want to have to deal with his crew that night. I found a bottle of Heineken and popped the cap off using the plastic end of a Bic lighter for an opener. He sucked the beer down in one long pull then gazed at the empty bottle and belched. "Look," he said, "I gotta go, but you could do me a favor."

At that time I was still a relative neophyte whereas R.O. was an icon among growers, so I was more than happy to help him out. "Sure," I said. "What do you need?"

"Would you go with me up to Serenity? I might have to leave in a hurry and you could sit in the truck." Then he added, "It's all right. You won't be in any danger."

If there wasn't any danger then why did he want me along? A question that in hindsight I should have asked him, but I wasn't thinking too clearly at that moment. In those heady days, I felt invincible. Whatever realm existed, I considered R.O. one of the Kings, so I said, "Sure, just give me a minute to get ready."

I could have gone along in the sweatpants I was wearing, but for some reason decided to change into my blue jeans. It was one of those insignificant actions that you do without thinking. But looking back on that night's events, that seemingly insignificant action may have saved my life.

The moon was full and directly overhead. The first full moon after the autumn equinox is the harvest moon and, owing to the path the moon takes through the night sky during that part of the year, it seems much brighter than it does at other times. In the old days the farmers found that it was bright enough to harvest their crops by, and they would work around the clock. Pot growers called it the "rip-off moon," and the smart ones stayed close to their patches for a few nights until it passed. The night air was cooler than I thought it would be, and wearing only a sweatshirt I had a notion to go back for a light jacket, but since I was going to stay in the truck I decided to forgo it. I climbed in behind the wheel but R.O. told me to slide over. He said we'd switch when he parked up top.

A barn owl flew across the headlights as we drove along the farmyard fence. I remember telling R.O. that I wasn't superstitious but being the full moon and all, I was glad it was an owl and not a raven. R.O. was preoccupied and I think we went the rest of the way lost in our own thoughts.

The road snaked up a steep hill through some sizable second-growth Doug firs and a blend of stately oaks and magical madrones. Halfway to the top of the ridge the terrain leveled out and we passed a rolling meadow. The road to Serenity Park was a hard right at the end of the first meadow and after making the turn, a quick left as the road dipped down a small incline and disappeared into a thicket. We stopped where a cable crossed the road, twenty yards or so past the first bend. Pulled between two posts, it formed a makeshift gate. On the driver's end of the cable was a combination lock, hooked to the post under a large "No Trespassing" sign. With a grunt, R.O. got out of the truck. He started to walk around the open door, and as I began to ask him if he wanted a flashlight he spun around and grabbed the steering wheel. My first thought was that he was goofing off, fucking with me, until the first shot went off catching him square in the shoulder and standing him up straight.

He looked back at me with a disbelieving face, and the scene began playing in slow motion. R.O had been hit with a shotgun blast! The pellets caught him on the shoulder in a spray pattern, as little dots of red covered his shoulder and chest. He had a dazed look on his face. The jolt must have knocked him unconscious.

I must have thought I was in a fucking movie, never stopping to think of myself as a witness. Another blast! The second shot was choked down and got him just behind the right eye. The back of his head exploded like a bloody sausage ejaculation, and his famous glass eye popped out and rolled across the dashboard. This macabre scene seemed frozen in time. The notion that I was also in peril seemed to take forever to dawn on me.

Seeing Bunny Eyes lean over the bloody body whisked me back into reality. Bunny apparently was expecting R.O. to come alone and didn't notice me until he tossed a sawed-off shotgun onto the front seat of the truck. I grabbed the gun and the door handle at the same time, but he grabbed the gun too. Rather than have a tug-of-war with the guy, I let go of it, jumped out of the truck, and started to run. I had only taken a few strides when Billy Wayne appeared from behind the truck with a tree branch. As it cracked on the side of my head, my world went black.

When I came to, I was next to the bloody mess formerly known as R.O. Mosby in the back of his own truck, bouncing slowly down the road below The Billys' cabin. R.O.'s head was busted to pieces and parts of his skull were hanging open like trap doors held hinged by flesh and gristle. I say "came to," but in reality I was closer to being unconscious than I was conscious. I heard talking, but I didn't know what the words meant. Before I could clear my head, the truck stopped and The Billys got out.

I heard the tailgate open and was dragged by my ankles out of the back of the truck like a sack of garbage. My head hit the bumper on the way down and I landed on the road in a heap. In pain, but conscious, I kept from moaning thinking that my chances of escape were better if they thought I was out cold. When they dragged R.O.

out of the truck he landed on top of me. I heard the truck drive away. Whoever stayed behind grabbed R.O. and started dragging him into the woods.

When I thought I was alone, I tried to stand up. I was semi-conscious but I couldn't get my balance and my first few attempts were unsuccessful. Spinning and falling, I crawled a few yards and tried again. This time I was successful, but it had taken too long, and I heard somebody returning. I tried to run and managed to get a short distance down the road, but my head was bleeding like hell and the blood was getting into my eyes, causing them to burn and making it impossible to see where I was going. I was caught before I made it fifty feet and pretended to pass out, but they weren't buying it and clubbed me again. This night was really starting to suck.

Chapter 7

Barrels

I knew right away where I was—the barrel yard I'd created the first year I worked at Serenity Park. I could sneak a few peeks and see what they were doing but didn't want to have my head bashed again so I played dead. Having been knocked unconscious twice it was amazing that I was even coherent at all. I must have been running on pure adrenaline. Panic washed over me in waves. I was determined to play 'possum for as long as I could, but my heart was pounding and just lying still was an effort. Maybe they would leave me there, but probably not. I thought if they just stuck me in the barrel thinking I was already a goner, I might find a way to get out.

Because of his bulk, they were having trouble getting R.O. into the barrel. Bunny Eyes was a Nam vet who still exhibited traces of "The Thousand-Yard Stare" and I'd heard that he slept with a knife under his pillow. Awake, he always wore a skinning knife. I had already begun to suspect the guy had a black hole where his soul used to be, but seeing him brandish that blade in the moonlight, he seemed absolutely demonic. He cut the clothes off R.O. like a surgeon in a field hospital. Naked, R.O.'s shoulders, stomach, and hips still resisted going into the barrel, but they squeezed him a little bit at a time until they finally stomped on his ass to finish forcing R.O. through the opening.

He was still too tall for his tomb. R.O.'s lower legs wouldn't fit so Bunny started filleting his legs like a butcher dressing a fresh carcass. Bunny lopped off his kneecaps and then severed the tendons and ligaments that connected R.O.'s legs at the knee. Once both legs were cut off and the pieces stuffed into the barrel, I closed my eyes and kept them closed. I knew it was my turn next, and I prayed they wouldn't do anything more than put me in the ground. From there I could figure out what to do.

I could hear them screwing the lid onto R.O.'s barrel when Bunny Eyes said to one of The Billys, "Finish the other guy off." Hearing that, I wanted to get up and run, but by now I was paralyzed with fear. I waited to be shot or stabbed, and with each shallow breath I could smell and taste the dust I was laying on, oddly reminding me of my childhood on the farm. I really must have been losing it. Why in the hell would I think of that?

In a moment of clarity, I thought to get up and run but it was too late. I felt myself being grabbed by the arms and dragged across the ground, and knew I was heading for a barrel. I felt the sharp edge of the opening as I was dragged across it. I didn't want to go in headfirst like R.O. so I let my lower legs flop into it as I was being pulled across, and Billy dropped me in. I slithered into the barrel like an eel.

"I told you to dust him!" snarled Bunny Eyes. "Here."

It sounded like Bunny Eyes had thrown the shotgun to Billy, who dropped it.

"Load this and finish him," Bunny Eyes was almost shouting. "You brought some shells, I hope. I asked you to bring the fucking shells, didn't I?"

"I b-b-brought 'em B-B-Bunny," Billy Wayne stammered.

"Then load the fuckin' thing and get it over with."

"But B-Bun…" Billy Wayne hesitated. I don't think he was as committed to doing me in as Bunny Eyes was.

"It's not personal son, it's business," Bunny Eyes interrupted.

The relativity of time was never so clear as it was over those next few moments. All along I'd kept some vague hope alive that somehow they were going to leave me in a position to save myself, but now I realized I was finished. I was nearly unconscious, and don't know if I would have reacted any differently if I hadn't taken the knocks to the head. But a weird feeling of acceptance and surrender came over me as the world turned to pixels of color then began to fade.

The blast was so loud I didn't hear it, but a moment later I felt its echo and the stinging heat in my hair. I remember thinking, "Wow, pain's different when you're dead."

The blast left me nearly deaf. I heard Bunny Eyes yelling, but it seemed a long way away, very faint, and the thought went through my mind, "I'm dead, what's he doing here?" Slowly I realized that I hadn't been shot after all.

"Jesus! I fuckin' can't believe you!" he yelled at Billy Wayne. Bunny Eyes flew into a rage. "You used the booby trap shells!" I was sure Bunny was going to reach down into the barrel and start stabbing me, so I sank as deep as I could. I guess he didn't think of that.

"Just screw the fuckin' lid on the thing. I got another idea. He ain't git'n away."

The barrel went black and I could hear the plastic ring being turned tight. My would-be tomb was absolutely dark and reeked of vinegar. Sealed in a barrel, with limited air and no room to move, I should have panicked. But for the first time that night since R.O. had picked me up at the gatehouse I felt safe. Until the lid went on the barrel I was sure they were still going to do me in somehow, but now my only enemy was an inanimate object. At that point I had two things going in my favor. One was that the barrel was made out of plastic. And two, they hadn't frisked me and found the Swiss army knife that was in my pocket. Thank God I'd changed my pants!

I felt the knife in my right front pocket, but I couldn't reach it with my right arm so I had to try and get to it with my left hand.

The way I'd landed in the barrel pushed my knees up under my chin and creased the pocket that the knife was in. To remove it seemed at first an impossible task, but I tugged and pulled and massaged the knife until it slowly squeezed out of my pocket. Even with the knife in my hand, I didn't know if I could cut the lid with it. I was nearly unconscious. I had the mother of all headaches. Every motion was agony but as the air disappeared, and as I lost more blood, I became disoriented. Nonetheless, I struggled and kept trying, and with some difficulty I managed to open the knife and start cutting at the barrel lid. One good thing about a situation like this is you stay focused.

The plastic was thick and hard, and the knife was prone to closing when I least expected it. It took some time, but I was able to poke a small hole in the lid before the blade broke. I used to have a big momma Swiss Army knife, but when I lost it I opted for a smaller, more streamlined model. The big one had two knife blades and a saw. If I'd had that knife with me, right now I'd be free. And if chickens carried 45s they wouldn't worry about red-tail hawks. I was fucked and knew it. All that was left at my disposal was a knife with a cheesy little pair of scissors and a can opener.

The scissors were too lightweight to help, but I figured I might get something going with the can opener. I stuck it in the hole that I'd managed to start but didn't have much luck making the hole any bigger. Then I remembered about the lighter in my left front pocket, and if I could get it out, I might be able to soften the plastic.

This pocket was really pinched off and at first I couldn't manage to budge the lighter. I was getting a little fresh air through the tiny hole, but not enough. It seemed as though I was fighting a losing battle but I thought of Carrie and my kids and knew I couldn't quit. By then the shock was wearing off and the adrenaline was kicking in. I went from feeling defeated, to being pissed-off. Fuck these crackers, I'm getting out of here!

I rested for a while and remembered the scissors. Moving inside that little hellhole was difficult, but I managed to open the scissors and manipulate them toward my left pants pocket. I was able to cut a hole in the pocket and free my lighter, suffering a few nicks to my leg during the process. It took a couple of minutes, but by softening the plastic with the lighter I was able to open the hole large enough to gulp down some much-needed fresh air. For the first time since this whole ordeal began, I allowed myself the belief that I was going to survive.

In the distance I could hear the sound of a diesel motor snorting to life, but what that meant wasn't immediately clear. I kept hacking at the plastic with the remaining small nub of the blade and the can opener. By the time the hole was big enough for me to get my hand through it, the noise of the diesel was getting louder and I came to the sickening realization that they were going to bury R.O. and me using the ranch caterpillar. Along with the sound of the growling engine I could hear the treads of the Cat as they squeaked and clanked on the road above.

By the time I had the hole big enough to get my arm through the lid and my hand on the ring that held it in place, it sounded as though the Cat had turned off the road. I could hear the sounds of tree limbs cracking. Small trees and bushes adjacent to the area were beginning to fall around the barrel. He was close, damn it! Frantically and with some difficulty, I unscrewed the lid and pulled myself out of the barrel just as the Cat pushed a pile of bushes on top of me. When the machine started backing up to get a blade full of earth, I forced myself through the brush that covered my would-be tomb and fled across the clearing into some whitethorn bushes. Fortunately, any noise I made was covered by the sound of the Cat. Scrambling on all fours as fast as I could, I cursed myself for not putting the lid back on, but under the circumstances, I was happy to be alive. I hoped that with a good enough head start I'd be able to get away.

I was about one hundred yards away when Bunny Eyes shut the motor off and lept off the machine.

"He got away!" He shouted as he ran back the way he'd come. "Wayne, run back to camp and get everybody! He got away! Wayne, you fucker, where are you?" Bunny's voice was fading as he ran farther up the road.

Since he didn't have a flashlight or a gun, I gained a few more minutes head start. On my feet now and running headlong through the underbrush, I could hear shouting from the direction of the camp, followed by the sound of a pickup truck starting.

I busted through the last of the whitethorn and into a clearing where I could do some open field running but knew my footprints would leave a distinct trail and these boys were hunters. At least I was on familiar ground and knew that abutting the clearing was a deep ravine.

The ravine raged torrents of water during the rainy season but would be bone dry by now. It occurred to me that if I could make it to the there, I could walk on the rocks without leaving a trail, so I ran to the edge and looked down. The walls of the ravine were dirt and gravel, and it was almost a sheer drop to the rocks about 15 feet below. There was nothing to hold onto so I lowered myself over the edge and let go. I tried to slow my fall and I still landed pretty hard but didn't break anything and was quickly back on my feet. My intent was to stay in the ravine and haul ass down the hill, but climbing over the rocks in the creek bed was slow going and I soon realized I wasn't going to outrun my pursuers. So instead of continuing down the ravine, I decided to double back.

Adrenaline is great for a burst, but my burst had passed long ago. I was spent. My lungs were on fire, my legs were cramping, and my side hurt so much it seemed as though my ribs were tying themselves in knots.

I heard The Billys racing down the road from camp and skid to a stop. Doors slammed and Bunny Eyes started barking orders. Above me, I could see an occasional beam of a flashlight sweeping the hillside. They were fanning out looking for my trail. My heart was pounding but I forced myself on.

At that point I was soaked in blood and my head was still leaking like a broken faucet. Heading down the ravine, I took off my soaked shirt and wrung some of the blood out of it, intentionally leaving a trail of drops for them to follow. After about fifty yards or so I scrambled up the embankment on the other side, taking pains to see that I disturbed as much ground as I could, making it look like I had climbed out of the ravine and disappeared into the woods. Then I wrapped the shirt around my head to stop as much of the bleeding as I could, and hustled back up the ravine knowing I needed to get as far away as possible before they found my false trail.

I heard the excited shouts of one of The Billys and knew he'd found my footprints across the meadow. Damn it—they were close! Figuring I had a few minutes before they would all be together, I forced myself to continue up the ravine. It was harder and much slower going up. I knew I had to make it past where I had entered the ravine because that's where my false trail started. At that point I didn't know exactly where I was but could hear them busting through the whitethorn into the meadow, so I crawled into a small cave on the side of the ravine.

Seconds later, they were at the edge standing right above me. I could see their moonlit shadows in the creek bed. Some small pebbles started raining down on me from above, and for one terrifying moment thought I'd been discovered. But they started walking again, following the rim and searching for an easier way in.

They climbed into the ravine about twenty or thirty feet below me, and immediately found the trail of blood. I'd hidden myself as well as I could in the shadows and looking down the ravine I saw all four of them with their flashlights. If they'd turned their lights around I would have been in plain sight, but they must have been convinced I was heading down the hill. Still fearing for my life, I held my breath and watched them disappear down the ravine.

When they were past the first turn, I quietly started climbing again. I didn't know how long my deception would work but didn't think it would be for long. I needed to climb out of the ravine without leaving a trail and took the first opportunity that presented itself. A fallen doug fir had created a makeshift ladder so I hoisted myself up its branches and escaped the ravine. No longer worried about leaving a trail, I just wanted to get the fuck out of there.

I hobbled up the hill for a while, but the terrain was steep and I needed to rest often. Due to my weakened state, I decided to stop climbing and walk side-hill. Going north made no sense since it would take me farther onto The Billys' piece of land. That meant going south was my only option but that would take me back to the barrel area, pretty much the last place on Earth that I wanted to be. Looking down the hill I could see a flashlight turn my way and guessed they were fanning out again, searching for my trail. Exhausted and in shock, I forced myself back into the whitethorn. I didn't pick a very good spot to enter, and for the most part had to crawl. If I was getting a second wind, it was maybe my third or fourth one. Finally, I found an animal trail and started to make better time. Luckily, before it petered out it crossed The Billys' driveway. Thinking I was well ahead of my pursuers, I ran down the hill as fast as I could.

I was only fifty or a hundred yards around the first bend in the road when I stumbled upon their truck, an early to mid-sixties Ford. Not surprisingly, they hadn't seen fit to leave the keys in it for me, but it was a stick shift and thanks to my days as a teenage rascal, I knew I could hot-wire the thing. The truck was a real pile of crap that had been wrecked at least once and I had to jimmy the hood to get it open. It finally opened with a loud metallic screech. Worried that I'd given myself away, I yanked a piece of wire from the horn and tried to rip it from the firewall, but it resisted my efforts. Then I noticed a crack in the fender well, stuffed the wire in it and pulled. It finally cut loose and I crammed the last few inches back into the crack, then pulled the wire again to strip the insulation off. It took a few frantic attempts, but finally worked. Next, I wrapped the bare wire around the positive side of the battery and hooked the other end to the coil. Glancing through the driver's window I saw that the dash lights had come on, so I quickly closed the hood and jumped behind the wheel.

I could hear a commotion in the woods behind me and sensed that the boys were close. The road slanted downward, but not steeply, and as I took the brake off the truck it reluctantly began to roll. I didn't want to pop the clutch too quickly but when Billy Bob and Billy Wayne appeared in the rearview mirror, running flat out and closing fast, I knew it was now or never. I slammed the truck into second gear, popped the clutch, and floored the accelerator. The engine roared to life!

At that instant, Bunny Eyes busted through the thicket next to the truck. With his shotgun in his right hand, he grabbed the side of the camper shell with his left hand and pulled himself onto the step side behind the cab. Luckily, he couldn't shoot me through the back window because the shell was in his way and the passenger-side window was rolled up.

I could see his reflection in the side mirror. Hanging on to the camper shell, he cocked his gun, aimed, and fired. That first shot took out the passenger side window. He leaned forward, put his gun through the window and took aim. He fired, but by then we'd reached the gate where R.O. had been blown away and I was able to scrape Bunny off by sideswiping the gate post. His shot took out the windshield, but miraculously it missed me.

I don't know if I killed him or not but suspected that in the future, he'd have some serious trouble maintaining an erection. Reaching the main ranch road, I was going so fast that I nearly spun out turning the corner but calmed myself enough to drive down the hill without incident. In retrospect, I should have continued up the hill to one of the other farms to get help, but wasn't thinking clearly, if at all. Running on fumes, my life on the line, I pushed on.

Chapter 8

Shadows

Five minutes later I was back at the gatehouse. The moon had settled behind the hills to the west and I noticed storm clouds gathering. It was dark, quiet and I was covered in sweat and blood. It must have been about three in the morning.

The cool water in the creek called to me, but I couldn't stop yet. I put the truck in the barn, closed the door, hustled to the end of the driveway, and opened the main ranch gate. If The Billys came down, maybe they would think I was gone.

I knew Curt had an old revolver somewhere. I went into the gatehouse and found the gun but it didn't make me feel any safer. The cold weight of it was a stark reminder of the nightmare I was living. My mind refused to accept what had just gone down. Like I said before, I wasn't a criminal, just an outlaw pot grower. At worst, I was a space case caught between a contradiction and hypocrisy. If I were a true criminal, I would wait until harvest time and steal somebody else's pot. Those motherfuckers hunting me down were hardened criminals, and they knew I just saw them kill somebody.

Murder had definitely NOT been in the game plan. I'd come out here to grow green bud, not to see some guy get killed, his legs cut off, and buried in a pickle-barrel. I was a hippie—Peace man! Smoke some dope, play some guitar, and make love all night was my mantra. In my darkest fantasy, I had never envisioned this scenario. But since some folks had some pretty fucked up wiring, I now had this shit to deal with. Four hours ago I was just another guy with a pot farm, now I was living in the shadows, fearing for my life. After the horrors of this night I'd never see things the same. The colors of my paint by number world had begun to bleed through the lines.

The events of the last few hours had seriously overheated my nervous system. I couldn't focus; probably in shock. I was playing hide and seek with my thoughts, suffering hot and cold flashes, and had that hair shirt feeling whenever my denial lapsed, and memory broke through. My head was cracked open and still bleeding, only just now beginning to scab over. Seriously dehydrated, my muscles were cramping from the hours of forced exertion without water.

I needed time to plan my next move. One thing I knew, it wasn't going to involve the cops. A few more weeks and my crop would be in, and the last thing in the world I needed was to have a murder investigation going on around me. Anyway, whatever came down, R.O. Mosby wasn't coming back.

I sucked down a few large glasses of water and then took a quick look around the house. Everything appeared to be as I had left it. The rolling tray was on the TV set and my sweatpants were in the bedroom doorway where they had been dropped.

I just turned out the lights when I heard trucks hauling ass down the road, correctly guessing that it was The Billys.

My nearest escape was the bedroom window. I opened it quickly and stumbled over the sill into the back yard. Closing the window behind me, I climbed the hill behind the house to where the woods were thickest.

To my relief, The Billys roared by the house and through the gate without slowing down, then kept on going.

I sat for a while in the safety of the trees, intuitively knowing they weren't coming back, or for that matter, even thinking of me.

The earth tenderly accepted my slumping body and I slept dreamlessly until the sun came up.

I awoke and for a bliss-filled moment my mind was blank, but soon the memory of last night's horror came rushing back. I dragged myself to the house, grabbed the phone and dialed Tex. Tex wasn't home, but Ethan answered and told me that Tex was at Jefe's place in Garberville. That was good news, Garberville was just up the road from me. I jotted the number down and dialed while rummaging through the medicine cabinet looking for peroxide and gauze. Jefe's wife Isa answered

"Isa, this is Duncan Easley, we've met a couple of times." My voice sounded weak. "I heard that Tex is there."

"Oh hi, Goomba, sure I remember you." She was a beautiful lady. In my delirium I almost imagined her flirting with me over the phone. Her voice had that certain bounce. "He's with Jefe. They're out behind the house, somewhere on the hillside shooting pigs. Anything I can do?"

I told her I had wrecked my truck and needed a ride to the hospital to get some stitches.

"I'll try to reach them with the CB," she said, "but why didn't you call an ambulance?"

I told her that it wasn't too bad, but to have Tex and Jefe meet me at the gatehouse ASAP. Hearing that, Isa knew something was up.

By the time I hung up the phone, I had located all manner of first-aid supplies. Kurt and Jenny's linen closet looked like a storage locker in a M.A.S.H. unit due to Casey's medical problems. They had cases of saline solution, boxes of gauze and tape; everything I needed to patch myself up.

Fading again, I started to play doctor. My head hurt too much to even wash the cuts, so I dug around a little more and found some pain pills. I chewed two or three, drank some more water, and then lay down on the bed to give them time to work. I started to nod out or maybe just drifted into a low-grade coma.

Nothing bleeds like a head wound. While I was sleeping, I must have pulled back the flap of skin that was masquerading as my right ear, and the whole mess started flowing again. By the time I was awakened by Tex and Jefe, the pillow was soaked with blood and sticking to my hair. I was dizzy, nauseous, and so weak I couldn't sit up.

"You stupid son-of-a-bitch," Tex growled. "Why the fuck didn't you call an ambulance?" Tex never was too good in pressure situations.

"Easy, Tex," said Jefe, in a cool, commanding manner. He was staring in amazement at my wounds. He put a hand on Tex's shoulder. "This guy's fucked up pretty bad." He leaned over me and said quietly, "We have to get you to the hospital."

I was having trouble staying conscious but managed to whisper, "Bunny Eyes killed R.O., I got away." Then I drifted back into the other world.

The Grateful Dead's version of "*Stagger Lee*" was playing on someone's car stereo and the music found its way through the window of my hospital room. The room was empty when I woke up, but as I started to stir and groan a little, my wife appeared in the doorway. I could tell she was worried and had been crying.

"Oh my God, what have they done to you?" she sobbed.

I just shook my head and waved the question off. It took me a while to understand where I was and what I was doing there. I couldn't speak; still too groggy and unable to focus.

She held my hand and gave me a gentle kiss, then whispered in my ear, "The cops don't believe the car wreck story. They think you were beaten up. Tex and Jefe told them that they found you wandering down Highway 101." She offered bravely, "Tell them you can't remember what happened."

"I don't." And at that moment I didn't.

By the time the doctors found out I was awake, they called the sheriff. My memory was more or less restored, but it wasn't hard convincing them that I was still too traumatized and incoherent to answer their questions. I really did look like shit. My head was wrapped in bandages, my face was swollen, and both of my eyes were black. They told me that when I was feeling better I could come in and give a statement, but as far as they could tell, no foul play had occurred. They went away and I asked Carrie to get me out of there.

She left and returned in a few minutes. "They won't let you go today. They say you might have some internal bleeding and need to monitor you."

I didn't mind staying. The nurses were doting on me, and I was on pain pills as needed. They released me the next day.

I stopped by the sheriff's office a few days later. The cop in charge of the case wasn't there and a desk sergeant and booking clerk asked me a few questions. Apparently, the cops were satisfied with the answers. The only thing they had on me was a blood test showing traces of pot. I had a severe head wound that I milked every time I couldn't come up with a good answer. I got a lecture on the evils of drug use, but because no traces of alcohol were found, they decided to let the matter rest. They told me if there were any more questions, they would give me a call.

A few days later, I still wasn't feeling great but a few friends were getting together to have a wake for R.O. His sister Judith and a bunch of Goombas were getting together to comfort each other and plan their next move. Tex and Jefe were there when I arrived.

Judith had already snapped a few back before I got there. Her grief had turned bitter and obnoxious. With my head wrapped in gauze and my face swollen and purple, her first impression of me couldn't have been any more positive than mine was of her.

They all knew R.O. had been whacked and wanted to know the details. I told the story in depth, except for the part where I scraped Bunny Eyes off the step side of the truck at the gate. If he hadn't survived, I figured the fewer people who knew about it the better. The evening went by and we quietly let our age of innocence pass. Someone had died, and we were just walking away. The stakes had been raised, but I don't remember anyone cashing in their chips and leaving the table.

It was as close to a wake as R.O. was going to get. We spent some time telling stories about him, and those who knew him best offered up some eulogies. In time, the talk got around to who or what was to blame, and what, if anything, we were going to do about it. I found myself in an uncomfortable position. I guess by my wounds and suffering, I qualified as one whose opinion counted. I found myself captain of the debate team, defending the career choice of nearly everyone in the room, and trying to reverse Judith's notion that pot was the cause of R.O.'s death. His sister was clearly running a "Partnership for Drug Free America" commercial in her mind. She had concocted a reefer-madness scenario, so I had to jump in with an alternative perspective.

"The violence in the pot scene is caused by the black market that surrounds the trade," I asserted. "There is nothing inherently violent about pot. If anything, it mellows people out. The violence is created by drug laws and not by the drugs themselves." Standard arguments at the time; nothing too esoteric. I was in a whole lot of pain and didn't want to exert myself.

Judith was losing steam. "You never read about pharmacists shooting people," she argued lamely.

I shot back, "When pot growers have the same protection as pharmacists, when they can keep their money in the bank and seek redress against bad debtors in court like any other businessperson, they won't be shooting anybody, either."

That should have been obvious but sometimes the obvious is hardest to perceive. In the end, I felt uncomfortable arguing with someone who had just lost a loved one, no matter what the circumstance.

I may not have changed her mind, but she realized the house was full of pot growers, and they were lining up with me. Eventually her militancy waned, and she went about grieving in a less vocal fashion.

I ended up feeling pretty much like everybody else, sorry it happened, but glad it wasn't me. Nobody was interested in getting the cops involved, least of all Judith. What remained of R.O.'s empire, and I'm sure it was plenty, now belonged to her. It was now all about an orderly transition and who would own what. All we needed to do was sit down around a big table and break a bunch of pencils and we could have re-shot The Godfather.

When I had some time alone with Jefe and Tex, I heard the full story of the alibi the boys were putting out. They told the cops that they had found me dazed and disoriented, wandering on Highway 101. I'd mumbled something about a car wreck but passed out before I'd given them any details. They told the cops that's all they knew, but to cover my story, they had driven an old junk heap ranch truck up to Shimmins Ridge and pushed it off the hillside in a place where it was sure to roll over a time or two. They didn't have any of my blood to smear on the interior, so the story was that I must have been thrown from the vehicle, and my injuries were sustained from the rocks and bushes that I'd landed on. Luckily, the first rain of the season had come since the accident and any blood at the scene would have been washed away. In the end, the cops never found anything and nobody said shit.

As for R.O., he stayed dead. His sister hired a reject from "Gurus R' Us" to perform some kind of New Age cleansing ceremony out at the ranch. Dressed in yoga pants and wearing a turban wrapped around his head, he looked like Mr. Peepers playing the Sheik of Araby. He chanted some mumbo-jumbo and waved a bundle of burning sage around. To whatever degree we needed our consciences assuaged, we let the ceremony suffice.

Judith took over R.O.'s business like nothing had happened. She shut down Serenity Park but kept his other farms running. Eventually she toned down the rhetoric and found something other than pot to blame for her brother's death. Bunny Eyes was either dead, paralyzed, or limping big time. Nobody ever heard from him, but no one found his body either. And The Billys were never seen again.

Chapter 9

Nazis

Harvest that year took place during the 1986 midterm elections when Reagan became a lame duck. He had already managed to accomplish the main parts of his agenda—rewriting the tax code for the rich and ramping up military spending—but he didn't have any legislative initiatives put forward for his remaining two years in office. In June of that year, the cocaine overdose death of basketball star Len Bias dominated the news and focused the public's attention on the evils of drug abuse, a generic term that lumped marijuana in with heroin and cocaine, but in general bypassed tobacco, alcohol, and prescription medication. With Len Bias's death as a backdrop, the drug issue became a central part of the 1986 election and put marijuana on the wrong side of the 90/10 polling numbers. The people running Reagan's campaign decided that getting tough on drugs would be their message. Nancy Reagan accidentally coined the slogan, "Just Say No" and for better or worse, the war on drugs began in earnest. Politicians from both parties tripped over themselves to see who could spend the most money on the drug war. This was the wrong approach and proved disastrous in the long run.

Despite the changing political climate, we growers continued living in a bubble, a world of our own creation. Owing mostly to the vast amounts of money that we spent around the county, the locals gradually accepted us and we gained a measure of goodwill. That we missed noticing the storm clouds gathering on the nation's electoral horizon is obvious; we were busy growing weed and having too much fun.

A few short years after the drug war began in earnest, the wholesale price of pot coming out of the Emerald Triangle doubled, leaping from $2,500 to $5,000 a pound, essentially increasing the reward so significantly that it easily outstripped the associated risk. It didn't matter how many growers were locked up, thousands more were waiting in the wings. At five grand a pound, growing pot indoors also paid off handsomely.

By 1995, even the arch-conservative William F. Buckley declared the war lost. However, nothing's ever over while the taxpayer is shelling out the cash and as of 1998, the War on Drugs has been the costliest war in our nation's history. An estimated 100 billion to 170 billion dollars were being spent annually, while social services were cut to fund building more prisons. For all those taxpayer's dollars spent to stop it, the use of illicit drugs mushroomed. Sigh, okay, you got me, that pun was intended.

It was about that time my marriage broke up. Carrie couldn't deal with the stress of our lifestyle and I couldn't blame her. She was starting to work in corporate America and I was an embarrassing anachronism. But in the end, it came down to her feelings for our children. She was a good mother, and though she worried about me, she knew she couldn't change me. The children were her first concern, and she wanted to secure a safer life for them. I couldn't argue with her and respected her for it.

Professionally, I could have gone either way at that point. I drifted in and out of a few business scenes, but nothing in the so-called real world piqued my interest. After much soul-searching, I found out what I'd unconsciously known all along—I loved growing pot! Now that my kids were older, I could live on my farm and concentrate on trying to grow the best bud in the world.

Honey Bear was up and running on all cylinders. The water situation was resolved, and I pulled in close to two hundred pounds my second year, the year CAMP had its first big impact on prices. Good pot was selling at $1,600 dollars a pound for as long as I could remember, but thanks to CAMP, over one dry summer it jumped to $2,500 a pound.

I started looking around for a vacation to take.

It had been a while since I had been intimate with Carrie, and I found myself longing to be with a woman. One of my pickers grew up among the privileged elite of Southern California. Through her I met a Hollywood producer's daughter who I absolutely fell for. Her name was Alexandria, but I usually called her Deb or Debbie, short for "debutante." Her mother was from Greece, and Alexandria was doing a pretty good imitation of a temple goddess. Tall, thin, statuesque, shoulder length brown hair so dark it sometimes looked black, gorgeous hazel eyes and as sassy as any Australian. It was lust at first sight. Having plenty of cash and stash, I decided to take the year off and hang in the Southland, hopefully to get to know her better.

While I was away from the Northcoast, I had a buddy of mine run Honey Bear. Garrett Nash had been a grower about as long as I had but had lost his crop and farm in a raid the previous year. I agreed to let him grow at my place for thirty percent of the year's haul. I could take a much-needed break and Garrett could get his feet back on the ground.

I stayed in Westwood and Beverly Hills for a while but the Los Angeles air gave me a headache, and Debbie was busy most of the time. So, I kept going south and hung out for a while in Puerto Vallarta, a funky artist colony about halfway down the west coast of Mexico. Puerto's air was pretty shitty too, so I drifted up the coast and ended up hanging at a place called San Blas, farther north near Sinaloa. I bought a forty-foot sailboat and some scuba gear and pretended to be running a dive charter operation. while I hung out with the locals waiting for Debbie to show up but before she arrived, a storm came up without warning and my boat capsized and sank.

Lonely and disappointed, I called Debbie and told her I was coming back to the States, thirty grand poorer than when I'd left. I needed to drive up to Mendocino anyway to grab some stash and money. She was working as a continuity director for a movie her dad was producing, and postproduction was winding down. I spent the last week of August in the city of Lost Angels, and in the first week of September we headed north in her 911 Porsche.

We got to my house on a Saturday. Sunday morning we drove out to the farm where I had my green bud and cash buried. Deb had never seen a commercial pot farm in action and early September was a great time to get a tour.

Garrett's tender was a six-foot, four-inch lug of guy named Big John, who'd been tending for years. He liked his cold beers, so we stopped in Willits and bought a selection of imported suds before driving out to Honey Bear. Garrett was taking the day off and Big John was busy doing his laundry in a plastic garbage can.

"Goomba!" Big John had a snaggled tooth grin that could light up the night. "I thought you were in Mexico!"

"I got home last night, Johnny." Debbie was following me down the trail to the cabin. I stepped aside and let her pass me. "John, this is Alexandria, but I call her Debbie for short. Debbie, meet Big John."

They shook hands and I handed Big John the bag with the beer. "Dig around in the bag Johnny, I brought something for you."

He pulled a six pack out and looked in the bag. "Copenhagen!" He looked at me grinning. "Goomba, you remembered!"

John liked his smokeless tobacco more than he liked his teeth, which he was losing rapidly as the seasons passed.

"How are the girls?"

John opened a beer. "First of the day!" He offered his typical salutation to the beer gods. He sucked down about half a can of Oly and smiled broadly. "The girls look great!"

I said to Debbie, "After I dig up some stash, we'll walk over and check 'em out."

Debbie was fascinated by the living conditions. The place looked like a battlefield headquarters painted green, brown, and black camo-patterned, and covered with camo nets. "You guys should turn this into a roadside museum."

"Big John can be the docent," I laughed as I walked out the back door and jumped down off of the deck.

My barrel was a quarter mile or so into the woods and it took me about a half an hour to get there, dig up some assets, and walk back.

John was funny and had Debbie laughing as I walked back into the cabin. "What kind of stories are you telling her?"

"Who's Blake?" Debbie giggled.

"Jesus John!" hanging my head in mock despair, "That's not exactly our finest hour."

"Who is he? John made me promise to ask."

"He was John's roommate." I looked at John, who was enjoying himself. "What-about two or three years ago?"

"At least," John nodded.

"John was living in the city and I had been on the East Coast. It was wintertime and I'd landed in a storm. The flight back had been a roller-coaster ride and by the time I landed, I was a basket case."

"Goomba doesn't like to fly," John offered.

"I wasn't carrying any stash, and when I got to John's place, I asked him if he knew any place around town where we could cop an eighth."

Big John jumped into the narrative. "I'd only lived in the city for a couple of…"

I cut him off, "What he said was, 'Don't worry, my roommate has a stash,' and a moment later came out of Blake's room with this beautiful gold Thai stick."

"I was trying to be a gracious host."

"Oh bullshit…"

Debbie laughed, "Sounds like two addicts lying to themselves."

"So anyway, I said, 'are you sure he won't mind?' And remember what you said John?"

"I think I said something or other about."

I interrupted him again, "You said, 'No problem, he hardly even smokes. He just has it for company."

Big John stroked his chin. "I said that?" He let loose a big infectious smile that Big John hid behind as deftly as a matador hides behind his cape. He got up and went into the kitchen to grab a fresh beer. "Anybody want one?"

It was early, but it was a brick oven kind of day. We both nodded yes.

"I wouldn't be telling this story if you hadn't shot your mouth off, so shut the fuck up and let me get on with it."

"Go ahead, I'm not stopping you."

I looked at Debbie and laughed, "See the kind of shit I put up with?"

Big John got back with the beers and passed them around.

"So, the upshot is we started pinching on this guy's Thai stick Friday afternoon and by Sunday night it was ashes. Each time we'd load a bowl, John would insist that Blake was that rare person who doesn't smoke the herb but chooses to break the law anyway."

Of all the rascal stunts I've ever been involved with over a storied career, this was one of the lowest. To me, ripping someone's stash is like stealing holy water from the Church to put in your car's radiator—a big taboo.

On Sunday night, around eleven-thirty or midnight, his roommate Blake appeared in the entranceway looking like a lost animal, soaking wet and dejected. He set his luggage down in the foyer and tossed his wet coat onto a chair, launching into the most mournful soliloquy I've ever heard.

He came in talking about how his favorite aunt died on New Year's Eve, forcing him to stay in Dallas an extra week. His fuckin' aunt died; can you believe this shit? There was a half bath in the hall and Blake paused a moment while he grabbed a small towel and dried his hair while he talked.

"I was supposed to fly out of Dallas this morning but ended up spending the morning stuck on the interstate because some big rig rolled over. By the time I got to the airport, my plane had been gone for two fucking hours." He looked absolutely miserable.

Blake slumped into an overstuffed chair and tossed the wet towel into the corner. "The airline couldn't get me to SF direct, so I spent dinner time in Las Vegas playing poker against a machine. I lost just enough money so that when I finally landed two hours ago, I couldn't even afford a taxi and had to take a damn shuttle bus in from the airport. I couldn't talk the fucking driver into bringing me out here, so I had to walk all the way from the Fairmont. It's raining cats and fucking dogs and I'm carrying my luggage, but with each miserable step, one thought sustained me." A Mona Lisa smile crossed his face as he closed his eyes and said, "I have a Thai stick at home!" Oh god, we felt like shit. Poor schmuck, his dream had literally turned into ashes, thanks to us!

In the blazing heat of Honey Bear, I lowered my head in shame while John roared his approval. He loved hearing that story. Debbie looked at us, shaking her head while she laughed, "You guys are terrible."

"It was a long time ago," I told her.

John grinned, "Blake was a big boy, he got over it."

The conversation meandered. A lot of what being a pot farmer is about is merely passing time, especially late in the year. Each day is its own little eternity. Once the plants have been tied, the grower is little more than a glorified baby-sitter.

John got up and excused himself, "I've got to finish my laundry. If you guys are hungry, help yourself."

"We're going to walk over to the patch. Is there any drinking water there?"

"Yeah, but it's warm. Take a cold bottle from the fridge."

Debbie took some things from her purse, put them in a fanny pack, and I grabbed the water. She was wearing a white, wife-beater T-shirt, so for camo purposes, I had her put on a Boy Scout uniform shirt that was hanging on a nail by the door.

It took ten to fifteen minutes to get to the patch and we walked it in ritual silence. The trail was well-worn and soft underfoot. Along the precipice, she commented on the view, but we were quiet as we neared the patch.

Debbie had a puzzled look on her face. The plants were camouflaged so well that she didn't even see them! When she finally realized what she was looking at, she was standing between two absolute monsters. Her head snapped back to see how tall they were and when she looked back at me her eyes were wide open, looking like a pair of cherry pies.

I recall a moment of satisfaction thinking the garden had really impressed her, but that passed the instant I saw what she was seeing. We'd walked up to a full-grown male mountain lion that had curled himself around a plant to let the water system cool him on a hot day. He awoke with a jolt and bolted from the patch like he was shot from a cannon. His ears were laid back flat and his tail was as straight as an arrow.

I grabbed Debbie's hand and we turned to run. Unfortunately, we chose a steep spot that was fat with mulch and slick as grease. We ran in place until we collapsed laughing in a heap. We composed ourselves immediately and sat up to listen. For a moment we could hear the big cat rushing through the trees and bushes next to the patch, but once it reached the meadow we never heard him again. What a beautiful animal, darker than I would have guessed, almost chocolate on top with only the long hair on his underside and legs the fawn color I had associated with pumas.

I lay back down in the mulch between two ten-foot pot plants. I softly tugged at her arm and Debbie followed me down. The beds were raised in the French intensive method. How apropos. Moist, soft, cool, the ground welcomed our sweaty, adrenaline-filled bodies.

In my arms she became Alexandria, and while making love with her I became completely intoxicated by rapture. Talk of addicting drugs, I was hooked. She was almost too good-looking. If she hadn't been so naturally playful, she would have been intimidating. As it was, the run-in with the lion and the inherent danger of the pot patch added a spice of arousal she could relate to as much as I could. We must have breathed the big cat's air, because we both started purring and growling, scratching and biting. We were intoxicated by the smell of fear as we melted into one another.

We used our clothing as a makeshift blanket. That only worked so well, but who cared? She was so lovely. Her face was only the crowning glory to her statuesque body. Her breasts were not too big, but pert and perfectly formed. Her nipples pointed slightly skyward, beckoning my lips. She was slender, but not freak show skinny. Her waist was athletic and solid, flowing gently and beautifully to the curves of her hips and butt. She had a bit of a wild streak in her, and what she had put in her fanny pack was massage oil. While she massaged the oil onto the appropriate part of me, she rolled over on her back and surrendered into a receiving pose. Her magic worked again. Her magic always worked.

Chapter 10

Snap

Alexandria stayed with me in Mendocino for a couple of weeks but had to go back to LA to start another movie. I tried to get her to quit, but she was one of those women who had never moved her dad off the mantelpiece. Carl Jung claimed that the children's story Beauty and the Beast relates to a subconscious maturation process within a young woman's psyche. "Confronting the beast," is a metaphor he suggests for the transferring of the pure non-sexual love Beauty has for her father, to the sexual, erotic love she has for the beast who, once confronted, of course, turns out to be a prince. Maybe? But hey, who's Carl Jung? Whatever the real reason, Daddy was her hero and everybody else was just a spear-carrier in the great play of her life. So basically, she split.

She had orders to fill when she got back to Brentwood, so on the morning she was to leave, we drove out to the farm to dig something up. She wanted a whole unit, but all I had left until we harvested was a couple of quarter pounds, or QPs. She was happy to get anything I had. She just didn't want to go home empty-handed.

We had just turned off 101 and were driving the long gravel road that passed Honey Bear before it disappeared into the mountains, when a frantic Garrett pulled us over.

I had a quick pow-wow with him, locked my hubs and got back into Big Blue. "I'm going to have to leave you here Deb," I apologized. "The shit's hitting the fan at Honey Bear and it's too dangerous for you." I shifted the transfer case into 4-wheel drive.

"Are you out of your mind?" Debbie didn't like the idea. "You're not leaving me here! It's the middle of nowhere!"

"Sorry, I can't take you with me." I leaned over her to open her door. "There's a driveway back the road about a half a mile. The people are friends of mine, John and May Belle."

"Fuck you, I'm not." She tried to slam the door, but I held it open with my left hand while I undid her seat belt with my right.

"You just can't come. It might be cops. C'mon, would you please move your ass?" I gave her a gentle push. She stumbled out of the truck and landed rather unceremoniously in the gravel. She was out of the truck, but she wasn't happy about it.

Gravel flying, Garrett and I raced to Honey Bear.

An hour or so later, we retrieved our pot. Getting our pot back was mostly good luck, but Garrett bullshitting the sheriff and getting away with it was pure balls.

I drove back to John and May Belle's farm to get Debbie. We kissed and made up, but it was never the same after that. We were both headstrong individuals and the more we got to know each other, the more it became apparent how fundamentally different we were. I was spoiled, but she was really spoiled and I don't think anybody had ever told her "No" before. She went home and we danced apart. Over the winter we made a couple of half-hearted stabs at getting back together, but in the end she was committed to her world, and I was committed to mine.

Garrett's crop had suffered from being picked a little early and from the abuse of being handled so roughly, but it was pretty good smoke anyhow. Garrett cleared enough to get back on his feet and I made enough to buy another farm.

Meanwhile, Kurt was tending for another Goomba, The Fat Man. If Kurt's stories were true, they were sitting on a mountain of pot. The Fat Man's place, aptly named High Anxiety, pulled an astounding six hundred and twenty-seven pounds that harvest. They had so much schwee, the smaller buds from the center of the plant, that they stored them in body bags until the tenders came back for spring work, then gleaned another twenty pounds of bud from it.

Kurt's ten percent cut came to over a quarter million dollars, and he wanted to buy his own farm. He knew I was looking so early the next summer we decided to join forces and started searching for the right piece of property.

Having blown it with water once before, I was determined to buy a place where I'd actually seen the water at the end of the summer. Blue lines on a forest service map are supposed to denote year-round streams, but I'd learned not to trust them.

We found a beautiful one-hundred-and-sixty-acre parcel with decent cover and the water was absolutely fat. Kurt and I were now in business together.

It had been a couple of years since the rip-off incident, but with the memory of a cop standing in my driveway and the fact that rip-offs had found the place once, I was feeling insecure about Honey Bear as a pot farm. I had a feeling that something bad would happen if I tried growing there again and in hindsight, should have listened to my gut. But it was springtime with a new farm and there was a lot work to do. Listening to my gut way down my list of priorities.

Kurt reminded me of Ethan. They were both big, easy-going guys who could work like oxen all day, but had trouble getting themselves started. Both of them needed a spark plug like me barking at them in the morning to get going. Kurt and I got along well, having known each other since our days living on the Russian River. We knew what to expect from each other, and our friendship filled the voids. The two of us formed an easy alliance and got along great.

While we had all sorts of water at our new place it wasn't yet developed, and the water needed to be pumped a long way to where it was needed. With some trepidation I offered up Honey Bear for our nursery, figuring that we'd be in an out by the end of May before CAMP started flying.

Our plan was for two hundred and fifty plants minimum, but we hoped for three hundred and fifty and needed about eight hundred starts to ensure enough girls and also cover any losses due to mice or bad breeding. The nursery at Honey Bear came in handy as it was established with well-built cold frames already camouflaged in. We had hundreds of six-inch pots, having moved on from the early days of Styrofoam cups, an automatic irrigation system, mountains of mushroom compost, and most importantly, seeds. Thousands to work with from several proven strains. Our first couple of weeks were spent at Honey Bear filling eight hundred pots with starting mix and deciding which seeds to plant.

The new place was a lot like Serenity Park on its first day, raw land that needed everything built from scratch, from roadwork to carving in the new garden. There was an old road onto the property that had washed out a couple of hundred feet past our gate. We wouldn't be able to get any road work done until the rainy season passed, and unfortunately the new patch was a long way from the gate. We ended up using something we called a pack-track, basically a large, motorized wheelbarrow mounted on a pair of heavy rubber caterpillar-style treads, to haul in our supplies. The machine could carry about a ton of materials and we used it to haul soil amendments, irrigation supplies, garden tools, fencing; basically everything we needed to get the patch going.

There was a dry spell in mid-April that year so we rented a Cat for a couple of weeks. Besides the mile or so of road work, we needed to install a few culverts and level off some pads for our parking spots and living scenes.

Before taking the machine back to the rental joint, I spent a day with it at Honey Bear. My driveway crossed the neighbor's land for about half a mile, but since I was the only one using the road and it was up to me to maintain it. The previous winter had been harsh by Northern California standards, and about a hundred yards of the road needed to be completely redone. It started raining hard the day after I finished cutting the grade and didn't stop for a week which meant I didn't have time to get the gravel down. For the next week and a half we had to hike into both places. Every few days I popped into Honey Bear to fill the generator with gas and check the babies and the mouse traps.

It was the end of April and we'd been sexing the plants for a few weeks. We hadn't finished and needed to move about five hundred starts from the nursery at Honey Bear to the new place. We only needed a few dry days to do this, but every time the road got nearly dry, the rain started up again. But the holes at the new place were ready to fill, and on the twenty-eighth of April we decided we couldn't wait any longer. We planned to pack-track the starts off the hill in moving boxes, then where the road was too muddy, walk them through the woods to my truck. It would be more tedious than laborious.

I pulled up the driveway to Honey Bear and parked Big Blue at the edge of the muck. It wasn't even 9 am yet, but already the temperature was in the mid-seventies. Today was definitely going to be warm. Kurt wasn't there, but that wasn't a surprise. He just wasn't a morning person. My dogs Faux Pas and Oola jumped out of the back of the truck and the three of us hiked the hill.

It felt like a privilege to be walking in nature on such a day. There were some high cumulus clouds, cotton ball white and widely scattered. The rain had washed the air clean and moistened the forest floor so that the leaves quietly padded our footfalls and no dust was generated. As the forest gave way to mountain meadows, the dogs chased dragonflies by the pond and I checked the progress of the wildflowers. An overall great day to be alive.

Until the cop put his gun to my head and told me to freeze.

I was thrown face down on the ground as half a dozen or so camo clad goons came at me from all directions with automatic rifles pointed at my head. All my gauges had needles pushing the red zone. I quickly appreciated what a fish feels like flopping on the riverbank and wondered why my dogs hadn't alerted me to the danger.

I was hauled to my feet after being cuffed and frisked. The lead goon politely said, "I'm going to ask you a few questions, but first I'm going to read you your Miranda rights."

"Let the record show, that I didn't crap in my pants," I said. The cops chuckled, more in amazement than anything else, but that's all I said to them other than, "It's time to let the lawyers do their thing."

A lifetime of being late for work finally paid off for Kurt. The place was crawling with cops by the time he got to the road leading into Honey Bear. He drove on by, pretending to be mildly curious. About half a mile up the road, he parked and spent twenty minutes tossing some firewood into the back of his truck then hauled ass to his house to get the word out.

I was taken to Ukiah and booked into the county jail. My dogs were kindly delivered to my house along with a search warrant.

Right away I noticed something, but what it meant wasn't clear at first. The cops didn't treat me like a criminal, they treated me like a customer. The whole ordeal was less like being busted and more like having a transmission repaired. I even talked to a deputy who told me I shouldn't even be there.

"Pot growers never give us any trouble, it's the speed freaks and the drunks," he said. Over and over that sentiment was echoed.

Growers brought a ton of money into the system. This was when it dawned on me that the law enforcement industry was awash in pot money. We were, in two words, good business.

They charged me with one count of cultivation, and one of possession with intent to sell since they'd found a half-pound of my personal stash and during a search of the house. My bail was set at $3,000 so I called a friend in the Goombata and told them how much I needed. Jenny showed up with the money about twenty minutes later.

Police departments tend to be models of inefficiency. Either that or they just like to punish while they process. I ended up spending most of the afternoon sitting on a stainless steel bench in a holding cell, while Jenny sat in the waiting room with the money. The scene of me getting arrested played over and over in my mind. I felt like I was on a sinking ship and on the verge of tears, but some macho instinct kept that bottled up inside. At some point I fell asleep. The bench was cold steel and sucked the warmth from my body. I woke up shivering and paced the holding cell for a while as time passed very slowly.

They cut me loose around five, and it was like going to my own wake. A very sad time. At that point we knew very little, and suspected that whatever bad could happen, would.

At home I surveyed the damage. Like curious weasels, they had snooped in every nook and cranny, but like buffoons, they had missed the big stuff. They took my computer but didn't find my coded records that were on a disc hidden in a book. They found my personal stash, but they missed the twenty pounds buried under the doghouse. They found a scale and my commercial seal-a-meal machine but missed fifty thousand in cash. So, on balance, I made out better than I had hoped.

Going back to Honey Bear a few days later, realized the extent of the looting. It was less of a bust and more of an Easter egg hunt. They took all the equipment on the property; several pumps, three generators, the pack-track, the four trax, all my hand tools, chain saws, climbing gear, our alcohol and walkie-talkies. They even took personal stuff; the television, VCR, videos, tape deck and music tapes, sleeping bags, tents, golf clubs, a hunting bow, and even clothing. Literally everything of value was pirated from me for the cops' year-end rummage sale.

I retained counsel. I could say I hired a lawyer, but for five grand I want to feel like I got my money's worth. It was a flat fee and standard at the time. I was never given a bill to justify the costs, and the lawyer easily made his five grand in less than eight hours of work.

I was assigned a probation officer and was sitting in her office when the local high school called. They had just expelled her daughter for bringing a bottle of Vodka to school. It's ironic that I, as the "Evil pot growing felon" had children who were academically gifted and accomplished, while the woman society had hired to represent law and order to the community had her own kid thrown out of school. But the ironies stack up faster in the Emerald Triangle than body bags on a Saigon tarmac. In her report to the court, my probation officer wrote eloquently that I "had been smoking marijuana for over twenty years, and 'risked' becoming an addict."

The DA in Mendocino was a most reviled individual who had an attitude and demeanor suggesting that at one time or another, someone had lubricated a three wood with Tiger Balm and shoved it up her ass. She was such an uptight bitch, that I had no doubt she would push for Flipper to do ninety days for splashing water on a tourist.

She wanted me to do state prison time. At the arraignment, the whole story of how I got pinched came out.

It all started when the owner of an adjacent property decided to harvest some timber and filed a Timber Harvest Plan (THP) with the state.

In California, the state agency entrusted with the husbanding of forest resources is the California Department of Forestry, or CDF for short. At the time I was busted, it was taken as gospel by the environmental community that the whole department was in the pocket of corporate robber barons, and about all the department really did was apply the K-Y Jelly while the timber companies fucked the environment. The cheese dicks who ran the place weren't cops, but they got to wear cute little cop-style uniforms and were technically officers of the court. They could trespass on your property under the aegis of the Supreme Court's open field search doctrine, kind of like how the Nazi brown shirts had free run in the ghettos. To tell you the truth, most of the CDF employees were probably pretty cool, but it only took one cop wannabe to put the whole group under a dark cloud.

I couldn't believe the little CDF motherfucker who ratted me out. He looked like a hippie. He had long brown hair like a brother, but he was about the shortest little runt I'd ever seen. I mean he wasn't even five feet tall wearing platform shoes. I was sitting in court being shish kabobbed by some asshole that was too small to wear a bunny suit on Halloween. The neighbor's dog would eat his dumb ass. Just another short white wimp trying to prove he's a big man. I jokingly whispered to my lawyer that this was a classic case of a Napoleon complex. It turned out the guy had dirty laundry of his own and, and in a small town sooner or later everybody knew who was fucking whom.

My massage therapist's husband worked with the schmuck and knew first-hand how screwed up the guy was. His wife left him over a rumored homosexual affair he was having, but the word on the inside was that he was molesting his own children. Whatever the truth was, he had a reputation for being a fucked-up psycho. The whole unseemly affair was kept hush-hush so he wouldn't lose his job or his pension, but it put him under a dark cloud at work where he became increasingly alienated. At some point he began a vendetta against pot growers. The coffee table psychologist in me believed it was just a crusade to rescue his masculinity. I'd also heard that during one investigation he became so enraged that he suffered cardiac arrest and would have died if his partner hadn't known CPR.

As in the Viet Nam era, the line between the good guys and the bad guys seemed to get blurred in a hurry. The day of my trial I saw my lawyer, the judge, and the prosecuting attorney sitting in a window seat at the courthouse telling jokes. Of course, they were laughing all the way to the bank. My lawyer was basically a warm body who knew how to find the courthouse. The judge and my lawyer were buddies. My lawyer said they had smoked pot together on several occasions. The assistant DA who tried the case was about as memorable as a bowl of soggy corn flakes, a lap dog of the system putting in his time. When it came time to argue over sentencing, he sat down and nodded to the head DA, an ambitious person with sights set on a higher office and clearly out to use pot prosecutions as one of her stepping stones along the way.

She stood up to address the court and informed the judge that the scurvy creature (Moi?) on trial before him was a diabolical menace to society. I can't remember him pounding the gavel, but I'm sure he did. I do remember that he asked me whether or not I was intoxicated, or under the influence of drugs. Maybe I'd burned a fatty on the way to court, but so what? The judge probably had too.

I got six months work furlough. That meant that I could go home six days a week, hang out in my wood shop, and enjoy a periodic tete-a-tete with the lovely woman who was watching the house in my absence. I liked to golf but the local course ran by the back of the jail. I couldn't risk sneaking out there for a round, so instead I just kept my short game sharp in my back yard and managed to get through the entire ordeal without any damage to my handicap.

Because of prison overcrowding, I got to walk in ninety days. So, for my heinous crime of growing pot, I did three months of Sundays at the local Graybar Inn. I wasn't going to win the Cool Hand Luke hard-time award, but I could live with that.

My lawyer got Big Blue and my computer back on a technicality, so in that regard he earned his five thou. But about $20,000 worth of my equipment found its way into the police officers' "retirement fund", or perhaps some cop's brother's farm, I never found out.

Big Blue was in sad shape. After three months of gathering dust in the impound yard, with a few tires needing a blast of air, Big Blue looked about like how I felt. To my surprise, he started up right away as if eager to get back into action.

On the dashboard were the real estate papers for the new piece of property and an ounce of stash was still under the seat. Kurt got lucky, and because I had a small percentage of his crop, so did I. It was time to let go of the dream and find my way back into the real world where I could pad my resume and get legit. With a heavy heart, I left the impound yard, feeling that I'd never again have a job that I loved as much as growing pot.

PART III

DEEPER INTO THE WOODS

Chapter 11

The Wilderness Years

It had been a couple of years since I'd been busted, I was living alone, getting back into carpentry and trying to take it to the next level. But being a full-fledged contractor didn't click for me. I could handle the work but wasn't the type of person willing to deal with bankers, architects, and building inspectors. After the freedom I'd had as a grower, kissing some suits' ass to get a contract wasn't my idea of good time. And lacking a significant other, it felt like I was twisting in the wind, untethered and without a course to chart. The itch to get back into the marijuana business was creeping in, and as happens so often, the opportunity came out of the blue.

I was at Doug the Slug's house watching The Godfather and toward the end of the movie there's a classic scene where Don Vito waxes philosophical about being a gangster. He tells his son Mike that he wasn't ashamed of the life he led and that he'd never be a fool, dancing on strings held by big shots.

I said, "Fuck, that's what I'm doing!"

The movie ended and musing over my own fate, off-handedly I declared, "Give me some steady water and a clump of manzanita, and I'd grow again in a heartbeat."

I was just blowing smoke and Doug knew it, but remember the old adage about watching out what you wish for, you just might get it? I got it.

In the1880s, Spanker Creek, California was a beehive of activity. At that time, seemingly endless stands of old-growth redwoods, some over three hundred feet tall, graced the wilderness; one of the truly exquisite natural wonders of the world. Stand amid these trees, and you stand with some of the oldest and largest living things on Earth. Most of these titans predated the dark ages. Others had been around since the days of Arthur and Guinevere. The small fry saplings only recently appeared in the last one or two hundred years. These were stands of trees so massive that they made their own weather. To chop one of these monsters down without a chainsaw would take two men a week.

A runt by comparison, the Douglas fir topped out at around two hundred feet and grew in countless numbers in the adjacent areas too arid for the mist loving redwoods. The northwest was a lumberman's mother lode for all time. Although there was timber to be had, the trees were so massive that new tools had to be invented and produced to cut them down, move them to a mill, and saw them into lumber. The men and women who made their living harvesting what seemed to be an endless bounty, did so with little more than gumption and hard work.

In the early days, lumber towns typically sported taverns, gaming halls, and bordellos, so the loggers played as hard as they worked. In that regard, not much has changed.

One hundred years later, their children's grandchildren were still at it, although the idea of an endless bounty was now no longer true. But generations of hard work and isolation bred a sturdy stock of backwoodsmen who talked straight, liked their beer early in the day, and their women any way they could get them. Whatever they did, they did frontier style—true grit with a dash of attitude.

I had some business to attend to in Spanker Creek, and while I was there dropped in to see a couple of guys I knew from the early days at Serenity. Spaghetti Freddie and Jay had worked at a farm called Tavern on the Greenbud, and were now land partners. We had a kind of Christmas card relationship, bumping into one another about once a year.

It was at their place that I met Fartin' Jack. With a name like that, I couldn't imagine what his enemies must have called him. Just twenty minutes with the guy would explain all you needed to know about how he got his handle. Like most of us, he was a combination of positive and negative qualities. Among other things, he was a good family man with a college degree in engineering. Though not the greatest worker, he was a hell of a businessman and kept a lot of irons in the fire. On the downside, he had a habit of screwing his partners. He couldn't help himself. He was just driven to make sure that every time the pie got cut, he got the biggest piece. He wasn't a big-time rip-off pro, just a small-time chiseler.

Freddie and Jay lived miles outside of Spanker Creek and neither had a phone. A paved road got you to within several miles of their places, but the last leg was over some rough terrain that demanded four-wheel drive. Living near the end of the known world, they were always happy to have company. Backwoods intellectuals, they spent their days playing chess and backgammon or droning on about Nietzsche. They could chew your ear off for hours given the proper inducement, and Freddie usually had a bindle of inducement stashed away for a special occasion.

Fartin' Jack dropped in while I was there, putting out the word that he was looking for someone to take over a guerilla operation he had started with another guy a few years earlier. Now neither of them wanted to hike in that far. They'd done well their first year, but since then it had been a lot of work for not much bud.

He knew who I was. We knew a lot of the same people and the R.O. Mosby episode branded me notorious in local circles. Our meeting was one of those synchronistic, serendipitous events that happen sometimes and left me feeling that there was still some magic in life. Jack hired me on the spot. He had to talk to his partner about the split, but aside from that, I was back in the business. Fartin' Jack explained, apologetically, that the patch was very remote and that working it entailed an enormous amount of hiking.

To me the place sounded ideal. "Don't apologize," I said, "I want to be remote, the farther out the better." Having been busted once, I was in no hurry to go through that trip again and figured that being so remote, if the patch was ever spotted, they'd come in from the sky to grab it and I'd have plenty of warning. I didn't think they would bother setting a trap to nail me like they did at Honey Bear. There was no place for them to land a helicopter, and it was a long way to hike.

Jack and I shook hands and agreed to meet again in a few days.

I drove back to Spanker Creek on Saturday morning. Feeling like a rookie on opening day, I was glad to be back in the game. The winter had been cold and rainy, but the day broke sunny and warm. Freddie was cutting firewood with another local guy named Mac the Bear when I got there. The mingled aromas of freshly cut wood, clear mountain air, and chainsaw exhaust were like temple incense to me.

Waiting for Fartin' Jack to show up, I sat on the woodpile with Mac the Bear, and Freddie went inside and rolled us one of the fattest blunts I'd ever seen. This guy rolled cigars! We were toasting that bad boy when Jack arrived with his business partner, Theo.

Theo Dank was a pale, pasty-faced, humorless Swede. Called either T.D. or Dankster, the guy had the appearance of a man in the early stages of a heart attack. He smoked cigarettes incessantly and carried himself as though he hadn't taken a crap in a month. For a guy who made a living in the outdoors, it was a mystery how he never sported a tan. But when he got excited, which was often, his face and neck turned bright red. He tried to be a straight shooter but had an unsettling edge about him that kept me from completely lowering my guard.

I had no idea what kind of offer the boys would make to have me on board, but figured I should get at least fifty percent since I'd be the one doing all the work. However, I was desperate to get back in the game and would have worked for carpenter's wages just for the opportunity. Growing pot wasn't just a job to me, it was a calling that combined my love for the farming life, nature, and counterculture lifestyle.

There was no industry standard and each deal was unique. They offered me sixty percent of the crop and I snapped at it. I had a reputation for bringing in the A-Plus bud and they figured the forty percent they'd get from my crop would be better pot and less trouble than if they stuck a pilgrim or some local fuck-up in the woods.

With the terms settled, the rest of the afternoon was spent drinking beer, smoking the herb and bullshitting.

As we parted, Freddie stuck his head out his window and yelled, "Get it in writing." Everybody laughed, except Fartin' Jack.

The trail to the outback started at Jay's cabin, so we agreed to meet there in a few days. I used the time to outfit myself for a summer in the wilderness. Knowing I'd be carrying a ton of supplies over the summer, I bought an expensive, internal-frame backpack that would carry as much as I could lift. I also bought a down sleeping bag, tent, camp stove, flashlights, a bunch of other basics, and most importantly, an air mattress. A grower works their ass off during the season, and a good night's sleep is about the only tangible reward until harvest.

Jay's home was a post-and-beam two-room cabin in the woods, built solely from timber harvested on his property. His only power tool was a chainsaw, and though unfinished, the place was beautifully rustic. The cabin had rough wood floors and mylar plastic covering some of the windows. It was the type of place you would expect to be full of antiques, maybe a butter churn or a spinning wheel. But instead, remarkably, in one corner of the main room was a Steinway concert grand piano. Living deep in the woods, I guess you never knew when you might need one of those things.

His elevation was one-thousand feet, about a third of the way up a three-thousand-foot ridge with a commanding view of the valley.

The trail to the patch started behind Jay's cabin and meandered for miles. Much of it was a tortuous climb to an escarpment two-thousand feet up. Beyond the ridge top, the trail disappeared deep into the woods. It could take anywhere from an hour and a half to three hours to walk to the patch, depending on the weight of the load being carried. On the first day, I had a carload of shit to haul, but Jack had a backpack as well, so we split the load and made pretty good time.

The first part of the trail was the worst, especially early in the season before my legs were in shape. The pack felt like it weighed a ton, and every step shot arrows of pain from my legs to my brain. Progress was slow, but after the first quarter mile or so, the incline became less severe and easier to climb. The hike became, if not enjoyable, at least bearable. Near the ridge top, the grade became very steep. The last hundred yards or so became known as the "thigh-master." Before long, I was buffed. The summer of hiking that incline with an average of fifty to sixty pounds on my back was extremely hard work, but it was the best pure exercise regimen I'd ever had to endure.

The trail to the patch was well-traveled, and I could follow it without being led. That was lucky because frankly, if you were hiking with Fartin' Jack, it was better to walk in front of him. The area was wonderfully wooded. Though we hiked for miles deep into the wilderness, there were few if any places where the trail was visible from the air. No concern for the average hiker, but a big one for a pot grower.

The first indication I had that we were near the patch was the sight of a large doughboy swimming pool that was being used as a water tank. Painted in camo green, brown, and black, and covered with tarps and camo netting, the thing was nearly invisible, hidden in a thicket between small trees that were pulled together with ropes to make the pool completely invisible from the air.

A few hundred feet down the hill from the tank was the patch. We were on a finger of land that jutted off the northeast side of the ridge, but the patch was carved in on the side of a gully with a southwestern exposure. The holes were spread over an acre, under a canopy of fifteen-foot-tall manzanita bushes and an assortment of smallish live oaks. So here I was, less than a week after my off-handed remark, looking at a clump of manzanitas with a steady supply of water. I was back in business!

The patch was overgrown and in need of tree work, but the holes were established and the irrigation system was in place. There were about fifty bags of steer manure and thirty-five bags of worm castings left from the previous year. I was lucky because it was too late in the season to start pack-tracking soil amendments that far into the hills. I still needed to carry in some oyster shells to adjust the pH, plant food, and Maxi-crop™, but as far as building up the soil was concerned, I'd have to make do with what was already in place.

The living scene out there was a real hoot. Constructed entirely from small trees and covered with camo tarps, it looked like the kind of place where Fred and Wilma Flintstone would send their son Bam Bam to summer camp. It consisted mainly of a drying shed, a field kitchen, and a few level pads as tent sites and was the most primitive setup for growing I'd ever seen, but to my eyes it was a perfect ten. Water was unlimited and the cover was total—I was going to grow some ass-kickin' green bud!

The water lines were in but had been drained for the winter. The ram pump had been taken out of the creek bed and hidden in some rocks. The thing ran on water pressure twenty-four hours a day and used four gallons of water to pump one gallon a minute. That doesn't sound like much, but that added up to 1,440 gallons a day. The patch was for 200 plants, and that was plenty of water for my needs.

Jack knew where all the tools and equipment were hidden and where all the valves were, so he spent the afternoon helping me get set up. By five or so, the water was running and I was ready to grow herb. Jack left shortly thereafter to ensure he made it out of the forest before dark, and I was left to myself, give or take a bear or two, for the first night.

The deep woods possess monastic serenity. My only companions that night were the forest fauna and my thoughts. The only sounds I heard were the wind in the treetops and the occasional rustling of an animal as it skirted my campsite. As darkness fell, the insect world came to life in song. The sound they made was surprisingly loud if you listened to it, but it was the kind of noise the mind could screen out. It was the sound of footfalls that took getting used to. From inside the tent, the noise that the deer, squirrels, and small birds made walking through the leaves could easily have been bears and mountain lions. There was a measure of nervousness at first, but the day's work had exhausted me sleep came quickly and deeply.

It didn't take long to get into the swing of things and feel at home out there. With few diversions other than eating, working ten to twelve hours a day became the norm. The deer moved into the camp and became my companions, possibly sensing that the big cats were steering clear of me. The little deer made a habit of sneaking up behind me while I was eating and nuzzling me with their noses. The first time this happened I nearly jumped out of my skin. But I adjusted to their friendliness and they learned to trust me, and soon they were eating snacks out of my hand. The owls were also very sociable and helped keep the mouse population around camp to a minimum.

Miles from anywhere, surrounded by the coastal mountains, it was a dream scene. The only drawback was a Forest Service fire lookout tower in the distance. Because of the tower, I couldn't build a fire or have lanterns glowing at night. My tent was covered with black plastic under the camo tarp so it didn't glow, and my flashlight had electrician's tape across the lens like a headlight on a World War II army vehicle. I played by the first rule of wilderness growing, don't let anybody know you're there.

Not only did that requirement preclude the use of lights and fires, it also meant no power tools. Handsaws and loppers were all I could use to do the tree work, and mattocks and hoes took the place of a rototiller. It took me a month to do what a pair of tenders with a tiller could have done in four days. Due to this, the babies didn't get in the ground until the end of May, remarkably only missing the ideal target of Mother's Day by a couple of weeks.

The biggest difficulty of that whole endeavor was the hike. On the days I hiked in, I was so exhausted by the time I got there, that I was only good for a few hours of light work. I could only pack enough provisions and growing supplies to last three or four days, so would hike back out, rest a day or two, and start the cycle all over again.

My patch was far more remote than any I had ever heard of, leaving me miles away from any kind of help. I tried using my mobile phone once but didn't get a signal. During those days a grower had to fend for himself, but as far as I knew, I was the only one out there who didn't carry a gun. Still being on probation partially affected my decision, but the reality was I never could relate to guns. Years ago, while living in Berkeley, my first psychedelic Guru advised me to go my way in peace and never carry a weapon. Those words resonated with me, so I never carried anything more threatening than a Swiss army knife and wasn't about to change.

My buddies knew about my aversion to guns and loved relating and embellishing any bear or lion stories they knew in an attempt to rattle me. But the few bears I did meet on the trail ran from me like I was the human plague, so I never worried. Ironically, it was Mac the Bear who'd had a scary run-in with a real bear, and the boys made sure I heard about it.

The story went like this; on the way to his place one day, Mac encountered a large male bear that instead of running away from him, turned and snarled a toothy warning. Mac usually packed a gun but happened to be unarmed that day. Manzanita berries are one of the bear's favorite foods and the bear was on a section of trail that looped around a two- or three-acre bowl of manzanitas. The bear must have thought that Mac was there to steal his food and came bounding down the trail toward him. Mac spun around and ran for his life! Thanks to a big head start, the bear lost interest and Mac got away. The bears had always run from me, but after hearing this tale, I was instilled with a greater respect for the majestic creatures.

After that story got around, everybody made sure their guns were loaded and handy. Except me. Before my next trip into the patch, a few of my pals offered to let me borrow their guns, offers that I declined. I did, however, decide some form of weapon was called for, and grabbed the pitching wedge out of my golf bag not knowing what I would do with it if I met up with a hungry bear, but if nothing else, it was good for a few laughs around Spanker Creek.

I hiked in without incident and after a few days of work, started my usual hike back out. Near the ridge top I heard noises off the trail to my right. From the sound of it, I could tell something big was out there, and I hurried to the side of the trail to get a look at what I assumed was a bear but instead found myself face to face with a large, wild pig. Luckily it wasn't a big ole tusker, but a full-grown sow, weighing somewhere around three or four hundred pounds. I hadn't been faced with that much man hate since I'd gotten into a traffic argument with a road-raged lesbian.

Me standing at the side of the trail with my pitching wedge failed to inspire the same respect in the pig that King Arthur got wielding Excalibur at his foes. With a snort of contempt, the sow charged. I'd failed to make my point and it was time to turn tail and flee.

Fueled by adrenaline, I set a new Olympic record for the 100-meter dash, but three more sows waited for me at the finish line, along with about twenty little wiener pigs. They froze. I froze. Luckily, the sow chasing me also stopped. Enveloped with fear, I found myself in one of the worst predicaments in nature, being caught between a pissed-off mama and her young. There wasn't time to think; it was all about instinct now. I let out a blood-curdling scream and charged the litter of piglets. Pandemonium ensued as piglets and sows ran squealing in all directions. I hauled ass up the trail as the pigs regrouped and ran off through the woods. Our paths merged and for a moment I thought that they were coming after me again. I kept running and they stopped, allowing me to pass unharmed. I don't know if I was ever in real danger, but that old sow scared me more than any bear ever did.

By the end of the summer, I had seen about a dozen bears, a rabid fox, nearly stepped on two rattlesnakes, had my run in with the pigs, and nearly got zapped by a skunk. But I never saw a plane or a helicopter anywhere near my operation. So, on balance, it was as anxiety-free as a grower could hope for.

When harvest rolled around, I was sitting on a bumper crop of some of the finest pot I'd ever grown. I didn't know who was going to pick for me, but the stars were aligned and everything was working out like it was scripted. In late August I was introduced to the locally famous picker, Purple Candy. She usually picked for another guy but he'd been busted a week before and she hadn't yet lined up another job.

Candy Hedges was a legend among pickers. She manicured pot so fast it made you dizzy to watch. She was a little cutie too, weighing in at about ninety pounds with a rock in her pocket and naturally funny. She could make you laugh just by asking for a cup of coffee. She typically woke up early, rolled about ten fat reefers, and got to work. I couldn't have processed pot any faster if I had tossed it into a snow blower. She averaged about seven pounds of clean buds a day. That year I grew a strain called Fuckin'A, and the buds were big, tight, and full of resin. Seven pounds a day was incredible. In comparison, the one time I did it, cleaning just one pound took me a day and a half.

My cut after expenses was fifty pounds and change. Except for about five pounds I kept for my own stash and for friends, I sold the whole crop to a guy from New York City in one pop for a cool quarter million. Other than all the hiking, it was the easiest year I ever had. When all was said and done, I essentially traded about fifty pounds of pot for twenty pounds of cash, which I tossed into the toolbox in the back of Big Blue, then headed home for the season.

Chapter 12

Rusty Greyhouse

After the success of that first year, I figured the second year would be party time, but my partners were funny. They seemed to hang together better when the chips were down. Success sometimes breeds higher expectations and having done well the first year, my partners thought I should do better this next year. It seemed to me that it was a classic example of the old adage, "If you do more for someone than they expect, then they always expect you to do more."

Instead of having a relaxed year with money in our pockets and a few new toys to play with, the second year became a pissing contest.

Having worked alone the first year, I wanted to peel off a few percent and get a helper. I had a few people in mind, but my partners insisted on one of their guys. I didn't care who he was, just so it was someone who could hack it.

Growing pot in the wilderness takes a certain blend of qualities. At a minimum, a grower needs to be independent, self-motivated, and hard-working. While I could teach a new guy what he needed to know about tending a garden, work ethic was something you either had or didn't. Think of it like this; a Ferrari is a great car, but if you're hauling gravel, a big old dump truck is preferred.

Rusty Greyhouse looked like a big old tattoo-covered dump truck. Unfortunately, he was as temperamental as a Ferrari and usually harder to start. As far as I could tell, his only real qualification for the job was that he knew Fartin' Jack.

I can't fault Jack entirely for choosing the guy. First of all, Rusty looked like a backwoods pot grower. He was big, ruggedly handsome, and seemed like someone who could do an honest day's work.

The guy could have been a professional wrestler but chose meth instead. He talked the talk. Could he walk the walk? It took more than wearing a cowboy hat and carrying a knife to be successful in the biz. Rusty wanted to be a grower but unfortunately, he just wasn't independent, self-motivated, or hard-working enough to cut it, and herein lay the rub.

Rusty was a con man with a con man's flair for self-promotion and no shortage of charm, in that loveable biker sort of way. But, having graduated with honors from a childhood spent within the California Youth Authority system, he had a history of multiple scrapes with the law and approached life from the dark side of the street.

Why would they hire a guy like that? The real question was, if a guy like Rusty doesn't work out, how do you fire him? Answer—you don't.

One of the locals I'd gotten to know the first year was Rasta Patti. She lived on a small farm in the valley, about halfway between the main road out of Spanker Creek and Jay's cabin. Patti had a few plants growing in the woods behind her place but she didn't like to work too hard and ended up spending most of her time hanging out. She liked company so her place became the unofficial meeting place. That's where I first met Rusty Greyhouse.

Looking like a Hell's Angel without the Angel, he immediately put me at ease with his warm, strong handshake and smiling eyes.

"So you're the famous Goomba," he said with a grin when we first met.

"I don't know about famous," I replied with a snort, "If fame is the same as notoriety, then maybe." Again the R.O. Mosby incident had been my invisible calling card. An Emerald Triangle secret that seemed like everybody and their first grade teacher knew. Juicy stories have a way of proliferating, as well as embellishing themselves. Anonymity is the desired status of a grower, and it always made me uncomfortable when I was reminded of past exploits.

"Everybody's heard of Goomba," declared Patti, "He rolls some of the prettiest, ass-kickingest hooters I ever smoked." She handed me a rolling tray and asked, "How's that for putting you on the spot?"

I shrugged and feigned sheepishness. "Everybody's got something they do well. I think I can handle it."

We huddled like conspirators in Patti's cabin. Nasty weather had moved in from the Gulf of Alaska, and the wind was blowing cold and wet. Branches of an Oregon Yew were slapping the side of the cabin. It was a drizzly, gray, mud-cake of an afternoon and we were happy to stay next to Patti's wood stove and talk about the season ahead.

"I hope you like walking." I said to Rusty while gazing past him at the flames dancing behind the mica windows on the door of Patti's stove. "It's a thousand miles between us and harvest," I added, "with 50 pounds of whatever on your back."

"There isn't a lazy bone in my body," he claimed, but I noticed a look on Patti's face as he said it. She gave a little eye roll that I took to mean that she knew Rusty better than Rusty knew himself and had formed a slightly different opinion. It didn't matter anyway, Rusty had already been hired by Fartin' Jack and good, bad, or indifferent, what I saw was what I got.

We spent the afternoon swapping stories, smoking dank, drinking beer, and listening to the Reggae music that Patti played without interruption. I had a long drive ahead of me, so after laying out a rough schedule and giving Rusty an idea of what he needed to live in the outback, I split. It was the first week of February, and while we'd hoped for an early start, we had to wait for a break in the weather. The soil in the garden needed to be renewed, and to haul the shit in was going to be a long, slow, arduous process.

The weather stayed shitty for another week, then turned warm and spring-like. It took a few nice days for the trails to dry out and firm up. Because we were going to use Big Blue for all the early hauling we needed a dry road.

On the appointed day, I bought a huge load of manure and other assorted supplies and drove to Spanker Creek, arriving shortly after noon. Behind Jay's cabin was an old skidder trail that I hoped Big Blue could navigate. My truck was fitted with a massive winch. Mounted to the front bumper, the winch was really an elevator motor capable of lifting eight-thousand pounds, enough power to pull the truck up into a tree. Outfitted with one hundred and fifty feet of aircraft cable, the truck could pretty much go wherever it was needed, as long as there was something to anchor the cable to.

Some sections of the trail were extremely steep. One place in particular rose at a fifty-five-degree angle for about a hundred feet. Our first attempt at conquering it nearly did us in.

I drove the trail until it got too steep and the wheels started spinning. It was time for the winch. Rusty grabbed the cable and struggled forward with it. I carried the mooring chain up the hill and wrapped it around a big oak we had selected as our anchor.

I could tell he was having trouble converting to work mode. As we were inching our way up the grade, he was slipping and cursing, bitching with each step. I listened to his complaining and thought to myself, "It's going to be a long, long summer."

With the cable secured to the mooring chain, we stumbled back down the trail to the truck. I fired it up but my heart sank when I realized the winch wasn't working. It ran off a second battery, which had gone tits-up since the last time I'd used it. Luckily, I had jumper cables and connected the two batteries, but now I couldn't close the hood. Not a deal killer, except that I couldn't see the road. At a rate of one mile an hour, it's doable but still a bit unnerving.

In due time we were ready for our first attempt. I reeled in the slack and as the cable tensed, the truck inched forward.

Our next unknown was the load. Could Big Blue handle it? We were carrying eighty bags of steer shit, and apart from the added weight, we weren't sure they would stay put with the truck pointing up that steeply. I had faith in Big Blue. We'd been through some amazing predicaments together, and he had always managed to get the job done. That truck was like one of the boys, a real brute. Between the 400 CID V-8 and the four-ton winch, he had all the power we needed. The cable supplied what we lacked in terms of traction, and soon we were well on our way.

The first two-thirds of the pull went without incident. The trail was steep, but not impossible. It was the last thirty or forty feet that were the most daunting. From where I sat, it looked like I was pulling Big Blue up the side of a building. The weight of the bags had shifted to the back, and whether or not the tailgate would hold was a considerable worry. About three thousand pounds of cow shit hung in the balance, essentially one and a half tons straining against the tailgate like a fat women's ass in Spandex pants.

The cable was strung as tight as a guitar string. Rusty stood safely to one side; eyes wide in amazed worry. The last few feet of the escarpment were now under Big Blue's wheels. Thousands of pounds of shit and steel, and one hundred and seventy pounds of human hung precariously by the spider's silk of an aircraft cable. The moment was pregnant with possibilities, and for an instant I believed we'd make it. As if on cue, the engine died. Talk about having your hard-on go limp! This was Sag City.

Big Blue thought he was out of gas, but it was just that the angle at which we were tilted was so steep, that the gas in the tank had shifted back and refused to be picked up by the fuel line.

I looked at Rusty, and I could see him cursing under his breath. Shaking his head, he started to say, "At least the shit stayed..."

I knew where he was going, and I held up my hand in the manner of a crossing guard, "Don't say it!"

As if on cue, sounding like a big steel cherry popping, the tail-gate tore loose from its hinges. Big Blue breathed a sigh of relief and bounced lightly, suddenly free of cargo. The cargo itself headed west, cascading down the embankment like lava from a cow crap volcano. The spare tire was with the load and, rolling at about fifty miles an hour, disappeared into the woods below.

Rusty sat down dejectedly, and I slumped over the steering wheel like a bad actor emoting despair. It would be dark in an hour and we still had work to do, so there wasn't any time to sit on our butts and commiserate.

Big Blue refused to start again until we were back on level ground. Without the engine running, the winch didn't have enough reserve power coming from the battery to even think about pulling us the rest of the way up. My only option was to unroll the cable and back the truck down the embankment. While I was engaged with that task, Rusty managed to clear the bags from our path.

We reached the bottom easily enough, but the battery was nearly dead. I doubted there was enough current left in the thing to turn the engine over. We had to reload the truck and jerry-rig the tailgate with ropes and chains, which took about half an hour.

It was getting dark by the time we were ready to try the engine again. I figured that if I could get the thing started, I'd switch over to the spare tank, which was full and would keep the gas supplied for the entire grade. Knowing the carburetor was dry and the battery was low, it was either going to start right up or not at all.

What saved us was a small can of chainsaw gas and a Taco Bell cup. I put about 6 ounces of gas into the cup and had Rusty sit on a fender well under the hood. He poured the gas slowly into the top of the carburetor while I turned the ignition. I could tell we had only one chance. The battery just barely turned the engine over, but miraculously it was enough. Big Blue coughed once and sprang to life. He idled roughly for a few minutes while whatever air there was in the fuel line was purged, and then purred like a kitten.

Once again we started up the incline, retracing our tracks from what seemed like a lifetime ago. This time we met with success. Rusty was a serious skeptic with a habit of expecting the worst from life, so it was important that we persevered and accomplished what we'd started out to do. It was the first day that we worked together, and to be defeated would have reinforced his victim complex, starting the year off on a real downer.

It was late evening before we had the cable rolled back on the spool, but not so dark that we had to use our lights. We were going into a wilderness area, and we didn't want to announce our unauthorized visit people in the valley. Feeling better about our situation, we lumbered up the mountainside and arrived at the hilltop without further trouble. An old skidder trail headed in the direction of the patch for about a quarter of a mile before it was washed out, so I backed Big Blue as far down the trail as I could. We had a hiding place already picked out and planned to stash the large pile of white bags until morning.

I knew the battery would be recharged by now but left the engine running just to be sure. It was late and I didn't want any more surprises.

But what I wanted didn't matter, fate dealt us one more fuck-you card. Over the sound of the idling engine came the hiss of escaping air. Big Blue's right rear tire was going flat. As far as I knew, the spare tire was now rolling through Spanker Creek. Stuck without a spare, we needed to unload in a hurry and get out of the woods as fast as we could.

It turned out that the tire wasn't punctured after all. While backing down the trail I'd hit a large, partially decayed stump and it turned out that some of the rotting wood was forced into the bead between the tire and the wheel. I tried franticly to remove the wood with a hammer and tire iron, but it was no use.

Rusty was tossing the bags off the truck as fast as he could. I hopped up and joined him. Our only hope was to get out of the woods before the tire was completely flat. Normally a grower would pull the bags under some branches, but we just dumped the load and left it in the middle of the trail. The tire was almost flat by the time we tossed the last bag off the truck. Without 'phlaging the pile, we hopped in and got the hell out of there. Bouncing down the trail must have caused the tire to partially reseat, because we still had air when we reached the bottom of the hill and the loud hiss was replaced by a barely audible one.

I was using Jay's place again for a parking and staging area, and he had begun to wonder about us. It was well past dark when we returned with our tale of adventure. Jay had an air compressor, so I could fill the tire and hope it would still have some air in it in the morning. All things considered the day had been a success. Rusty and I, for better or worse, were now a team. We were on our way.

Rusty had his enduro motorcycle parked at Jay's, so after a hit off a reefer and one or two beers, he rode home. I told him that we had to get our manure pile moved to a better hiding place and wanted to head out at first light.

"Not a problem," as he liked to say. "I'll be back at seven or seven-thirty in the morning."

"I'll have the coffee on," I replied as Rusty fiddled with the strap on his helmet. He gave me the thumbs up, and kick started his bike.

As he disappeared down the driveway, Jay remarked that he'd consider it a minor miracle if Rusty made it back before noon. "He's just not a morning person." The way he said it made me wonder if I'd ever see Rusty again.

I crashed on Jays' sofa, a dusty, hair-covered collection of over-stuffed cushions that I shared with two cats and a ferret.

I've always been a morning person, being hexed with the day-light curse. For some reason, when the earliest hint of daylight rolls around, my eyes automatically spring open. I can't help it. By six-forty-five am I had the coffee water boiling and a fire going. Jay slept in the attic and needed a blast on an air horn just to rouse him. There was no need for him to get up, so I went about my morning business in monastic silence.

Seven-thirty rolled around and still no Rusty. I put on another pot of coffee.

Jay moseyed down the stairs around eight thirty.

He saw me sitting alone by the wood stove. "No Rusty?" he yawned. "I'm not surprised."

When Rusty still hadn't showed up by nine I refused to wait any longer. I left instructions with Jay for Rusty, in the event that he'd get there after I had gone. With food and water packed, I started out while muttering a few expletives aimed at my no-show partner.

It was a beautiful late February day on the north coast—sunny, but cool. A wonderful day to be working again. Normally it was a brisk, forty-five-minute hike to where we'd dropped the bags, but at the top of the mountain I had to detour by Mac the Bear's hiding place and collect his pack-track. It hadn't been used all winter and took a few minutes to get started but soon I was heading down the trail to collect the manure.

Moving a ton and a half of manure was tedious work, made more so by the fact that Rusty had apparently decided that he needed a vacation after one day of work. It was about a two-mile round trip to the patch from the end of the skidder trail where we'd dumped the load. The easy part was the first half mile or so because the trail was wide enough for the machine. But at a ravine's edge it became impassable, so I started a new pile and returned for another load. It didn't require a lot of physical power to perform this chore, but took six round trips, each one taking over an hour to complete. Moving eighty bags that far into the woods took me the whole day and nearly fifteen miles of hiking.

The last two days were tough. I was glad they were behind me, but sobered by the fact that this was only the beginning of what promised to be a long summer.

It started getting dark around five as I neared the trail's end with the last load. Tomorrow the real work would begin. Each bag would have to be carried one by one through the ravine and around a rock outcropping where the trail was decent again, allowing us to use a wheelbarrow for the last leg of the journey. At four bags a load, the eighty bags required twenty, one-mile round trips. Hopefully, Rusty would magically reappear, and armed with two wheelbarrows we'd split the work and each do ten trips. If you've never pushed a wheelbarrow through the woods, even though the thing is empty for the return leg, ten miles of it is a long goddamned day of work.

Rusty was at Jay's place when I arrived, well past nightfall, with some lame excuse that wasn't worthy of remembrance. He had a puckish quality about him, so it was hard to stay mad at him for long.

I was too tired to be pissed off, but told him in no uncertain terms, "Tomorrow is going to be a ball buster. If you flake out on me, you can spend the summer pulling green chain at the sawmill. I don't give a fuck"

He seemed sorry, but as the summer passed, I figured out that things with Rusty weren't always what they seemed to be. For the time being, however, the work got done and all things considered, he pulled his weight.

The next day, he was almost on time. We set off on our trek around 7:30 am and arrived at the new shit pile site about an hour and fifteen minutes later. With bandanas wrapped around our faces as breathing masks, we looked like we were getting ready to rob the Tombstone stage.

If any one activity defines the life of a backwoods pot grower, it's walking side-hill with a heavy bag of steer shit on your shoulder. We'd each made a dozen or so trips through the ravine and around the big rock when I left Rusty to finish the job and started wheeling the bags to the patch. Luckily it was downhill to the patch, so I had the aid of gravity when the wheelbarrow was loaded. While the trips back were uphill, the fact that I was pushing an empty wheelbarrow made it almost bearable, but it was still grunt labor.

It was our first full day of strenuous work. Busting our humps all day long was hard enough, but our bodies still had that hibernating bear quality and letting us know of their displeasure at being awakened. In short, our legs and lungs were singing burning arias, with our arms and shoulders doing background vocals.

Counting a day off to recover, the first eighty bags took four days and demanded something around fifty miles of hiking. Stationing in the rest of our material took three similar loads, and owing to the vagaries of weather, another month to complete. By the end of March, we were busy working the soil and establishing the nursery.

Rusty missed a couple of days over those few weeks, but by and large held up his end of the deal pretty well. He reminded me of working with Ethan, slow, but strong and steady. I helped him out financially, about a hundred bucks a week plus smoke, and he was grateful in his own way. Unsolicited, he began seeing himself in the role of my personal bodyguard. I guess I was flattered, but slightly uncomfortable. Rusty was unpredictable and I questioned myself about the potential downside of his services. It wasn't long before I had my answer.

Fartin Jack's partner Theo didn't come around much. He lived out of the immediate area and didn't have much interest in the business other than getting his share of the cash. His personality was grating. Most people who'd dealt with him would rather gargle razor blades than repeat the experience. He left a trail of hard feelings behind him wherever he went and in some curious blend of bad luck and karma, Theo and Fartin' Jack seemed to be joined at the hip. Between Theo's rage and Fartin' Jacks chiseling, the two of them had alienated practically everybody in the business and were left with only each other through a process of social osmosis.

If I was surprised to see Theo's dusty Bronco in the driveway when I got to Jay's, I was flabbergasted to see his face. He'd either been in a serious accident, or somebody had done some heavy pounding on him. The latter proved to be the case, and the somebody was Rusty.

Theo looked like he was suffering an allergic reaction from soaking his face in an over-cooked huckleberry pie. Most known shades of the color red were represented. His lips looked like two pink water balloons. A blood vessel in his eye had erupted, leaving the would-be white looking like a broken traffic light.

His other eye was swollen shut, bearing an uncanny resemblance to a nasty vagina in a dial-a-porn ad. If I didn't know better, I would have guessed that a Brazilian soccer team had used his head for a ball. He reminded me of one of those monster characters that would be driving the hot-rods on a Big Daddy Roth T-shirt.

He didn't care. He was in a rage, spitting a barely understandable stream of expletives through a gap created by the forced exodus of several of his teeth. "Nat thun-ob-a-bith!"

With Theo there wasn't much room for pity. If he possessed one constant, it was his abrasive personality. And with such an extremely short fuse, it followed logic that whatever misfortune he encountered, he more or less deserved it. All that aside, it was hard to look at him without some degree of sympathy.

On Jay's kitchen counter a jumbo bud of last year's gold was steeping slowly into tea. Sensing where this was leading, especially if Rusty showed up, Jay was making some "Mellow Yellow" tea for Theo. Talk about going to war with a peashooter!

Nodding toward Theo, I said to Jay, "He looks like he could use a quart of morphine."

Although it was painful to talk, Theo had come for a reason and was intent on being heard.

"You god do fire nat munner fusser!" he raged.

I had to bite my lip. His brains were all but hanging out of his nose, but the resulting image was in a macabre way, comedic.

"Fire who?" I asked. It's not like I had any employees.

"Nat munner fusser Russny," he garbled. "Hoon na fuss you thint?"

"Fire Rusty? I didn't even hire him. You guys did" I shot back. Seeing where this was leading, I began to get irritated. "You can't fire him anyway and you know it. What's to stop him from ratting us out?" I tried to reason with him, but that just pissed him off worse.

He ranted for a while, but I could tell he was in too much pain to keep it up and held my ground. He was asking something that was ridiculous to the point of being absurd. Ghandi would rat you out if you tried to pull this kind of heavy-handed jam job. The fact that he expected Rusty to accept being fired magnanimously was too much to consider. Theo was clearly deluded.

The tea had cooled off a bit and Jay managed to convince Theo to have a cup. He sipped it through a straw.

We all knew Theo had a blood pressure problem. When he got excited, his neck and face lit up like a plastic Santa Claus. The strain on his facial features over the last hour or so had caused some of his wounds to open, and as the blood began dripping, his face became horribly grotesque. Having shot most of his wad and realizing that I wasn't backing down, Theo begrudgingly let the matter rest.

Knowing that it would be the last thing Theo wanted to do, I invited him up to the garden to check out the babies. As expected, he declined. At that point I could have hung out at Jay's if I'd wanted to, but instead excused myself saying that the plants needed water.

As soon as I was hiking again I felt better. But Theo was a hard-headed Swede, I knew that too many months were ahead of us for this to be the last chapter in the book of Rusty and Theo.

Returning to the patch, I was surprised to find Rusty there and working. Given his penchant for transforming most of his life's events into an excuse to take the day off, I fully expected him to milk this one as well. He had some swelling and small cuts on his hands but aside from that, he apparently had the better of the exchange with Theo.

When I commented about it, he just smiled and said, "I'm very good at what I do."

"What exactly do you do?" I asked, then quickly added, chuckling, "You don't have to tell me if you don't want to."

"I'm like a re-po man," he shrugged, "only I don't do cars."

"Why did you tee off on Theo?"

"I was sticking up for you," he said. "Those guys are fucking you."

Then the story came out. Rusty had been drinking heavily and was holding court in a local bar when Theo ran into him. He knew Rusty was a risk when he was oiled, and figured he better get him out of there before the whole town knew what he was doing and for whom. It was obvious that Rusty was too drunk to drive, so Theo offered him a ride home. On the way out to Spanker Creek they started arguing, and it quickly escalated into a fight. The genesis of this particular argument was that Rusty didn't like the terms of my arrangement with Jack and Theo. It really wasn't any of his business, but looking back on it, I think it was just two drunks looking for a reason to rumble. There had been bad blood on and off between the two of them for years, and my deal with Jack and Theo was just the latest convenient excuse. Theo was behind the wheel and basically had the shit kicked out of him before he could get the car stopped.

I tried explaining that hit men were supposed to wait to get a contract before they went out on a job. I was flattered to think he wanted to be my protector, but who was going to protect me from him if his feelings for me changed?

As spring became summer, I was buffed and feeling good. Pot growing is farming with attitude, with a tendency toward the extremes. The environment I was working in was a beautiful and remote little world, far removed from the concerns of the average working stiff. No bosses, timecards, paperwork, or jockeying for a better cubicle. It can be as peaceful as a dove but there is always a hint of danger in the air. The very nature of the game breeds anxiety, and in the end, more things can go wrong than can go right. Stack

Theo and Rusty's little war on top of what already existed, and you can just predict an explosion.

While I was waiting to hear the bang, I was blind-sided by more lethal type of explosion.

Chapter 13

Felicia

The life I led was inherently dangerous but worry seldom reared its ugly head. I was just doing a job and my mind was consumed by the day-to-day requirements of running a pot farm. Growers are like high-rise window washers, focused on the task at hand and oblivious to the danger all around them. Rusty's pounding of Theo's face was a wake-up call. Realizing that I was dealing with a loose cannon had me on edge. So, the universe loaded up a spitball and threw it at my head.

There's no rhyme or reason for love, there just isn't. It appears when you least expect it only to disappear when it will hurt the most. My relationships have all ended up on the rocks leaving me leaning toward cynicism but my inner self keeps hoping. If it wasn't for the love I have for my children, I could become a hermit without much prodding.

Since my breakup I had been dating a few women casually and convinced myself that it was enough. I try to keep the emotional shit tucked away, but I'm Old School Sixties, Love is my badge. Sometimes it feels like beating a dead horse, but the dream never dies. It was burned into my psyche, and there's no removing it. Jung thought that the Arthurian legends constitute the physical under-pinnings of the collective unconscious while forming archetypes that describe the human condition. If I was a dreaming Percival, Felicia became Blanchefleur and her kiss woke me up.

Somewhere in the philosophical concept pile lies the idea of duality. Good and bad, pleasure and pain, day and night, Jesus and Satan. You can't have yin without yang. Philosophically speaking, that's just the way it works. Shakespeare said something like, "There is no good or bad, but thinking makes it so." Everything has a polar opposite, but our mind's eye often misses the big picture and sees just what it wants to see. My memories have faded with time, and it seems like a dream to me now but clearly l had lost my way. When I needed to be in the "Now" I was in the "Then." Whatever I was thinking about, it wasn't "The Big It."

I was working in the forest with someone who seemed to be a beast, not knowing that I was about to be blind-sided and destroyed by an angel. Work is work, but the bullshit that comes with the pot business in general and the bullshit of my situation was wearing me down, and when my feet needed to be on the ground, they weren't.

Not everybody has the same Big It. Money, fame, and power are probably the big three but there are others, but my guess is they are subsets of money, fame, or power. My Big It is Love. has been all along, even before I was a Hippie. I was girl-crazy in elemen-tary school and going through puberty only made it worse. That Sixties' thing—the pot, Acid, and free-love—just turbo charged the dynamic.

Although an individual's persona can change with the seasons or be set in plaster, it is voluntary, self-selected. It is what he or she chooses to show the world. Eric Clapton seems to change his per-sona with each new set of strings. Sometimes he wears a beard and long hair, and sometimes he's clean-shaven and wearing spectacles. Willie Nelson, on the other hand, has had the same salt and pepper whiskers and long braids and played that same gut-string Martin with a hole in the soundboard for thirty years. These choices are freely made, a matter of personal taste.

The personality on the other hand, is innate. It's who you are, whether you want to be or not. It's a combination of one's genetics and early environment. Out of that jumble arises the personality. The first order of business is to decide "What's my motivation? What's my Big It?" In the secret recesses of my mind, I feel that my life has been a quest for Love. It is the prize I covet above all others and an endless cause of despair because of my ability to royally fuck up a relationship. Don't get me wrong. Other drives such as wealth, fame and power play a part in my makeup too, but we all know inside ourselves what means the most. In my own mind's eye, I would gladly trade everything, even my life, for Love, knowing, believing, that the divine is Love and that possessing that Love, one possesses transcendence. Some heady shit, but I'm an old hippie, so maybe you can cut me some slack.

Have I been a fool for Love? Oh sure, lots of times. Take the story of Paula McKnight, my high school sweetheart.

High school sweethearts come and go like swallows from Capistrano and little teenage hearts get broken all the time. In most cases the pain wears off quickly and kids get on with being kids until they grow up. In my case, the pain didn't wear off quickly, as a matter of fact, it didn't wear off at all. Don't know why, it just didn't. Some psychologists refer to it as The Fisher King's wound. If that's what I was dealing with, the only thing I knew for sure about the wound was how it happened, I never understood why.

I met Paula when I was a sophomore in high school. The few neurons I'd ever devoted to my emotional side were quickly vaporized. As I said before, I hadn't had much experience with Love. When I met her my nervous system melted down. My love for her was all consuming. In a typically adolescent way, I loved her without measure, without hesitation, without suspicion and without regard to my own health or safety. In short, I was fifteen.

I didn't know it, but I was a balloon floating in a rose garden where the flowers are more easily noticed than the thorns. The tragedy is that once the balloon is popped, it has no future. It becomes like bits of latex scattered on the wind where it loses its ability to think, or even care.

Decades after the experience, dreams of Paula would trigger bouts of depression. Paula became my in-house obsession, taking permanent residence in the dark attic of my mind. I would find myself standing at the door of that room in my dreams, a door kept closed by fear. The truest indicator of the depths of neurosis to which I'd descended is that I still loved Paula, even after all these years. I admit it. As far as Love is concerned, I'm one sick puppy. I put Paula on a pedestal in my mind and there she stayed, until the moment I met Felicia.

It was an evening destined to be perfect in every way. The day had been warm, maybe hot, yet gentle breezes from the Pacific had cooled things off a bit. Los Lobos was playing at a riverside park in Garberville and somebody had come up with a few tickets. I went to the show with Spaghetti Freddie and Mac the Bear. When we got there, the roadies were still setting up equipment, so we had some time to kill.

Freddie had gone off somewhere and Mac and I were drinking some Red Tail Ale, talking about one thing or another. The conversation turned, as it often will, to women. In particular, Mac's bad luck at hooking up with one. It had been a couple lonely years for the guy, while I had been fairly lucky since Carrie and I had split the blanket. I was trying to cheer him up, so out of the blue I pointed at a woman standing alone, waiting for the music to start.

"That woman over there seems to be by herself." Looking at him I asked, "What do you have to lose?" We were maybe twenty feet behind her and couldn't see her face, but she had a beautiful figure and that big hair look that causes a man to fixate, and indicated to me that at least she wasn't ashamed of her face. "Go up and stand next to her casually. See if she'll talk to you," I encouraged him.

"I don't know," he mumbled, rearranging some dirt with his toe. "I'm not too good at breaking the ice."

"Come on, I'll go with you," I said playfully. "It doesn't cost anything to window shop."

We refilled our beers, and without fanfare, strolled up next to her. Mac was beside her, and I was next to him. She must have sensed our presence. As she turned her head toward us, poor Mac might as well have been invisible. She looked at me and our eyes locked.

She was breathtakingly beautiful. Ringlets of gold framed her face. Her eyes were a mixture of sapphire and jade. Her high cheekbones and soft mouth awoke something within me that had been dormant for years. Thank God, I didn't faint. She was the goddamned daughter of Aphrodite. You think I'm exaggerating-I'm not. I can't describe how I felt. There are no words.

Poor Mac was having a tumor removed from his brain. Her eyes and mine locked to each other's, created a laser beam that burned clean through him. Without a word he peeled away like a fighter plane leaving formation, allowing the two of us to be alone together, pondering the mysteries of each other's souls. It happened that fast.

Our auras enveloped us and transported us to some mysterious place that only the two of us could enter. We were in a crowd of people, but they existed in some other world. I don't think they saw us either.

The entire evening lasted one heartbeat.

Her name was Felicia, and she was from France. It fit, she sure as hell wasn't raised on a shrimp boat in Albania. She had a casual elegance, an earthy style, a New Age panache. She had to know how beautiful she was, yet she was amazingly approachable, sweet, and friendly.

And smart! Thank God I'd read something other than the sports page. I can't remember our first words to each other, but she worked in an art house in Paris and through Lady Luck I remembered some ancient bit of trivia, a one-time collaboration between Picasso, Jean Cocteau and Erik Satie. I think that surprised her. Apart from the physical attraction we obviously held for each other, our minds seemed to meld together like ingredients in a soufflé.

Love at first sight? Is there any other kind?

Los Lobos came on stage and launched into a set of original material and Rich Valens covers. Rock and roll with a side of gua-camole. The music was good, but my attention was glued to the woman dancing next to me. As we swayed to the music, our arms would touch and a feeling of euphoria would well up from within.

The band changed tempo and played a love ballad with Spanish lyrics. Spanish happened to be one of the five languages she spoke fluently. As she interpreted the romantic lyrics to me, we began to dance. With our arms around each other, her head on my shoulder, her lips near my ear, she was softly translating the words of love the band was singing. Within me a voice was screaming, "Don't let go!"

Einstein, in trying to explain his theory of relativity, said this. "When a pretty woman is in your lap, an hour will seem like a minute. If you sit on a hot plate, a minute will seem longer than any hour. He was right! The evening passed at light speed. As the crowd dispersed, we hooked back up with Mac and Freddie. We were heading in the same direction, so I gave Mac the keys to my car and told the boys I'd ride home with Felicia. Each moment was ecstasy. I didn't want the magic to end.

I began to learn about her life. She was half-Russian. Her grand-father had been a colonel in the Tsar's army and had migrated to France after the revolution. Because of her abilities with language, she worked as an interpreter for an international art house in Paris, but she wanted to be a writer. We talked about our favorite authors. She had just finished "The English Patient." I told her I liked a lot of the old guys, D.H. Lawrence, Nabokov, Thomas Hardy. Because she had never read anything by Hardy, I promised to find something of his for her plane ride home. I could not get enough of her. We'd bought a cheap bottle of wine to drink on the way home, and now the bottle was empty.

She dropped me off at the foot of Jay's driveway, and we parted. I wanted to kiss her, but I wanted to own her soul more. I gave her a hug and we said good night. I promised to call her in the morning.

On the way up the driveway, my feet barely touched the ground. The song "Some Enchanted Evening" got stuck in my head, and I made a mental note to buy the soundtrack from "South Pacific." What a fucking idiot, I was that far gone.

It was past two a.m. when I finally made it to bed, but I was awake by six, with visions of sugar plums and Felicia dancing in my cabeza. It was still too early to call. Chafing at the bit, I made it to eight o'clock, but could wait no longer. Risking that she would still be asleep, I dialed. To my delight, she answered before a second ring. Her voice was absolute nectar. We talked for a minute about the previous evening and what a great time we'd had, but all I really wanted to know was when I could see her again.

Unfortunately, her mother had made some plans for the day and her father was coming to town. She had family up and down the West Coast and they were all on their way to a family reunion. Hopefully she would have all her family dues paid by tonight so we could get together tomorrow.

The sands of the hourglass were now mixed with honey, and time seemed to stand still. I walked up the hill to water the plants, but nothing I did would release my mind from thoughts of her.

Tuesday morning found my heart palpitating as I dialed her number. Once again she answered the phone quickly. And again she told me that family responsibilities would keep her tied up, but she had told her mother not to plan anything for Wednesday evening. For those few precious hours, she would be with me.

Rusty would be on the hill that week looking after things, so I decided to drive to the Mendocino coast. On the off chance I could get together with Felicia sooner, I wanted to be close by. Melody

Austin, one of my pickers, lived in nearby Caspar, so I had a place to stay.

Melody was beautiful and possibly the sexiest women I ever met. She was a dear friend, and it's one of those mysteries of life that we didn't fall in love with each other. We slept together a few times, but somehow it never really clicked. We ended up liking each other as friends very much and that was enough. Her current boyfriend was the lead singer in a local band and his group was playing that night at the Caspar Inn. Not having anything better to do, I tagged along.

I was alone at the band's table when Felicia walked in with a guy that I later found out was an old friend of her mother's. I wasn't jealous, just dying to be with her. She was happy to see me, but unfortunately was waiting for the rest of the family to show, and couldn't dump the professor. She gave me a hug, "I can't wait for to-morrow. Call me at my mom's at five." She gave me another squeeze and then walked across the bar to be with her growing party.

Seeing Felicia, but not being able to be with her was too much to take, so I told Melody that I was going back to her place.

The music must have stopped at midnight, because Melody and the band strolled into her place around twelve-thirty. They had all seen "my Felicia," and were duly impressed. Felicia had star quality. She seemed to be bathed in light. She was the kind of woman who had the power to turn a dreary little watering hole into someplace special.

The bass player was busy loading the refrigerator with beer, and Melody was checking her answering machine.

"Melody, its Cheryl," began one message. "I can't make it to the Dead tomorrow. Something has come up. Call me."

Cheryl was the sister-in-law of one of the Grateful Dead's drum-mers. She always got backstage passes when they were playing.

This was not good news for Melody and she voiced her displea-sure. "Shit." She had lost her license after her last DUI conviction, so she needed a ride to Mountain View to see the show.

Everybody in the room heard the message, but they were playing another gig that night and couldn't make it. It came down to me. "How's about it, Goomba?" Melody cooed provocatively. "Take me to the show and we'll do the Dead in style!"

"Fuck," I laughed trying to sound disgusted. "Isn't that just like life? You can't get a goddamned thing without paying the price for it." Shaking my head I told Melody that the price of a date with Felicia would be a backstage pass to see the "Dead." I did some quick math and thought of Felicia. Cheap at twice the price.

On Wednesday morning I drove out to Spanker Creek to take Rusty some provisions and to check "the girls." It wasn't completely necessary, but it helped the time pass more quickly. I was back at Melody's in Caspar by 3:30, still plenty of time to get cleaned up before I was supposed to call Felicia.

At five I called, but nobody answered the phone.

I decided to head out to Mendocino and hang out in the Mendocino Hotel bar. It's about a ten-minute drive or so, and I called again when I got there. Still no answer!

At first, I naively figured she was running late, tres chic. But by 5:30 I'd ordered my second gin and tonic and started to worry. By six I knew the deal was dead, and by 6:15 I had finished my third G&T. Dragging my tail, I left. I should have been pissed-off, but I was just hurting. The anticipation of being with her, and the realization that now I wouldn't was a heavy hit of blue chagrin.

I got back to my car. A copy of Thomas Hardy's Far from the Madding Crowd sat on the dashboard mocking me. Sucker.

I backed out of my parking place, pulled a U-turn and headed for the highway. Mendocino is a small town. The businesses are mostly on one street. Before I reached the highway, I saw Felicia's mom's car parked in front of a small, local cafe. I couldn't believe it!

I pulled into a no parking zone in front of the fire station. This wouldn't take long. I grabbed the Hardy novel and went inside.

She wasn't there, but the waitress said I could check their deck out back. Walking through the restaurant, I caught a glimpse of

Felicia and her family through the window. Everybody was talking and laughing without a care in the world. I finally allowed my hurt to transform into a mini rage. They didn't see me coming until I tossed the book at Felicia. Unfortunately, it landed in her soup which splashed over her and her mother. Startled, the whole family gasped and turned to look at me in disbelief.

I didn't have a speech planned. I just launched into a diatribe.

"I know it doesn't matter to you, but I've been waiting three days to be with you and we had a date tonight. You could have waited at home to have the decency to break the date when I called. Instead, I had to sit like a fool in a hotel bar. Well fuck you and the horse that pulled the pumpkin wagon you rode to town on! I could have been backstage with the Grateful Dead tonight. Instead, I'm going through this.," searching for a word, "insult!"

About this time I began to focus on the faces at the table. They were speechless, their mouths agape, staring at this lunatic who I realized was me. Felicia and her mom were covered in minestrone, and I had basically said enough. So I spun on my heel and stomped off, as much as one can stomp wearing Birkenstocks.

A fireman was writing down my license number. He started to give me a lecture about blocking a fire lane, but I was on fire myself and I told him to go pet his Dalmation. I pulled out into traffic and slowly made my way toward the highway. From behind me, I heard Felicia shouting my name, and in my mirror I could see her running up the street. I probably should have sped away, but of course I stopped.

She was panting and out of breath when she reached the car. "Let me explain," she pleaded. "My mother went to so much trouble to get the family together. She would have been devastated if I didn't come with them." She went on, "Some of these people came from Oregon, others from LA. I caved in, but it's not my fault."

I could see she wasn't too good at accepting responsibility, but I didn't care. She had chased me down and was standing by my car, leaning in the window. God, was she beautiful. I never had a prayer.

"Give me another chance. We can go out tomorrow," she was almost pleading. But she didn't have to.

Leaning in the window the way she did revealed some of her left breast and the small black rose tattooed on it.

"Nice tattoo," I sighed.

She wrapped her arms around my neck and put her face by my ear and whispered, "Tomorrow?"

With another sigh, knowing the torture I would face for the next twenty-four hours before I saw her again, I nodded "Tomorrow."

She moved away from me slowly, her eyes and mine lost for a moment in each other's. Her arms gradually released me and slid across my shoulders like a python.

I patted my cheek with my index finger, indicating that I wanted her to seal the deal with a kiss. She obliged, but before her lips made it to the side of my face, I turned quickly and accepted her kiss on my mouth. It was good. She smiled.

"I'll call you at five," I whispered.

"And I will be there." Her voice and the promise it held made me quiver.

The next evening, the same bartender recognized me. "Given' it another try, eh?"

"Hey, hope springs eternal." I smiled and gave him the thumbs up. "Yer talkin' to a Giants fan."

He had the Tangueray ready. I set my wallet and sunglasses on the bar, took my drink, and walked into the lobby to use the phone. Felicia answered, but she was running late. She had been shopping with her mom and they had let the afternoon slip away. I told her where I was, and she said she could be there by six. I hung up and called the Cafe Beaujolais, a noted local restaurant, and made reservations for two.

"Any luck?" queried the bartender. My little two-day drama had become a soap opera for him and a few of the locals.

"Yeah," I said with a grin, "at least she was home."

One of the hometown wags chimed in, "But who's she with?"

They had a few chuckles at my expense, but I knew they wouldn't be chuckling when they saw her. I sat at the bar and nursed my drink for an hour that seemed like a day.

The bartender was returning with a tub of ice. He set it down behind the bar and whistled softly. "I think your date just arrived."

I looked up in time to see her reflection in the mirror as she walked up behind me.

A Paris original.

She was wearing a black pants suit with fine gray pinstripes and wide lapels. It had that 1930's zoot suit look with wide shoulders. It hugged the contours of her Monroesque body. Her big blonde hair flowed across her shoulders, waiting to be spun into gold chains. With the minimum of makeup, her face absolutely redefined the word beauty.

I left the barkeep a pot grower tip and he never said a word. I held her hand as we walked out of the hotel into the warm evening air.

Strolling along the storefronts with her, I felt as if a long-lost piece of my soul had returned to its rightful place. I was overcome with a feeling of renewal.

The café lobby was packed when we arrived, but the masses parted for us. We were walking in a force field of desire. Our table was ready, and as we were led into the restaurant, the place became quiet. I can't describe how it felt to have every pair of eyes in the place looking at us. I'd like to think that I added something to our appearance, but it was Felicia-she commanded the moment. No one seemed to breathe until she had been seated.

The murmuring resumed and the casual dining atmosphere returned. The place had its reputation for a reason, but the dinner, though superb, still placed a barrier between me and where I wanted to be. We enjoyed the meal as we explored the depths of each other's eyes but got our dessert to go.

We left the restaurant and walked back to the car like high school kids. The sun was still a few degrees above the ocean as we left the town of Mendocino to find a nice beach. The sunset promised to be spectacular. We drove south to the Navarro River and found a beautiful and secluded strand.

Having four-wheel drive, I was able to get far enough down the beach to ensure that no Land Captain would sail his Winnebago up next to us. I parked facing the sea. Enya's "Watermark" was playing on the CD player, and the sun was nearly down. The sky was crystal clear, a rarity for that time of year.

I said, "Let's look at the sun as the last bit of it disappears below the horizon. Sometimes you see a flash of green."

"Why green?" she teased, obviously more focused on me. She put her arm around me and gave me a soft kiss on my neck.

"I don't know," I said with a shrug. "Maybe it's because you see the light through the ocean water. Maybe it's because the sun is really green."

"You're telling me the sun is green?"

"Watch."

Only the tiniest sliver of sunlight remained over the Pacific, and it faded from view quickly. As the line of light compressed in length as well as width to a tiny rectangle, barely visible above the horizon, it changed from orange to gold to white and then emerald green. A crystal of kryptonite flashed and then faded.

Neither of us said a word.

My arm was around her and her head rested on my shoulder. I slid my hand under her hair and gently massaged the back of her neck. With my left hand, I softly stroked her face until she looked at me. I had been living for this since the moment I met her, and now, serene as a high diver poised to take the plunge, I resisted for an imperceptible instant before I melted. Her mouth was soft and delicious and our souls were hungry. We feasted on each other's lips like suckling infants.

Time, you bastard! Give me back the suffering hours so I can relive them at my leisure.

Her jacket was rather restricting, but once she was free of that, the lacy silk blouse she wore beneath breathed with her and became part of the sensory parade. It was one of those delicate pieces of clothing that seemed to unbutton itself a little bit each time she laughed. We laughed. We held each other. We kissed each other on our mouths, on our bodies, wherever it elicited a sigh or a moan.

"You're a Scorpio, aren't you?" Confident in her intuition, she said, "I am too. I can always tell a Scorpio."

If there are eighteen steps to arousal, we were on fourteen when the banister broke. I didn't need the armrest anyway, and it supplied a really great excuse to get in back.

It didn't take me long to find out why sports utility vehicles are all the rage. I practically lived in mine; it was outfitted with a foam mattress, sheets, blankets, pillows, the whole nine yards. If you can spare the two minutes it takes to put the seats down, you have a bedroom on wheels.

The Enya CD was playing over and over. It captured and defined the moment and we let it run on. Parked on the beach, one song was especially poignant, called "On Your Shore." It contained the lyrics, "I cannot hold you long enough." Felicia was leaving for France in twelve hours and I was flying on wings of wax, knowing what the sunrise would bring.

The moon was almost full. It had risen in the east at sunset and was now setting over the ocean. The blue-black sky of night was losing its power to blind, replaced by a soft, misty gray.

The rhythmic pulsing of the ocean, the barking baritone of harbor seals, the atonal melody of seagulls singing. The two of us were in harmony with the world.

The promise of that which sustains life, below the moist plankton, parted by the nose of the sea lion, deep in the wet darkness, over and over he dives until satisfied.

The two of us nestled together as one. She dozed off, but I never did. I would not surrender one moment to the mystery of sleep.

She was my cologne. Her parfum lingered, but as sure as sunrise, she was gone. I never saw her again.

Chapter 14

Ripoffs

I let her go. Shit. A really stupid move on my part but what else could I do? I was locked into my life, and she was heading back to hers.

Harvest was six weeks away, and like most years, I'd already blown most of the cash from the previous season. Besides the two hundred plants and Rusty depending on me, I had a halfway remodeled house, an ex-wife with a shopping fetish, two teenaged kids and a zoo full of critters. It wasn't like I could load my backpack and just split like back in the hippie days. I was wired into the so-called Real World and it was going to take me a couple of months at least to get my affairs in order before I could head to France. Until then it would have to be phone calls and love letters.

And business. We were in the rip-off season. The plants were covered with immature buds, still too early to harvest. But for the kind of low-life slime-balls it took to be a rip-off, then it was show time! Happened every year. Sometimes they got away with it, sometimes they didn't.

On the way back from Mendocino I noticed an abandoned vintage '60s Mustang, parked in a grove of redwood trees at the turn-off to Spanker Creek. I didn't think much of it until I saw a sheriff's car parked at Rasta Patti's, sending my worry meter into the red zone. I quickly drove on, pretending not to notice, and sped up once I was a turn or two down the road. I wanted to get up the hill to Jay's place and see if he knew what the hell was happening.

It seemed to me that half the people in the valley were there when I arrived. People I hardly knew, their kids, and dogs. It looked like the Fourth of July, but it didn't take me long to notice a few guns and nobody was smiling.

"What the fuck is going on?"

Jay met me where I parked. "It was a rip-off," he said solemnly. "They hit Tag and Andy's."

Tag and Andy were gay and two of the nicest guys you'd ever meet. They were pretty quiet and generally stayed to themselves.

"Who called the cops?" I asked. Rip-offs were usually dealt with "in-house."

"Wait 'til you hear the whole story," said Jay shaking his head. "God, what a day!"

I followed Jay to the cabin. Tag and Andy were there, along with Rusty, Fartin' Jack, and a couple of guys I didn't know. Andy was the more emotional of the pair and burst into tears when he saw me.

"Oh Goomba," he sighed sobbing, "it's over for us. We're finished!" He came up to me, and I put my arms around him. He was taking it hard.

Tag was feisty, pacing quickly back and forth. "Are the cops still in the valley?" he asked.

"Yeah, I saw the sheriff's car at Rasta Patti's."

"They're looking for Rusty," he said, pointing at Rusty with his thumb.

I glanced at Rusty and he looked like a kid with a bad report card, having to face his dad.

"Guess I got a little carried away." He feigned repentance, but I could tell he was savoring his role as the enforcer.

Jay began to narrate the story. "Two kids from down south ripped Tag and Andy this morning at dawn. Lucky Larry," he gestured towards one of the guys I didn't know, "was on his way to work, and he caught a glimpse of them running from their parked car with ski masks and backpacks. He called Patti from the store and got the alarm out."

I said, "Guess that's why he's called Lucky," and the others agreed by nodding their heads.

I introduced myself to Larry and his buddy, and we shook hands. "Rusty was there and…"

"Wait a second," I interrupted, "Rusty was supposed to be up the hill."

Rusty shrugged and slunk down in his chair.

"That's between you guys," Jay said, waving it off as unimportant, "thank God we had some muscle when we needed it."

Rusty jumped in to defend himself, but I told him to relax. "Let Jay tell the story."

Tag continued the narrative instead. "They topped me an' Andy's crop and had two backpacks full of green bud when we caught 'em. Me an' Rusty were waiting at their car, and we grabbed the little rip-off motherfuckers."

We could see Tag's blood pressure rising as he choked an invisible rip-off.

"First, we got our buds back, and we has 'em lay on the ground. At first everyone stayed cool," he shrugged, "but when one of 'em started talking shit, Rusty came unglued and started pounding on him. The other turdball took off in a panic. I had to keep Rusty from killing the guy."

To defend his violent actions, Rusty jumped up with a good deal of animation and began to recite some sort of biker oath, then everyone starting talking at once.

"Slow down," I counseled. "Just finish the story."

"OK." Jay patted Rusty on the back like a corner man. "Easy Champ, we're getting to the good part." Rusty went to the kitchen and grabbed a six pack of cold beer and started handing them out.

Tag continued the story. "So I pulls Rusty off the guy, but now he's really pissed. Rusty picks up a huge piece of firewood and starts bashing in the kids' Mustang." Apparently, this was the one I'd noticed driving into the valley. "He busted out all the glass, dented all the doors and panels, climbed up on top of it and started caving in the roof. It was fuckin' cool!" Tag was obviously getting some pleasure out of the retelling.

Half-jokingly I said, "That car is a classic."

"Not anymore," said Rusty, sounding like Peter Sellers in the movie, The Pink Panther.

We all laughed.

Jay took over again. "Some asshole heard the commotion, thought somebody was being killed, and called the cops." Nodding at Andy he went on. "Luckily, he stopped at Andy's to use the phone, so we knew they were coming."

Tag added, "It's an hour at least from the donut shop in Willits, so we had enough time to clear out the rest of the plants and get them hidden someplace else before the cops arrived."

"So it wasn't a total loss then," I said. "From the way Andy was acting, I thought you guys lost your whole crop."

"It wasn't ready to pick," he shot back angrily. "You know the weight won't be shit and the quality won't beat Mexican."

The conversation was interrupted by the sound of another car coming up the driveway. Rusty started to bolt, but I said, "Relax, it sounds like a Volkswagen."

It was Rasta Patti, and everybody ran to meet her.

"Somebody roll me a reefer!" she said with a grand wave of her arm. Patti was agitated over having to deal with the cops but was enjoying her moment in the spotlight. Seeing Rusty in the crowd, she chirped, "Hey big fella, the cops want to talk to you."

"What?" Rusty lumbered through the crowd. "Didja tell 'em my name? Ya didn't tell 'em my name, I hope."

"Relax. They think you're somebody named Mike," she said playfully, pretending to be straightening an invisible tie. "Maybe you should spend a few days at your office."

I voiced my approval. "Fuck'n A, maybe a few weeks!"

"Anyway, the cops are gone, and they took the rip-offs with 'em. They sure weren't gonna drive!"

Hearing that the cops had left the valley put everybody in a better mood. Jay put Another One Bites the Dust by Queen on the sound system and cranked it up. A beer run was hastily arranged, and we spent the day partying. It was OK with me as it helped take my mind off Felicia.

The late summer days dragged on. There wasn't much work to do once the plants were tied, just watering and waiting. I wasn't counting the days to harvest; I was counting the days until I could fly to France. I spent hours writing letters to Felicia, writing poems and songs about Felicia, daydreaming about Felicia. I'd think of her as I fell asleep, and in the morning when I awoke. I called her whenever I was off the hill. My phone bill was over three hundred dollars that month. Because it was eight hours later in Paris than California, I'd call her at midnight my time and reach her while she was getting ready for work. Then I'd set my alarm for four am so I could talk to her again when she stopped for lunch. I updated my passport and booked a ticket to France for early November.

The plants had been pumping the juice since the beginning of August. It was now the middle of September, the traditional beginning of harvest. The clear trichomes were turning milky white, and some were getting the amber hue prized by growers. The buds were now hard to the touch, the pistils were browning out, and the calyxes were swelling. Our crop would be ready in less than a week.

Unfortunately, I had completely forgotten about the old hair up Theo's ass. It had been five months since he'd gotten into it with Rusty, and I figured he would be happy to get his share and let the old matter rest. He probably would have, except that Theo was a magnet for trouble with an uncanny sense of timing.

A nearly permanent fixture in his local taproom, not much happened in Theo's neck of the woods that he didn't know about. Late one night, a casual acquaintance of his, Cilla Owens entered the bar, battered and disheveled. I didn't know Cilla or her husband well, but he was a local white-trash shithead named Marvin. He was a hulking mass, with a reputation for being a surly bully. I can only guess about Theo's real motivation, but he later claimed that he was only being a good neighbor. Hard to believe given Theo's track record, but the upshot was that Theo ended up taking Cilla home with him for about a week, and at some point he started screwing her. Before long everybody but her husband knew what was going on, but nobody dared spill the beans. While Marvin tried franticly to find her, the rest of us were busy getting harvest started.

I tried to keep Rusty up the hill as much as I could, but he was a meth head and could only stay clean for so long. He got wind of Theo's secret while taking a day off. Being a natural born shit disturber, he found a way to let the juicy tidbit slip to Marvin.

In a rage, Marvin loaded his 30-30 and hiked up the hill to Theo's place to settle the score. In a stroke of good fortune, Theo had decided to get Cilla out of there earlier that same day. He was taking her to a battered woman's shelter in Willits when Marvin arrived. As I heard the story, he hid in the woods above Theo's house, waiting for him to get home. After several long hours, he had cooled off a bit, or maybe just got bored. He decided to go home, but just so the trip wasn't wasted, he set fire to Theo's prized Harley-Davidson.

I didn't know any of this was going on at the time. I wasn't really in on the local grapevine. The only thing I knew for sure was that Rusty went away for a day off, and three days later, still hadn't come back.

We didn't have a phone at the camp, so after three days in the wilderness, I didn't have a clue as to what was going on. My provisions were depleted, so about an hour before dark I headed down the mountain. Halfway down, Theo stepped out from behind a tree and scared the hell out of me. He had been hiding there all day with a gun, waiting to ambush Rusty. He wanted to know if Rusty was at camp, and I told him I didn't know where the hell he was.

Theo brought me up to date on their latest soap opera plot twist.

"I don't need this shit, man." I let him know in no uncertain terms.

"Well, there wouldn't be this problem if you'd fired Rusty when I told you to." Theo, like most losers, started blaming everybody but himself for the mess he was in.

I said, "Look, I didn't hire Rusty in the first place, and I'm not the one who was putting the wood in Marvin's wife."

"I didn't fuck Marvin's wife!" he interrupted.

"I don't care if you did or didn't. He thinks you did." I took my backpack off and dropped it at the side of the road. This whole thing was absurd. "In three weeks I'll be in France. You'll have your cut, and you can do anything you want with Rusty."

The guy was a mess. He didn't know what to do. He really felt like smashing something. "Did you hear what happened to my bike?"

"We've been over this shit already." I said. "Let it go." It was nearly dark. "C'mon, I've got some cold ones at Jay's."

We walked down the hill together and got to Jay's well past dark. We drank a few beers and went over Theo's problem a few more times until he started to sound like a broken record. I left around ten. I had a long drive, and I wanted to be home in time to call Felicia before she left for work.

After the two-hour drive, I was exhausted. I grabbed a beer and went upstairs to my room to call Felicia. Phones don't ring in France; they issue a tone. The phone toned as usual, but to my complete surprise, a man's voice answered the phone.

Taken aback for a moment, I stuttered, "I, er, uh, is Felicia there?"

"Oui," I could hear the sound of the phone being put down, and him calling her name in the background.

She came to the phone, but her voice lacked the usual sparkle. "Hello, Duncan?"

"Yes, it's me, who answered the phone?"

"Fellipe. I told you about him before." Fellipe was her old boyfriend.

"What's going on?"

She paused a moment and in that pause I knew all I needed to know. "He wants to get back together," she said with a sigh, "He's asked me to marry him," and then trying to sound upbeat, "We can still be friends Duncan. The French can be very accommodating."

"I'm not French," I said softly, feeling hollow and dejected. Slowly the picture was coming into focus and my voice was withering. "I told you before I'm not interested in a three-way relationship."

She had a hard time with responsibility. Trying to make it easier for me she started "It's not so bad."

I cut her off, "My plane just crashed in the Atlantic. It's bad, it's *real* bad." She started to say something, but I just hung up the phone.

Tears cascaded down my face. Whatever I'd been holding inside, getting busted, the misery and shame of my failed marriage, the immeasurable love I'd felt for Felicia, the tension I had been feeling in Spanker Creek that summer, all exploded and I broke down. I'd never been laid so low and what remained was a tattered shell of my former self.

The colors faded, and my world turned gray. Fascist bombs dropped around me, horses in pain, wailing women, bleeding wounds of misplaced desire. In the mirror was reflected the dazed face of a bull. Colorless home movies of Guernica with "Death of Arthur" as a soundtrack.

I guess you could say I didn't take it very well. And to make matters worse, the rainy season came early that year.

A full seven-gallon tank of propane weighs about the same as a sack of concrete, filling a backpack and leaving your hands free to carry four bags of groceries to camp. After walking a mile uphill with one, you feel like your knees are connected to your ankles. By the time you reach camp, two and half hours have elapsed and the discs in your spine are tenderized and compressed. Exhausted, wet from rain and sweat, you sink into a chair with a cold beer. If you're lucky, you can hang around the pickers' tent awhile. There's always a fatty to burn and coffee laced with Bailey's Irish Cream. If your help has flaked, you pull an all-night shift in the drying shed. We called them Dr. Pepper drills. At ten, two, and four we rotate our plants to ensure that the ones nearest the heat don't get too crisp. This process goes on for two or three weeks and the propane lasts two days, max.

It all seemed to fit my mood quite well, actually. I was feeling like an unindicted co-conspirator who was paying some sort of penance, being flagellated by nature because I was too nonfunctional to do it myself.

The first ten pounds went off the hill at $4,500 each, and I could start paying the helpers.

Once Rusty got his first infusion of cash, he copped a stash of meth and tweaked big time. The pickers became uncomfortable having him around when I was gone, so we reversed roles. I had him do the hiking for provisions while I stayed at camp to tend the dryer, and make sure the pickers had everything they needed.

The trouble was that you were never quite sure when you would see Rusty again once he'd left camp. The only thing for certain was that when he finally made it back, he would be high on meth, spinning tales of intrigue and convenient coincidence-things like "aliens ate my dog after my dog had eaten my homework stories."

Really transparent bullshit sagas, but I just wanted to get the year over with. I didn't have the energy or the desire to fight anymore.

Mercifully, the season ended and nothing got killed except for my ego. The crop was OK by industry standards, but not mine. The weight of the crop was about twenty pounds lighter than the year before, and because I didn't have my heart or my head into what I was doing, it wasn't correctly dried either. By the time I got the energy to set up a small dryer to re-dry what I had left, some mold was starting to appear. I nearly lost my whole stash and two more miserable days in the wilderness getting it dried correctly, re-weighing, and repackaging my share. I lost a pound of weight culling the moldy buds, but I was beyond caring. It was a year that ended fittingly.

A few weeks later a friend of mine visited from Southern California. The weather was great, so we went out early one morning and shot eighteen holes of golf. Upon returning, there was a message on my answering machine.

"Hello Duncan, Goomba, it's Felicia. I've just moved to the south of France and my number is 33..." Then a computer-generated voice said, "End of tape." And that was the last time I ever heard her voice.

Chapter 15

Estelle

This was going to be my final year in the wilderness. After all the bullshit of the previous year, it's a wonder I even went back. I don't remember why I did it, but I think it was because Fartin' Jack and Theo didn't want me to. It's amazing the way our minds are wired. Even when it's obvious we should let go, we hold on tighter.

I had been divorced for a few years, and in typically male fashion, was going forward with my life, concentrating mostly on business while ignoring my inner emotional life. My fling with Felicia had awoken some long-dormant feelings and torn a hole in my emotional gunny sack.

This isn't meant to be some sad tale of woe. I've enjoyed a wonderful life, but at one time or another we all question our existence—how'd we get here and why?

Human beings are a curious breed. Are we evolving or devolving? Going forward, backward, or around in circles? A few thousand years ago we seemed to know it all, what with sages, witch doctors, oracles, and priests running around spouting the "Divine Word of God." The truth was dispensed from sacred fonts and incense burners like so much penny candy. The rest of us mere mortals replied by kissing their hems, paying tithes, and singing sacred songs. These songs were designed to keep the singers on the good side of the Almighty, and whether they worked or not, is known only by the dead.

Somewhere along the line, perhaps about the time of Pythagoras, a handful of thinkers decided that all the mumbo-jumbo the wise ones were pontificating didn't really cut it. The few people who learned to think for themselves decided to create a new class of teacher. Teachers who brazenly admitted that they didn't know what the hell Truth was, just that whatever it was, they were busy looking for it. They needed a name to describe this truth-seeking activity, so out of a couple of Greek words meaning loving and wisdom, they came up with the word philosopher.

These smart people sat around thinking about stuff and one of their cool ideas was that mankind can be roughly divided into three classes of people. In no particular order, they are dogmatists, those who claim to know the "Truth" and are perfectly willing to cram it down your throat. Next are skeptics. They think there is a Truth out there somewhere, but the one you believe in is probably bullshit. The final group are cynics, people who believe there is no Truth to find and think that groups one and two are wasting their time.

The dogmatists gave the world religion; the skeptics gave the world science and art; the cynics gave the world what? Rampant hedonism? Unbridled narcissism? Acquisition lust? Does such a thing really exist?

By the time I reached high school I was a card-carrying cynic. Moving around so much growing up left me a little bit bent. Being the new kid on the block is OK if it happens once or twice, but I was going through that every couple years. My dad was on the fast track to becoming a corporate big shot. Sadly, Fortune 550 companies didn't care anymore about the welfare of their employees or their families than the military did at that time. Along the way I quit trying to make it with the penny loafer crowd and started hanging around with the bottom feeders—greasers, punks, and a group of serious misfits that we called Grubs who were themselves only a year or two away from being labeled Hippies. I was an early adopter. The years spent as a malcontent had me primed and ready, so when the opportunity came to rub Aladdin's lamp I jumped at the chance and rode the magic carpet out of Dodge. I never went back, but I never got completely free of the emotional ties.

The Comet Felicia ripped through whatever belief system I had concocted in my mind, and I was left in moon dog misery taking a pity bath. From the shadows I went about the bio-vegetative commerce of my life, but I was a long way from caring about anything. I knew I had to find a way to care, because in this business you either keep your shit in one bag or you end up wearing your ass for a hat.

I must have had a morsel of self-respect left because at some point I decided to try and make some sense of where I was and how I got there. I spent the winter trying to get my feet under me, but it wasn't easy to find the help I needed. Having done so much acid in my formative years, I didn't think I could find a therapist I could talk to. I felt I needed someone who'd tripped the light fantastic and wasn't completely clueless as to what my head had been through. But I went ahead and tried a bunch of New Age crap anyway; Reflexology, Kinesiology, and something called the Bach Flower cure but through it all, nothing managed to work. In time I found myself on the couch of a Hypnotherapist.

Her name was Estelle Friedman, a board-certified clinical psychologist who I thought was a channeler and quickly won my trust. Talking to this woman produced the most unbelievable contact highs I've ever experienced. She liked to sit in an overstuffed chair with her legs crossed in the yoga position. With a blanket wrapped around her shoulders, I saw her office transformed into an Anasazi pueblo, and she, a blanket-wrapped sage, sitting as if on a cloud. To me she was a cross between Don Juan and Yoda. Estelle was a holy woman and in a trance state guided me through my past.

My past included over one hundred experiments with large doses of LSD, and I was certain that one particular trip was the key to understanding what it was that made me tick.

LSD is a mental rocket ship and I was one of the early test pilots. There had been some tragic accidents with its use, but fueled by excess optimism I took off anyway. Being one of those cats who thought consequences were for other people, I never worried about outcomes; and after I went over the edge, nobody who knew me was surprised.

By the time I got around to blowing my mind, I had been doing acid for about three years— maybe fifty trips. Up to that point, I had always bought a round-trip ticket, but this time it was one-way straight to the top—The Omega Point. Known by other names such as Seeing God, and achieving Satori being two of the most common, but Acid Heads called it "The Experience of the Light."

I went to Estelle thinking this blown mind business was the cause of my mental anguish. Both awake and later under hypnotism, I went into detail about my White Light trip. I described how I got there and what that world was like, from beginning to end. She listened, took it all in, and agreed that it had important significance, especially as to how I chose to live my life. She was interested about my time in Berkeley. When I mentioned having read P.D. Ouspensky, she nodded and said, "You're of the Fourth Way School, that much is obvious."

I smiled ruefully. "Yeah, I flunked out of the other three. I'm a B-forces kind of guy."

She frowned. "You're being too hard on yourself. I see you on a quest for authenticity..." she paused to consider, "that's not a bad thing."

But she wasn't convinced the White Light trip was the genesis of my depression. The incident fascinated her, but by then I'd seen her half a dozen times and by then she'd heard my whole life's story. She zeroed in on an episode from my early teens; being dumped by my first love, Paula McKnight. I'd never gotten over her and decades later she was still showing up in my dreams. Estelle concluded that it was the unrequited love I held for Paula that was at the core of my depression and relationship issues. Estelle thought I had what Carl Jung called a "Grail Castle experience," a traumatic emotional shock, sometimes referred to as The Fisher King's wound. She believed that I needed to go back to St. Louis, find Paula, and tell her how I felt. In shrink vernacular it's called facing the dragon. Inject some reality into my fantasy. It was the worst idea I'd ever heard, and I needed some prodding. It would take all the courage I had.

I have trouble understanding my gender. It's not that we lack courage. We'll run across a minefield toward a machine gun nest before gathering up enough courage to ask a pretty girl to dance. Death before rejection? Doesn't make any sense.

After that session, Estelle gave me a book by the artist Alex Grey, called Sacred Mirrors. She told me there was a triptych inside that reminded her of my description of my White Light experience and then said something remarkable, "Concerning your experience of the light…, I've been an analyst in this hippie hamlet for over thirty years and you're the fourth person who has told me the exact same story."

Inspired by Estelle's insights, I spent the winter traveling down the back roads of my past. Taking the scenic route to the Midwest, I waxed my skis and pounded moguls at Alta, Utah for a week, then went on to Aspen, Colorado. My unconscious hopes of hooking up with a snow bunny in Aspen came to naught, as I ended up in Colorado during National Gay Ski Week. I was on a fucking roll.

I finally reached St. Louis on the Friday before Super Bowl and checked into the Chase Park Plaza Hotel. Kind of a snooty place, but I didn't want to meet Paula at anyplace less than the best. I knew she'd married but didn't know her new last name. On Saturday morning I hired a private eye to help locate her. I was embarrassed, but he assured me that what I was doing wasn't at all uncommon.

The phone woke me on Sunday morning.

"Hello," I said, trying to sound awake and blasé, but succeeding at neither.

It was the P.I. "Good morning, Duncan, I hope I didn't wake you up."

"No, I'm up," I lied.

"Your Paula is named Paula West now." He gave me her phone number. "If there's anything more I can do for you, be sure to give me a call."

I thanked him and said if it all worked out, I'd invite him to the wedding.

It had cost me two hundred and fifty bucks, but at least I had her phone number. I didn't have the nerve to call her yet, but it was still early so I decided to take a bath and order room service. By nine-thirty I was clean and fed, so I touched my third eye and dialed her number.

The call went to her answering machine. I don't know if I was disappointed or relieved, but nervously, I put a message on it. Something to the effect that she probably didn't remember me but was in town and would love to see her.

I sat back in a chair and wondered if she'd call back.

It was five or six hours before the Super Bowl kickoff. The pre-game show had been on for a while but my mind was only on Paula. Finally, the phone rang, and it was her.

"Duncan is it really you?" she began. "Of course I remember you."

Not wanting to dump thirty years of angst over the phone, I told her that I was passing through St. Louis, and on a whim decided to call some old friends. A lie for sure, but what could I do? After so many years, and driving this far, I had to see her again.

"I'm at the Chase. Could I buy you lunch?"

Without hesitating, she said, "Yes." I gave her my room number and told her to call me when she got to the front desk.

After years of heartache, it was coming down to this one mo-ment. I agonized over what to wear. I'm a jeans and tee shirt kind of guy but I was trying to look my best for Paula, so opted for standard-issue Yuppie camo: a dark blue silk jacket, gray slacks, light blue oxford shirt, and Ferragamo loafers. I looked like a Nordstrom's window display, but it was either that, blue jeans, or ski pants. I wanted Paula to know that I'd tried.

All I could do then was pace the floor and worry. What if she turned out really ugly? What if she weighed two hundred pounds now? What if she looked like a coke whore and her teeth had turned brown and were falling out? What if she had become the local president of the Partnership for a Drug Free America? It's amazing how much negativity the mind can churn up when worried.

The phone rang. "Mr. Easley, this is the front desk. You have a visitor."

"Tell her I'll be right down."

It seemed like a mile from the elevator to the front desk. I didn't dress up often and the shoes I was wearing hadn't been properly broken in. They had that new leather sole squeak and it's hard to be cool when your shoes are squealing like a satchel of baby mice.

I recognized her at once. She was still thin, maybe too thin, flaxen hair dancing at her shoulders, a long black wool skirt and a white silk blouse under a black wool blazer. She wore make-up that she didn't need, and too much jewelry for my taste, but her bangles were nice pieces, all gold with some assorted rocks. Along with earrings, she wore a necklace, lapel pin and bracelet on one wrist, a gold watch on the other. But no wedding ring. That was cool.

I wish I could say that we fell into each other's arms like long-lost lovers in the last scene of a romance movie, but it was more like meeting a business associate for lunch. I think we shook hands, maybe gave each other a gentle hug, but that was about it.

She was just as beautiful as I remembered, and her eyes were as captivating as ever. I can't remember meeting anyone with more gorgeous eyes. Miniature blue rosettes, constructed with slivers of sapphire and covered with a lens of diamond. Her eyes sparkled like the night I met her.

We settled on a sofa in the corner of the lobby. It was a quiet Sunday and we had the whole place to ourselves. We talked about old friends, how our lives turned out and what we were doing now, but luckily she didn't ask what I did for a living, although I'm sure she could tell I was doing all right. She let me know she was going through an ugly divorce and I sensed an aloofness, not necessarily towards me, but toward men in general.

After some small talk I found an opening in the conversation and decided to level with her. I wasn't just passing through town. I had come back expressly to see her again and tell her that I still loved her. I related that dreams of her left me depressed for months on end. We talked about my sessions with Estelle and how it was through her urging that I found the courage to return to St. Louis and let her know how I felt.

She was polite but unresponsive, even a little suspicious. I think at one point she wondered whether her husband had put me up to this. It seemed absurd from my point of view, but perfectly possible from hers. I gathered that she had suffered years of neglect and abuse, and the thought of that broke my heart.

We went into the dining room and had a snack and some coffee. In a distant vault where my memories were stored, I still loved her. I would have done anything to stay with her, to love her and to try and make her happy, but that wasn't going to happen. Probably for the best, we were both damaged goods by now and our worlds were very different. In the end it was one of those east-west things, and our twains would never meet.

I walked her to her car. We gave each other a kiss on the cheek and said good-bye. That's the last time I saw her. I wrote her two lame letters and left a couple of messages on her answering machine, to which she never replied, leaving me feeling sad but I couldn't blame her for not responding.

I drove to Florida to visit my parents and play a few rounds of golf with my dad. I stayed for several days but wasn't very good company. So far, the winter sucked. Between Felicia and Paula, my emotions had been run through a psychic garbage disposal but on the plus side, thirty years of angst had been off-loaded and I was feeling marginally better about the future.

Leaving Florida I drove to New Orleans for the start of Mardi Gras. The place lived up to its reputation. I got rip roaring drunk on Hurricanes, ate great food, traded beads, enjoyed the sights, and heard some fantastic music. The Big Easy, what's not to love? But alone and blue in a crowd of people enjoying themselves somehow only poured salt on the wound of the Fisher King. After a few days in The City, just another invisible presence in the crowds, I finally said, "Fuck it." and drove back to California.

Home for a few days, moping around, killing time, trying to figure out what to do or where to go and finding no answers, I put the movie Dr. Zhivago on the VCR. If I had to compare Paula to anyone, it would be Julie Christie. Paula was much prettier, but they looked a lot alike, especially their eyes. I started to cry when the overture began. I know men aren't supposed to cry, but finally reaching a catharsis, bawled like a baby for the entire movie.

I'd done what was needed. I hadn't been able to move forward without knowing what was in her heart, and now I knew. That winter took its toll on me but left me feeling like I'd scraped some major shit off my shoes. The therapy worked—I never dreamed of Paula again. I do, however, think of her from time to time but it no longer depresses me. The feelings turned out okay, bitter-sweet, but okay.

It was springtime in the Emerald Triangle, and ready or not, it was time to get back to work.

Chapter 16

Goons

Year three with Jack and Theo started on a sour note. Facing another year with Rusty, coupled with my lingering personal angst made it hard to imagine a positive outcome.

In the world of illegal pot growing, it was almost impossible fire someone once they were on board, even in the best of circumstances. I was determined to ease Rusty out, but what would keep him from dropping a dime on me? Luckily, I never had to answer that question. Before our first meeting in the spring, he got pinched in some bar room brawl and had to do one hundred and twenty days at the Gray Bar Hotel in Sacramento. Because of his long criminal record, he risked getting six months just for looking like he'd done something wrong. I hated to see anybody get fucked by the system, but in this case it helped me out of a serious dilemma, so I didn't lose much sleep over his misfortune.

I started off the year without a helper but wasn't worried. In the Triangle, pilgrim tenders seemed to crawl out of the woodwork and before long a young gun stepped forward and asked for a job.

Zack Skinner was a local rascal. The "System" had branded him incorrigible, but he was really just a pretty average high school grad who was still kickin' around his hometown, living party to party. His problem was he got busted a lot. He was smart, quick-witted and hardworking, so what if he liked to smoke pot and let off some steam once in a while? What twenty-three-year-old doesn't? He had the balls to ask me for a job and worked his ass off. As an employer, I couldn't have asked for more.

We had a great time working together and until August, the summer passed without incident. Then the cops came and started banging us hard. From that point to October were some of the longest days of my life.

Pot farms came in all shapes and sizes back then, from a few plants on the back porch to a dozen or so in the back yard, to a few hundred or even thousands. At that time, 109,000 plants in a series of indoor sites was the single biggest bust on record. There was also a fool who tried growing sixty thousand plants in a corn field but gave himself away by running his water pump non-stop.

Most growers despised the large-scale greedy bastards as much as the cops did. Around Spanker Creek, most of the farms were mom and pop operations, real small-scale grows roughly between fifty and one hundred plants, basically rent money. Hometown people scraping by.

But the Logans were different. A roughneck clan, they were the greedy, over-the-top, large-scale growers that gave regular, every-day outlaws like me a bad name.

Tim Logan was born bad. He looked like he'd stepped right off a "Wanted" poster, and while not a big man, he was grizzled and mean-looking. His face had that dried leather quality that cigarette smokers get, he always wore a sweaty old cowboy hat and was never without some sort of drink in hand. He tried to be friendly but had the kind of poker player face that never allowed what he was really thinking to show. He and his brothers and a few assorted other Goombas formed a tight-knit gang and fortunately for us, kept to themselves.

Nobody knew exactly how many plants Tim Logan and his brothers were putting in, but we knew their op was huge. It turned out they were growing a mind-numbing six-thousand plants and when they went down, they nearly took everyone in the valley down with them.

Tim's growing methods were brutal. He randomly cleared out large areas of the forest and packed as many plants into the clearing as he could, then crisscrossed wire high over the patches then hung branches, leaves, and camo nets from the wire to hide everything. This worked well for him on a smaller scale the year before, probably owing more to CAMP not hitting our area very hard than his growing practices.

During the summer, growers typically walked the hills around their operation daily, becoming intimately acquainted with the forest. Any small change not attributable to animals was noticed and analyzed. In late July or early August, Tim or one of his workers found a trail that had been cut through the bushes near one of their patches. Strangers had put it in, and they figured it was probably someone planning to rip them off. They picked up the trail and followed it off their property. It ended at an old logging road on an adjacent parcel of land where they poked around for a while, and found a pickup truck hidden in some undergrowth. Tim saw red and left a .45 caliber bullet on the dashboard as a message to the assumed rip-offs.

Unfortunately for Tim and the rest of the valley, the truck belonged to narks. Whether it belonged to the DEA, CAMP, COMMET, or HMET didn't matter. The bullet crossed a line and the various law enforcement agencies united, making Spanker Creek their new target of the War on Drugs.

Thanks to this singular action, things escalated one day in the middle of August to a level that nobody could believe. A convoy of over a dozen vehicles—sheriffs' office 4X4s, confiscated grower's trucks, a 3-ton flatbed stake-side, and a mobile donut cooker—entered the valley shortly before breakfast. Their arrival was announced by three noisy choppers consisting of a big Nam-era Huey used for goon transport and plant hauling, a Bell 400 for support and surveillance, and a Hughes OH-6 (also called a Loach). All in all, it looked like a wad of green puss dripping from the cock of the police state, coming to slime us.

They went after Tim Logan's operation first, taking nearly three days to cut down 5,000 of his 6,000 plants. His place was so big and spread out that they missed over a thousand plants. But they must not have been very good at counting, because they reported to the media that they found 2,700 plants. While the bust was going on at Tim's, aerial surveillance combed the valley, finding most of the farms on the west side, and a few others on the east.

Zack and I shifted into high gear and quickly buried our patch in camo. We made sure that the mulch below the plants was thick and covered them all in camo as best we could. I cut down most of a big bay tree, and we spread the branches around the patch. We did what we could, and fortunately were ahead of the game since we'd been serious all that year keeping our girls 'phlaged in.

For the ones that were out in the open, we cut down small manzanitas and tied them up around the plants to hide them. We also stuck one-gallon plastic bottles in the ground, filled them with water to keep the foliage green longer, and sprayed our fake trees with a product called Cloud Cover, usually used to keep Christmas trees green.

Luckily, the cops left the valley at the end of the week without ever coming close to us, apparently content with taking out Tim Logan's large farm and over a dozen smaller ones. The official word given to the media was that their total haul was close to 4,000 plants. But we knew they got 5,000 from Tim Logan's farm alone, and by our reckoning, took out 3,000 more plants than they reported.

By the time the weekend rolled around, most survivors were feeling frisky. CAMP had all of California to cover, and less than two months to do it before our plants would be safely out of the ground. We relaxed a little, thinking they wouldn't be back.

Tuesday morning came and changed all that. In the pre-dawn hours they raided Tim Logan's place *again* and arrested him in his bed. They must have wanted him badly and found he had a quarter pound of cocaine, several ounces of meth, thousands of dollars cash, and twenty pounds of clean buds in his basement. I'm sure if Tim had it all to do over again, he'd have used better judgment but after hearing about the amount of hard drugs around his place, I realized he didn't have any judgment to use. Fortunately for us, Tim was looking at twenty-five years in the big house and the valley was glad to see him gone.

The cops stayed in the valley the rest of the week, concentrating on the east side this time. Zack had the day off and by the time I realized what was happening, they were all over me.

My patch was on a bluff with western exposure. Flying from the east, a chopper would be hard-pressed to see me, but hovering in circles was a different matter entirely. I was running flat out toward the patch when the chopper started to circle above me. It was the big Huey at treetop level, covering every inch of the hillside. At a mere fifty feet above the patch, the exhaust sounded like artillery fire. We had done a thorough job of camouflaging, but some of the plants were over ten feet tall, and four 10-footers were in a row standing gloriously proud in the sunshine.

I had a razor ring in my daypack, a handy item growers wore for cutting string while tying plants. Fishing the ring out, I arrived at the patch and ran through, cutting the strings that held the four plants up. The chopper passed over only moments before and headed down the hill away from me. Then I heard the distinct sound of its Doppler shift and knew it was turning around and coming back. I climbed a small tree and cut the top wire with my hand-pruner then jumped down and started cutting string again. With the top strings cut, I bent two of the plants into neighboring bushes to hide them from view. The third one was brittle and its stalk snapped, effectively killing the top of the plant.

The Huey was combing every inch of the hillside and heading straight for my patch. As I took hold of the fourth plant, I saw the spinning rotor of the chopper, then its nose appeared over a small fir tree at the far west end of the patch. All I had time to do was fall back into the nearest bush, pulling the pot plant over me for cover.

The front floor of the Huey was clear and I could see the pilot and co-pilot scanning the hillside. They didn't notice me or they would have stopped. The Huey then slowly passed over the patch and headed in the direction of my camp. Moments later, I heard the chopper turn and head back for another look. Figuring the jig was up, I bounded over the patch's fence and ran like hell into the woods.

I took cover in a thicket; my heart pounding, racing at over forty beats in fifteen seconds. My heart rate, usually in the low 60s, was running at over 160 beats a minute. The chopper was back at the patch, only this time it sounded like they were hovering.

Thinking to myself, "So this is what it's like to be chopped." I began feeling nauseous and weak, but the feeling passed and so did the chopper. I don't know how they missed me, but they did. I sat on the trail for a while, too rattled to do anything, and the chopper didn't come back.

Zack came back that evening and the next day we redoubled our camo efforts.

In two more days of raiding they took out another thousand plants or so. They got Tag and Andy, Rasta Patti and some others, and when the Good Morning America crew showed up we figured it was all a media stunt. Stunt or not, the cops had probably taken about ninety percent of the valley's cash crop out and left the locals shell-shocked.

An eerie calm settled over the valley. We didn't hear another chopper for two weeks and slowly began to breathe easier. Thinking we were in the clear, I had all but forgotten the goons when suddenly they appeared again. Driving into the valley one morning in early September, I spotted the flatbed truck, Big Red. Half full of plants and parked in the landing zone, I had an uneasy feeling.

Shit! There weren't many targets left. I stopped at Rasta Patti's to find out what was up and the news wasn't good. She had been in a funk since her own patch's demise, but the look on her face as I parked my car told me volumes.

"They've been working the hill up behind Jay's place all morning," she said sadly. "I guess I won't get to pick for you either."

As far as we knew, my place was the only one behind Jay's.

I let out a sigh, and grimly tried to be philosophical, "It ain't over 'til it's over," but the words sounded hollow, even to me. With an eye out along the treetops for choppers, I drove slowly to Jay's, not knowing, but pretty sure what news awaited.

Zack was supposed to meet me at Jay's, and when he didn't show up I feared the worst. Jay had heard the same chopper as Patti and had come to the same conclusion. He didn't know about any patches other than mine in that direction and didn't know where Zack was.

Jay rolled a fatty. I busted out a couple of cold beers and we waited. I wasn't really in the mood to walk all the way out to the patch if the crop was gone. Jay and I must have been shooting the shit for the better part of an hour when we heard Zack's footsteps in the woods above Jay's cabin. He'd been marching double-time, and when I first saw him, he wasn't smiling.

"What's happening?" I shouted anxiously when he was within earshot.

"You ain't gonna fuckin' believe what happened!" he said, shaking his head with a big frown on his face. My heart sank.

Zack dropped his pack and gave it a disgusted kick. "A fucking bear got into our pool and tore the liner. We lost a whole fucking tank of water!"

Jay and I looked at each other and shook our heads.

Zack started apologizing for being late. "I had to put the spare liner in the pool and..."

Smiling broadly, I interrupted him, "But what about the chopper?"

"Chopper?" Zack asked quizzically. "I heard one this morning, but it never came near us."

We were still in the ground! Amazing. Jay and I started whooping. I shook a beer and sprayed Jay and Zack, while Jay danced a jig and Zack looked at us like we were nuts.

The bust was somebody else's patch. I felt a lot better now about the hour-and-a-half hike to the camp. Whoever went down must have been a "Pirate." Pirates are even lower on the grower social caste than carpetbaggers. A carpetbagger was a grower that lived out of the area, but paid tribute to whoever owned the land he had to cross. Pirates came and went in the night, sneaking in and out, paying tribute to no one. Still, I felt bad for whoever the guy was, at least he wasn't ripping anybody off.

Zack left for a couple of days off, and I started hiking up the hill. There were two other operations on the hill, but they were over a mile away from me in another direction. We used the same road up the mountain though and shared the cost of a lookout. The lookout was a friend of Rasta Patti's, and his tent was where the road forked at the top of the hill. I wanted to talk to him about the chopper Jay and Patty heard, before hiking back to my camp and was whistling for him near his tent when the Huey landed about a hundred yards from me and began disgorging goons.

The hilltop was a wide-open flat. It had been leveled by a bulldozer years before to use as a skidder pad for loggers and served the Goon Squad quite nicely as a heliport. I'd walked across that same clearing only five minutes earlier.

I forgot about the lookout when I first heard the chopper. He wasn't at his tent anyway, and I quickly got the hell away from it, scrambling deeper into the forest. I figured the odds were pretty good that the goons had spotted my patch and they were getting ready to hike in. This was the closest place to my operation that they could safely land.

The chopper took off after a few short minutes on the ground, making a colossal racket. As the noise abated, I heard the engines of a couple of Four Trax ATVs start up. They had ferried them in on the big chopper to conduct an open field search of the area. My first impulse was to get the hell out of there, go home, and let the goons go about their business. But another part of me wanted to hightail it back to my patch and rescue some plants.

My adrenaline started pumping and primitive territorial instincts took over. I'd worked hard for that crop and was determined to save what I could. I don't remember thinking. I just remember acting.

A smaller chopper landed disgorging more goons. The sound it made drowned out the noise the ATVs were making, and I didn't hear them coming up the trail toward me until they were near where I was hiding behind a tree. They must have seen the lookout tent from the air because they stopped near it and went into the bushes to check it out. They parked less than twenty feet from me, but to my relief walked off in the opposite direction.

The second chopper was a Bell 400 and the ear-splitting noise it made taking off allowed me enough cover to creep deeper into the underbrush. The 400 stayed in the area, hovering at treetop level and scanning the ground below for the patch they knew was nearby. The chopper drifted off to the east, then the ATVs started back up and headed down the trail in the direction of my place.

A lot of growers drove ATVs around their farms. The ones the cops rode most likely were stolen from growers on previous raids. I never used one for work, having been an old-school fanatic about keeping my trails invisible. "Pack it in, pack it out," as the old Boy Scout saying went. Keeping a trail camouflaged takes constant vigilance, and I'd pissed off more than one tender by making him rake leaves and scatter branches during the hot summer months. For the time being though, the extra work seemed to be paying off.

The cops on the ATVs reappeared after about twenty minutes. They must have stopped at the canyon, because they hadn't been gone long enough to make it all the way back to my place.

They milled around the hilltop for a while, then headed in the direction of Mac the Bear's place and Fartin' Jack's new operation. The Hughes had been looking in that vicinity and was now turning tight circles. I figured, correctly, that Fartin' Jack's farm was history.

Stashing my pack in a gully under a fallen log, and using a baby doug fir as a ladder, I disappeared into the canopy of a massive old oak. It wasn't until I was thirty or forty feet up that I felt safely hidden. The oak was infested with mistletoe, so I knew I was invisible from the ground.

The Huey landed again with another load of goons. The hillside was crawling with them. They assembled at the trailhead and started hiking east, and while they didn't walk directly under the tree I was hiding in, they went by close enough that I could see them. Wearing camouflage uniforms, bulletproof vests, and carrying walkie-talkies and automatic rifles, they looked like a bunch of Boy Scouts playing army. It was a chilling sight. A line from a Dylan song, "I saw guns and sharp swords in the hands of small children," flashed through my head.

I stayed hidden in the tree for an hour or so. I had my glass pipe with me, packed a bowl, and smoked some herb. Smoking pot in a treetop is one of life's simple pleasures and despite all the madness going on around me, I felt peaceful, even serene.

The Huey was now over Jack's place, and as the cable was being lowered to take out the first full net, I decided it was a safe time for me to move along. I worried that some stray goons might still be on this side of the hill poking around, so with the stealth of an assassin I climbed down out of the tree, retrieved my pack, and hiked deeper into the woods, reaching my place in a very roundabout way.

The chopper could take a load to Big Red much quicker than the ground crew could fill another net, so with the surplus time, the Huey continued aerial surveillance. The pilot must have had a hunch about my general area because just like clockwork, he reappeared every half an hour until dark. Having western exposure, the late afternoon was the worst time for me to get flown. I knew how the sunlight bathed my plants in the late afternoon, when the shimmering iridescence of their leaves seemed to jump off the forest floor. Luckily, the smaller choppers had departed, and I only had the Huey to worry about.

Vietnam-era Hueys were loud and terrifying by design and rumored to be that way to scare the shit out of the enemy. The exhaust was directed at the ground and sounded like cannon fire. It was one thing to use them against the Viet Cong, but another thing entirely to use them against our own people. Due to their size, they're lousy at surveillance and they're so big that when they get close to the ground, their prop wash creates camo.

What really got a grower's heart pumping was being at your patch with a helicopter circling overhead. Typically, choppers cause paroxysms of fear, and all work comes to a halt.

Usually, the time is spent hiding behind trees with binoculars, but I couldn't afford to stop. I had come this far, and anything I could do to keep from getting chopped down, although insignificant in terms of the whole summer's work, would be as valuable as all the rest of the effort combined.

I worked feverishly covering the trails around my camp. The trail to the pump was bare, and while I was working on it, I thought about the noise the water-powered ram pump was making. It didn't have an engine, just the weight of the water moving through it. It pumped a gallon a minute, twenty-four hours a day, and was pretty quiet. But like the beating heart in Edgar Allen Poe's A Tell-Tale Heart, our pump made a constant thumping noise that could be heard by anyone walking by. I ran over to shut it off, knowing that if I didn't it would be game over.

On the way back, I raked leaves over the trail as best I could but before I was able to finish the job, I heard voices in the creek bed near the pump.

Two cops were walking the dry creek bed looking for pipes. I'd shut the pump off just in time. They were about a hundred yards back down the hill and I had an unobstructed view of them.

The cops appeared bored. To my horror, one of them sat down on the pile of rocks that the pump was buried under, and the other sat on a fallen log that was hiding the pipe. If they started poking around, I was a goner.

They sat there for what seemed like an eternity, but in reality was only long enough for one of them to smoke a cigarette or two. They didn't seem all that motivated, it was late in the afternoon, and I had the impression they believed they were on a wild goose chase. In the two years that I'd been growing out there, I had gone to extreme lengths to ensure that the area surrounding my operation remained natural and pristine, and so far, my efforts were paying off.

The cops stood up and continued walking down the creek bed, passing a drain valve installed at the line's lowest point. It was only sort of hidden, and they would have seen it had they been paying attention. Instead, they just walked right by it talking to each other.

When the cops were no longer in sight, I beat it back to camp. If they turned west to climb out of the creek, they would walk right through my operation. I figured the odds of that happening were about fifty-fifty so I quickly wiped my fingerprints off anything I could find, loaded personal items into my pack, then beat a trail up the hill back into the thick brush.

I'd been on edge all day. Worn out and emotionally spent, I hunkered down to wait for the safety of nightfall to avoid the risk of being spotted. I never saw those two snooping goons again and figured they must have turned east at the bottom of the hill. The choppers worked until dark and then split.

I stayed hidden for another hour. Heading back to camp by moonlight I detoured to the pump and turned the water back on. I could see that the cops had stuffed out a cigarette butt inches from the rock that covered the valve that operated the pump. Fucking slobs. They probably didn't realize it, but that filter would be there for about fifty years. I got the impression that even if they knew it, they would leave their crap anyhow.

The environmental argument wasn't one-sided. We growers shouldn't have been out there either. We tended to be slobs too and had killed a lot of rats and mice that would otherwise go to feeding the owls and hawks. I'd much rather have grown pot out in the open on a proper farm than halfway to nowhere in the middle of the wilderness. Legalization couldn't come fast enough. The whole thing was a mess.

Cautiously I returned to camp but was too exhausted and nervous to eat. I unrolled my sleeping bag, but it was too hot to get in, so I undressed and lay on top of it.

Back then, growers spent much of their time agonizing over the wait. The last weeks were crucial in terms of quality and each day was its own eternity. Hanging in until the plants were ready was a grand game of chicken, and sometimes you felt like your only friend was the darkness. Darkness kept the choppers away, and if the sun didn't come up for a week, it would have been all right with me.

I was floating in the nether world, not asleep but hardly awake either when I heard the chopper returning. At first, I thought they were flying home, having never heard of a chopper doing surveillance at night. But the damn thing started to circle over me as its searchlight knifed the darkness. I was up and dressed in a New York minute and in a panic, bolted to the trail. This was too fucking weird.

The chopper drifted east and didn't return. It hovered a mile or so away, and after thinking about it, I figured the two cops I'd seen in the creek must have gotten lost and were being picked up.

I crept back to camp. Fully clothed, I lay back down but I couldn't sleep. Every deer or woodcock in the bushes sounded like an approaching enemy. Around four in the morning, I finally drifted off for about an hour but awoke with a start just before dawn. I quickly rolled my bag and strapped it to my pack. If they were coming in, I was going to be somewhere else. Hoping against hope that they had finished their work the night before, hearing the tell-tale *wukka-wukka-wukka* around seven am confirmed it was going to be another long day.

I stationed myself near the lower gate at the back of the patch, still having visions of saving a plant for stash. I had food in my pack for a couple of days, and if they showed up, was set to grab a plant, and disappear into the heart of the wilderness.

Like the previous day, the choppers were around every half-hour. It seemed as though they were working closer to me, and I wondered who had a patch left to raid. By eleven am the noise was taking its toll on me. The continuous overflights frayed my nerves. Time was standing still and I no longer cared. Every time the chopper got near my patch I thought to myself—just get it over with! But they kept teasing me, over and over, flying in, then backing away. It was driving me crazy.

When the raids started in early August, a friend of mine who had a foot in the world of Native American mysticism, advised me to hold a ceremony for the Great Spirit of the woods. She suggested that I smudge some organic yellow corn meal with burning sage and sprinkle it around my patch as an offering, asking the Great Spirit for protection. I had done the ceremony a week earlier, so at least I had that going for me.

It quieted around noon but I guessed, correctly, that they were only stopping for lunch. After a quiet hour they started pounding on me again. All three choppers were in the act by now, and at one point I thought I heard a fourth. They were buzzing around my hillside like flies on dead meat. The Bell 400 was checking the backside of the small knoll my patch was on, and the army green Huey was in the canyon below. Slowly the 400 began swinging around the north side of the hill, checking out every bush. If it continued on its course, it would be over my patch in a minute or two. The Huey hovered above as I hid under a large fallen log, no more than a hundred feet from the north side of my patch. I was being pelted by leaves, dust, and pebbles that were kicked up in the prop wash. At the same time, the Bell 400 was heading straight up the hill and I thought they were going to run right into one another. But at the last instant, they spotted each other and veered away in opposite directions. I was sure one of them must have seen the patch, but they hadn't. The corn meal was working, thank you Great Spirit!

The sound of the helicopters faded, and just as I was starting to believe they were gone for good, another helicopter, a dark green military job smaller than the Huey, flew in and did a quick circle over me before leaving the area.

I stayed hidden for an hour or more before daring to go back to camp. It must have been after three by the time I got back to camp, and I didn't hear another chopper the rest of the day. My nerves were totally shot and I realized that I hadn't eaten since breakfast the previous day.

Our cooking scene out there was pretty disgusting. We called it MTV, short for Mouse Turd Village. It consisted of one six-foot by ten-inch board that held our camp stove and cooking gear. Secured between two trees, directly below the stove was a plastic barrel for food. The bears had never gotten the lid off, but they had tried more than once, so the plastic was scarred by nasty-looking teeth and claw marks. Usually I'd do some clean-up, but not today.

I boiled water, ripped open a couple packs of Raman noodles, and rummaged around in the barrel for a sleeve of Ritz crackers. The food helped, and I slowly got my legs back under me. It was only then that I remembered the plants hadn't been watered for a couple of days, so I headed to the patch and ran the systems while watching the sun set over the coastal mountains.

Then I walked back to camp and collapsed.

Despite the previous day's events, I woke up the next morning feeling pretty good. Since the choppers had knocked off early I figured they were out of targets. The morning passed quietly, as did the afternoon. I had another pool full of water by early evening, so I mixed in a third of a bag of 10-52-10 and some Maxi-crop™ and watered the girls. By the time the water stopped running, I was packed and more than ready for the hike down the mountain.

When I got to my parking spot near Jay's, there was a note on my windshield. "We got whacked. Let me know if you need any help. FJ."

Poor bastard. He's even calling himself Fartin' Jack now.

"Goomba!" Jay heard me close the car door and called to me from his deck. "Did they get you too?" He hopped over the railing and trotted down the trail toward me. I didn't say a word, but he could tell by my broad smile that I had made it.

We reached each other about halfway between the parking spot and his cabin, and gave each other a high five, and a good brother abbraccio.

"If you didn't make it out tonight," he said, looking serious over the top of his glasses, "we were going in to look for you with a search party in the morning."

Doing my best Elton John imitation I sang, "I'm still standing, yeah, yeah, yeah."

We went in to get a couple of cold beers and fill each other in on what we knew.

"I got a note from Jack," I said. "Guess he got taken out." I sat down and Jay handed me a rolling tray. "But I had that figured out. There were three choppers on the hill for nearly twenty-four hours."

"You had more than that dude," Jay intoned solemnly. "You had a thirty-man narco task force on the hill with you all night!" He started listing the agencies involved. "You had CAMP, COMMET, DEA, fuck, you even had some little cheese dick from BLM." He took the joint I'd rolled and lit it. "They got Jack on Wednesday afternoon."

"I know. I watched him go down from the top of an oak tree." He handed me the number and I took a hit.

Jay continued. "Before they finished with Jack, they found Mac the Bear's patch. They camped at his place overnight so he couldn't go in and rescue anything."

"Those motherfuckers!" I finished my beer and went to get another. "I once read that there is no condition of human misery that can't be made worse by the addition of a police officer."

Jay snorted his approval. "Actually, that's an old Irish saying."

"Who would know better?" I asked rhetorically.

"Yeah. They chopped Mac's crop down first thing Thursday morning and found 700 more plants in four gardens along Kern Creek."

"No shit?" Kern Creek was just south of where the choppers landed. "I figured something like that was happening. They were close to me for hours yesterday morning." Then I remembered the fourth chopper. "How many choppers did you say there were, three or four?"

Jay shook his head and frowned, "There was a fourth chopper Thursday, but it wasn't the cops."

It turned out that during all the craziness, two of the valley's growers had been involved in a tragic accident. They were partners, and when the patches close to theirs on Kern Creek went down, the one who had been acting as look-out hopped on his motorcycle and headed down to inform the other. At the same time, the kid down in the valley hopped on his bike to ride up to see what was going on. Somewhere in the middle, they collided head-on. Neither was wearing a helmet, and one guy was fucked up so bad he had to be airlifted to the trauma center at Santa Rosa hospital.

Disgusted, I shook my head. "Those fucking cops, why don't they get a real job and leave us alone?"

The valley was having a summer to remember but this week took the cake. Besides the ten or so vehicles and three choppers the goons brought in, there was a ground ambulance, a helicopter ambulance, enough sheriff's cars investigating the accident to film a Blues Brothers sequel, and a news team from the local network affiliate with all their equipment. Everybody wanted in on the action.

Against all odds, I somehow made it to the end of harvest in one piece. Wrung out and with a serious case of survivor guilt, I couldn't even get my head around what had happened. I had no idea what my future held but knew I was done with the wilderness. Hiking out to the middle of nowhere to grow herb was one thing, but everything that came down this summer changed the dynamic, pushing it from a game of Cops and Robbers to full-scale warfare.

I was also sensing a building resentment as one of the few growers to make it out with a crop that year. As the scene degenerated into an exercise in finger-pointing and name-calling, I realized I didn't need the grief.

I was still only a carpetbagger and no longer felt comfortable there, so I started thinking about where to work next year. I could have quit, cashed in my chips and walked away. I could have bought a new piece of property and started again from scratch. I did consider that option, but it was too late to look for land and besides that, with the green-gold rush on, good land was getting hard to find.

But I still owned Honey Bear. Years had passed since I'd been busted there, and at some point over the winter, despite all that had gone down that summer, I realized how much I was committed to the cause and still loved being a grower.

It was then I decided to give Honey Bear another shot.

PART IV

THE RIVER RUNS ONE WAY

Chapter 17

Back to Honey Bear

I should have had my head examined. Honey Bear hadn't been farmed for six years, so I figured it was safe to work there again. Not much was needed to get up and running; a couple of tenders and the equipment taken as evidence when I was busted.

With the right guys, it would be easy to get the spring work done. Big John was looking for work and Zack was ready for another whack at the piñata. The only downside I could see was that Honey Bear put me back near Serenity Park. It was widely known that Serenity Park was starting up again with Judith Mosby replacing her dead brother, like a dictator's wife taking over the country after an assassination.

She must have blown the millions he left behind or she wouldn't have returned. She arrived back on the scene with a measure of goodwill that didn't last long. In the first place, with her grating personality nobody was thrilled with her showing up, but she owned Serenity Park and could do what she pleased. Secondly, even though Judith still garnered some sympathy, she was her own worst enemy when it came to running a pot farm. She assumed control of the enterprise but just wasn't cut out for it, and before long alienated herself from the rest of us. Her style was to stir the shit, and hope something good came from it.

Judith. Not a name we heard much those days. Most women with that name went by Judy or sometimes Jude. In her case, the name really fit. She was the kind of woman who married Casper Milquetoast and ruled the plantation from a rocking chair on the porch.

Judith might have been pretty once, but chain smoking and bourbon drinking was clearly accelerating her aging process. Though not particularly overweight, she was a little on the big-boned side, and whatever trace of femininity she possessed was disguised by the baggy and rumpled clothes she wore. As such, she looked the part of a ranch wife but that's about as far as it went.

Judith's significant other, Joe Ruggels, was getting along about as well as any man without a backbone could. As invertebrates go, he did all right. The limit of his involvement in life was to clean house and do the shopping. To him, cutting coupons out of the newspaper was physical labor. On the upside, he was a big-hearted guy and a fabulous cook. Judith liked to eat and that's probably why she kept him around. There were no freeloaders in Judith's world, and he'd really earn his keep come harvest time. Until then, he was like your little sister playing right field, basically a warm body you hope never has to handle a hot one.

Putting together a crew of tenders is an inexact science in the best of times, and rapidly escalating war on drugs, these were not the best of times. It's not like you could run a help wanted ad in the local paper, or post a sign at the union hall, or even pick up a few foreign nationals in front of a strip mall. Still, crews seem to arise out of thin air like a honeybee mating ritual.

Typically, a crew was assembled from friends or acquaintances that had expressed an interest in growing herb. Like mushrooms, they sprang from the ground after the last rains of winter. Hopefully, everyone's karma was clean and their stars properly aligned, because the last thing in the world you needed was to go through a season with a couple of baggage toting ducks. Since it was almost impossible to fire somebody once they knew your business, you needed to be confident about who you brought in.

With R.O.'s past connections, Judith should have been able to pull together an all-star crew, but she seemed to be operating with the same combination of hubris and rose-colored glasses as Tex. Her choice of tenders that year led to disaster.

Malcolm Gant was from Perth, Australia. A sheep rancher's son, he was your basic dog-loving Aussie. Underneath his macho-man exterior, he was a manipulating ass-kisser, but he did it with such style and humor you hardly noticed it. He also trained dogs for the Shasta County sheriff, but we didn't know that until later. Funny how a detail like that would slip by, but for our line of work I could see how he might not want to put it on his resume.

His running mate was a Canadian named Harry Cook. Dark and brooding, he was the type of guy you would imagine going on cross-country crime sprees, instead of a happy hoser who spent his summers growing pot.

Crews tended to hang by themselves, so it's likely I wouldn't have met any of these guys had it not been for the third guy she hired.

Chet Hogan, known as Cruiser, was an old friend of mine from the Russian River. We'd met playing softball on the locally notorious Panama Red Sox. He was called Cruiser because of how he cruised the outfield. He was tall and fast, but he was so graceful it never looked like he was hustling. Our shortstop used to say, "Look at Chet, he's cruising again," and the name stuck.

Cruiser's girlfriend at the time, April, was a size four piss ant on a hot rock, and cute as a bunny. She was hired on to cook for the boys and water the plants, but Judith should have put her in charge. April was a no-nonsense pragmatist and the only one in the group who had experience with plants, having worked a number of years in a commercial greenhouse. In spite of her small stature, she more than pulled her own weight.

One bit of business Judith and her crew had never dealt with was R.O. He was still out there in a barrel, silently reminding us of how far shit could get out of control. Early in the year, a debate raged over whether he should be exhumed and given a proper burial and, if so, how could that take place without cops, newspapers, or morbid curiosity-seekers having a field day? Nobody wanted to be infested by the maggots from trailer-trash TV, so after much soul-searching and debate, the matter was put on the back burner.

As so often happens, it came down to conflicting interests, with the human reflex to cover one's ass winning out. I think the whole debate had more to do with a lingering sense of survivor guilt than any serious intent. I don't believe for a minute that any of the principals involved had ever thought seriously about digging R.O. up. They just didn't want to **not** do it without talking about it first. They also kicked around the idea of a tree over the barrel, but never got around to doing that either.

In the years since Ethan and I had busted in the first two-hundred and fifty holes, four more large scale operations had arisen. The ranch now sported five full-blown marijuana plantations-Serenity Park, Tatum's Place, The Fat Man's place, known as High Anxiety, Tavern on the Greenbud and a new place Fartin' Jack bought that came to be known as Fartin' Jack's Place. In all, between four and five thousand plants were growing on that one hill.

Honey Bear got up and running quickly, and being in close proximity to ranch, I spent some time doing a little consulting and tree climbing for a couple of the new places. That kept me in the middle of a situation that brought back more than a few bad memories and seemed to be quickly overheating.

The ranch road that spring season seemed to have as much traffic on it as Hwy 101. Mountains of supplies were being transported up the hill at all hours of the day and night. There was always the sound of a truck grinding up the hill, a rototiller working the soil, a pump, or a generator droning on. After a while, it all became background noise, like the sound of trains that people living near a railroad track learn to screen out.

Judith ran Serenity Park from her home in Santa Cruz, which is to say, she let the day-to-day operation be run by an incompetent neophyte. That's usually a formula for failure, and this case was no different.

It doesn't bother me that the universe has a sense of humor. I find comfort in it, but it's so dark and twisted sometimes the way things work out, that I often wonder why The Tibetan Book of the Dead isn't dedicated to Rod Serling. The person with no management skills at all can become the one who ends up leading. In this case, April was the one who should have been running things because of her years working with plants, or maybe Cruiser because of his easy-going yet hard working style. But they were the ones least connected to Judith and were never considered for the straw boss role.

Judith opted for the person she felt most comfortable with, Malcolm. The decision wasn't based on any knowledge he had, but the fact that Malcolm was a world-class brown-noser, a real live Eddie Haskell who knew how to pour on the Aussie charm when she was around. In reality, he held her in extremely low regard and would bad-mouth her in the most creative ways when she was away. The crew saw through his act and were put in that all-too-familiar dynamic of having to take orders from someone they didn't respect. He may have been adept at training dogs, but his gift didn't translate to dealing with people. Malcolm kept a ferocious German shepherd named Kaiser on a chain, with the implied threat of turning him loose if anyone questioned his authority. He must have been feeding the dog steroids, because the damn thing was as big as a St. Bernard and meaner than mamma wolverine.

As spring turned to summer, the hard work completed, all the farms across the ranch settled into an easy routine. The Emerald Triangle is truly one of the most beautiful spots on Earth, and even boneheads like Malcolm and his mate, Harry, came to realize how lucky they were to be at such a fabulous place. People started to relax and in time, even the mood at Serenity Park improved. The workload greatly diminished after the plants were in the ground, and people started getting creative with their free time. Fueled by large quantities of green bud and adult beverages, folks tossed horseshoes, shot hoops, opted for archery, shooting, swimming, or any number of ways to kill time. Replace the camouflage clothing with shorts and white T-shirts, and you could have been at Camp Gitchee-Goomee.

Tavern on the Greenbud was going into its seventh year. It belonged to Fartin' Jack's brother-in-law, Detox. Detox brewed beer for a hobby and had double fermented a trash can full of bock. It was going to be ready to drink around the Fourth of July, so a big party was planned with all the farmers on the ranch and a select list of their friends. It was to be the event of the season, and it was decided that it would be held at the ranch house.

Tex and Jefe came with their crews. I brought my crew and a woman I was seeing at the time, a pert little rock and roll singer named Deirdre. Doug the Slug and his wife Samantha showed up, as well as a bunch of Goombas from around the county, plus some harvest helpers and pickers who lived in the area. A couple of local bar bands came and set up. In all, well over a hundred people were there. The party started on the 3rd and when I split on the 5th, it was still going on.

Most of the crews on the hill came down on their 4-Trax Hondas. Six or seven of them were parked by the barn. Little races were going on all afternoon, and it was only a matter of time and intoxicants before the Big Race materialized.

The trashcan of Bock that had started it all never made it down the hill. It was decided that we would race up to Tavern on the Greenbud where the contestants would stop, and swim across Detox's pond. Waiting for the contestants on the dock would be a pint of bock and a bong hit of finger hash. After chugging the brew and taking a bong rip, the racer would swim back across the pond and race back down the mountain. The only rules were that the driver had to be sober enough to stand and had to wear a helmet. But that second rule was observed mainly in the breech. Kurt had a Forty-Niner's helmet, and some wore those little bicycle jobs. Big John raced wearing only the 'Niner's helmet and a jock strap. Several of the women went topless, and Malcolm's girlfriend, Angie, who happened to be a stripper anyway, rode totally nude except for a helmet and tennis shoes.

It could have been a recipe for disaster, but it turned easily into the most fun I've ever had on a pot farm. Crap in the pants laughter carried the day, and by the love of Ja, nobody wrecked.

Judith Rose even had fun, and her guy Joe organized a barbecue that would make the foo-foo white wine and Brie crowd blush. The feast was sumptuous and without end. The guy sure took his food seriously. He must have been preparing the grub for a week. He barbecued burgers and weenies, chicken and baby back ribs, standard barbecue shit, but that was just his jumping-off place. He filleted a ten-pound salmon, and baked it stuffed with garlic and herbs. He put out cracked crabs and sourdough bread for appetizers, along with prawns I swear were the size of beer bottles. Just in case that wasn't enough, he baked a ham, and a twenty-pound turkey in a pair of Webbers. He made several salads, ambrosia, baked potatoes, baked beans, and corn on the cob. Most of the guests had brought potluck dishes too, so there was more food than any of us knew what to do with. It looked like backstage at a Rolling Stones concert. It seemed to me that after all these years, a sense of community had evolved on the ranch.

The music wasn't too well organized, with assorted wannabes pounding out cover tunes, but a few well-known musicians showed up and a respectable jam evolved after dark. The evening ended with a searing rendition of Fire on the Mountain that the band dedicated to pot growers everywhere. Blotter hits and mushrooms went around after dinner, and about half the crowd partied hard through the night. In the morning, Joe Ruggles whipped up another feast, and we had a ranch breakfast nearly as memorable as the prior night's dinner.

As parties go, this was one to remember. But as summers go, it turned out to be one to forget. Malcolm's dog and his girlfriend both played key roles in the unraveling.

The party generated quite a bit of good feeling between the different operations on the hill, but at Serenity Park the good feeling was an illusion papering over an ever-widening rift between Cruiser and April on one side, and Malcolm and Harry on the other. I got wind of it while shopping at the Safeway store in Willits.

"Well look who's here!" I recognized April's voice and as I turned, Cruiser was reaching out to tap me on the shoulder.

"Hey you guys, did the zookeeper let you out for the day?" I teased.

"Fuck the zookeeper," Cruiser said rolling his eyes. "He doesn't have much zoo to keep anymore."

April said, "You better tell Goomba what happened."

"I guess you better!" Looking amusingly conspiratorial, I asked, "You didn't put Malcolm in a barrel, did you? That wouldn't be very diplomatic."

"He shot Kaiser," she said not waiting for Cruiser.

"I thought I was supposed to tell him," Cruiser said with a mock pout.

At first I didn't say anything, but as I considered the consequences, I think my jaw dropped a bit.

"I told him if his damn dog ever got off its chain, I was going to kill it." Holding his palms up he shrugged his shoulders and asked, "What would you have done?"

"So," I asked, "did the dog get off the chain?"

"No, but it was only a matter of time. The fucking mutt went into a frenzy anytime April walked by."

Trying to voice my concern, but still keep it light I said, "All the boys go into a frenzy when April walks by." I winked at April.

Cruiser put his hand on my shoulder, "That dog was a menace. If it had gone after April, it would have been over that quick," he said with a brisk snap of his fingers. "I would have ended up killing that Aussie cocksucker,"

"That dog was like family to Malcolm, Cruiser. Better not let him walk behind you," I warned.

"Whatever he does, the dog'll still be stiff." Cruiser bit back a grin and looked away.

Cruiser and I had been friends for a long time and I knew he was serious. Like a lot of easy-going guys, Cruiser had a blue steel core. He wasn't the type to act capriciously.

"How's Malcolm taking it?"

"How do you think?" bubbled April, laughing nervously. "We're not going back there for a few days."

Cruiser added, "We're driving out to Mendocino for the weekend."

"You know you're welcome at my place," I offered.

"Actually, we were going to ask you a favor," said April while Cruiser nodded. "Would you go talk to Malcolm for us?"

Cruiser added, "He really likes you. Maybe you could reason with him."

My mind silently revisited Serenity Park, and a feeling of unease fluttered through me. "The last time I went to Serenity Park to do somebody a favor I almost didn't come back."

"We know," April said sympathetically. "If you don't want to, we'll understand."

"I'll think about it," I said with a sigh. "Call me Sunday when you get back from the coast. We'll figure something out."

I'd forgotten all about it until the phone rang Sunday afternoon. It was April saying they were back in town and if it was still cool to come over, they would grab a pizza and a few beers and be over in a bit.

"Tell Cruiser, no anchovies."

We talked about their predicament while we shot some pool and ate pizza. I wanted to help them out but was more than a little uncomfortable about going out there alone. So we agreed that they would spend the night at my house, and we would go out to Serenity on Monday together where I would try to mediate the dispute.

In the morning I had shopping to do for my crew. They needed living provisions and garden supplies. I went out early and got it over with. The crew could go through a hundred dollars' worth of food and beer every few days, so I shopped a lot. After the groceries, I stopped for gas. Big Blue had twin tanks and took about 45 gallons to fill. I also filled four, five-gallon gas cans for the generator and pump, and a large propane tank for the house. Our refrigerator, hot water and stove all ran on propane. It was early August and we were changing over to high phosphorous, so I went to the grower's supply and got a few twenty-five-pound bags of 10-52-10 and a five-pound bag of Maxi-crop™. By nine o'clock, I'd spent over five hundred dollars, about average for a Monday.

April and Cruiser were up when I got back to my place, and April had whipped together a few eggs and toast. We ate breakfast and rolled a couple of fatties for the drive.

It was early afternoon by the time we finally reached the ranch. We found Kurt taking the day off, and figuring there was safety in numbers, we talked him into going up the hill with us. He hopped in with me and the four of us went up to see Malcolm.

Malcolm's partner Harry was at the cabin when we arrived.

Cruiser asked, "Where's Malcolm?"

"He took Angie to see the patch," Harry said without emotion.

"Took who? Where?" Cruiser was becoming agitated. Angie was Malcolm's stripper girlfriend, and Cruiser knew that, but there was a strict no visitors rule. It was Judith's rule, and Cruiser wasn't going to let the transgression pass unnoticed.

The lifestyle must have agreed with Harry, because he was mellower and more upbeat than I'd remembered him. Or maybe he was just happy to see Cruiser and Malcolm going after each other. Whatever the case, I was glad that he wasn't taking sides. We busted out some cold beers and waited for Malcolm to reappear. It didn't take long. He roared into camp on a 4-Trax, with Angie hanging on for dear life.

Malcolm went right after Cruiser, as Kurt and I tried to get in between them.

"You motherfucker!" was yelled by both of them several times, as we danced around camp looking like a Rugby scrum.

It seemed to me that trouble had been brewing between these two for longer than this weekend, and I entertained the notion that the best course would be to just let them have it out. I was sure Cruiser would have the better of it, if no weapons were involved; but cooler heads prevailed. Kurt brought an 8-ball of toot along, so he chopped a few rails and packed our noses. I hadn't known Angie very well, but it turned out she was a big-time snow bunny.

There was more arguing. Cruiser shouldn't have shot the dog, and Malcolm shouldn't have brought his girlfriend Angie to the farm and shown her where the patch was hidden, yadi, yadi, yada.

Within an hour, everybody was tuned up and talking over one another, so I figured it was safe to leave. I collected Kurt for the ride down the mountain.

"What do you think?"

I was lost in thought and Kurt's question brought me back. "About what?"

"Do you think we've heard the last of it?" I could tell by the way that he asked the question that he didn't think so.

"My guess is that when the coke wears off, they'll beat the shit out of each other."

"Killing somebody's dog is heavy," he concluded. "It's like flipping off the Hell's Angels."

I sighed, "It's going to be a tense few days." I had no idea.

Buds. Big buds. Autumn's aura, late summer heat and the juice is flowing; a sensory delight, and an orgy of anxiety. At one level it's a pure adrenaline rush. Rapture among the sticky, resin producing trichomes. You can almost hear a sultry moan at sunset, as evening's gentle breezes bring a feeling of peace. I love this time of year. The plants are between eight and twelve feet tall and are blossoming into womanhood. Pumping parfum onto the flowers. Well-formed crown colas (the top bud on a single leader) can be as big around as a forearm and eighteen inches long. The girls are getting dressed to go out, looking sexy! Going caterpillar hunting, finding space creatures and imbuing them with a sense of time, or what's worse, making stressed-out people relax without Valium.

Pot growers have more names for marijuana than the First Nations People of Alaska have for snow. Be it ganja, green bud, dank, kind, Humboldt gold, or plain old weed, I was sitting on a couple hundred pounds of kick-ass pot. Among the best in the world, or maybe not, but at this level the distinctions became blurred. I guess it ain't braggin' if you can grow it.

Honey Bear was looking good. Sporting a pond and an improved well, the plants, for a change, had plenty of water. It was the height of the CAMP raiding season, but so far we hadn't been spotted. A nervous time of year, but we were becoming cautiously optimistic.

Little did I know, on a lonely stretch of two-lane highway somewhere between Redding and Chico, the CHP pulled over a speeding white 1967 GTO. Inside the car, a tweaked-out stripper named Angie was trying to stuff an ounce of coke down her panties, but the baggie got hooked on something while she was pulling it out from under the seat, and she left a trail of white powder leading right to her snatch.

In custody, she started singing like a meadowlark.

Chapter 18

The Raid

Kurt had only a thirty-second warning. The helicopter swooped into the canyon behind the house and began to circle tightly. Less than a minute later, one of those ubiquitous task forces made up of state and federal agencies crashed the gate. It was seven am, Wednesday, October 1, but from where Kurt stood it looked like June 6, 1944—D-Day. Vehicle after vehicle rolled by the ranch house as the helicopter hovered overhead.

Kurt's first impulse was for the safety of his family, however, before he had time to act a cop was at the door with a stack of warrants. Handing them off, the cop nodded to Kurt, got back into his car and sped up the hill.

After the cop left, Kurt grabbed the walkie-talkie to alert others on the ranch and shouted, "Fire drill! Fire drill! It's the real thing, campers. Run, fire drill, fire drill!" He then loaded Jenny and Casey in the car and beat it out of there up the 101. He drove to Leggett and called me from his parents' cabin and I told him I could get there by early afternoon.

Up at Serenity Park, the boys and April missed the alarm but heard the chopper, followed by the sound of cop cars racing up the road. Cruiser grabbed a backpack and told April to get away from camp, "Go hide in the woods, I'll find you." He gave her a quick kiss and ran to their big patch.

All over the hilltop growers were scattering like tenement cockroaches.

Cruiser reached his patch just as the raiding party reached the cable gate, the same gate where R.O. Moseby had been dusted, and Bunny Eyes had gotten his ass scraped off the running board. The patch was just above the road at that point, maybe one-hundred feet into the woods. The CAMP team cut the cable and raced by, heading straight for the cabin. Cruiser had a pair of plant cutters with him and he raced from plant to plant, cutting as many crown colas and big buds as he could. His heart was pounding so hard he could hardly hear the goons in the woods around him. When his backpack was full, he cut the strings off one of his most prized plants and cut the whole thing down. He was escaping through the back gate as the goon squad reached the front.

The lead cop shouted, "Freeze!" For a moment they faced each other across the patch. Then Cruiser said, "Yeah, right!" He gave the guy a head bob, did a full one-eighty, and disappeared through the gate like an All-Pro running back. He knew the trails well and had too much of a head start to worry about the ground team catching up with him. But they had seen him and must have radioed his position to the chopper, because in no time at all, it appeared like magic in the sky above.

The patch offered great cover, but along the trail the trees were spotty at best. The tall trees petered out and Cruiser was left trying to hide under small bushes without much luck. The terrain, however, was too rough for the chopper to land, and Cruiser was in overdrive. He ran in and out of arroyos, under the trees for a moment of peace, and then made another mad dash to the next hiding spot. It's what's known locally as The Mendocino Steeplechase.

On the hilltop it was every man for himself. After the cops secured Serenity Park, Tatum's place went down. Bud Tatum and his crew managed to hack a few plants before the cops secured the area, then they hid in the woods for the day. The Fat Man found cover in the forest as his gate was crashed. Since last year's crop netted him over a million dollars, money wasn't an issue, only saving his ass.

Detox and his crew sprang into action and did the smart thing. They pulled the water lines from the tank so the cops couldn't use them to find their network of patches. With cops all over the hilltop, Detox and his boys slipped in and out of the bushes pulling pipes and covering trails. Their quick thinking paid off; they were able to save most of the operation.

Fartin' Jack decided to get the hell out of harm's way and hopped on his four trax. His place bordered the north side of the property, and he thought he could find a back trail off the ranch. He rode between the trees to the property line and once he reached the adjoining parcel, quickly found an old logging road. Figuring it had to lead off his neighbor's property, he followed it for about a quarter of a mile until he ran into the old geezer who owned the place. The old dude was cutting firewood and shut the chainsaw off when he saw Jack.

The guy had a pistol lying on a tree stump. He picked it up and slipped it into his belt as Jack shut the four trax down.

Trying to smile and waving both hands above his head, Jack walked slowly toward the man. "It's OK, I'm your neighbor, I own the place over there," he said pointing back down the trail in the direction he had come. "Sounds like someone started a war below me, and I was scouting for an alternate route from my place."

"Well, this here's private property." The old fellow was stern but not rabid. "Who are you?" he asked.

Jack introduced himself, and the woodcutter said his name was Harold. After a few uneasy moments, he decided Jack was alright. The two of them sat down on a log and talked for a couple of hours. It seemed he was an old moonshiner and once he warmed up, he regaled Jack with stories about the old days.

"Me an' my pappy wuz runnin' 'shine outta here for years, right up to the end of Pro-hi," he began. Scratching his head, Harold got a sentimental, faraway look in his eyes. He obviously had some fond memories of his childhood. He spit a coffee-colored stream of tobacco juice, "I wuz just a kid, younger'n you. Me 'n pap wuz takin' a load to the city. I guess it wuz '31 or '32. Highway 101 wuz jus a dirt road mostly, and when we got out there near Ridgewood Ranch, one of our neighbors waved us down. Told us the revenuers wuz waiting for us down by Willits. You know, where Seabiscuit died."

Jack nodded. He knew the road south quite well.

"They knowed we had a still, but they wuz too lazy to hike around and find it. Somehow they got tipped off that we wuz bringin' a load, and they set 'emselves up a roadblock." He stopped long enough to reload his jaw with Red Man, spit a couple of times and laughed. "They wuz so dumb! Hell, everybody up here wuz related somehow."

Jack was enjoying the conversation. It helped him forget that his farm was probably gone. "So, did you get away with it?"

"We turned onto the Reynolds Highway. In them days it wuz just a wagon path, but it hooked us up to the old stagecoach road down on Tomki Creek. We got to Redwood Valley as easy as pie."

As they talked, they forged a kinship that bridged the differences in their ages and backgrounds. Although Jack never told him he was a grower, he didn't have to. The old geezer liked him instinctively and before they parted, he explained to Jack exactly how to get off the mountain, inviting him to stop in at his ranch sometime if he was going out that way.

Jack thanked him and started his machine. Harold wished Jack good luck and flashed him the peace sign. What a cool old guy.

Jack rode back to the property line and hid his machine in a thicket. He could hear a chopper taking off, and as he watched, it pulled a net full of his pot into the sky. Also in the net were a seven-hundred-dollar rototiller and an expensive extension ladder. They must have finished his place with that load, because he sat and watched for several hours while the chopper activity moved farther down the hill. It looked like they were working High Anxiety and Serenity Park at the same time, pulling nets full of marijuana from both places in an alternating scheme.

All over the mountain, growers were hiding in the bushes, sweltering in the afternoon heat. They had hours to do the emotional grief-work of mourning the loss of their summer's labor and the end to whatever fantasy they had concocted over what they would do with their money. Mostly they were stewing in their juices. The lucky ones had water. Most did not.

After being chased over hill and dale for what seemed like an eternity, but was closer to twenty minutes, Cruiser managed to escape long enough to hide his stash. He set off trying to find his real treasure, April. Although he had a general idea where she might be hiding, the mountain was crawling with cops, so his progress was excruciatingly slow. He finally took cover in a deep ravine.

The last chopper load went out around five-thirty and the caravan of cop cars and trucks followed, a few at a time. It was impossible to tell if they had all departed, but man by man, the tenders from various crews reassembled, and crept back to their respective camps to survey their losses.

It could have been worse. No one was arrested. Serenity Park and Tatum's place went down totally, but the goons missed Fartin' Jack's altogether, thinking his cabin went with Bud Tatum's garden. All Jack ended up losing was his tiller and ladder.

Detox was able to save over half of his gardens including his best spot. Fat Man lost three gardens but held on to one. Because of the scale he was growing, he got away with over a hundred and fifty pounds.

Cruiser had found April around noon and the two of them hiked down to the ranch house to wait things out.

I rolled into Leggett around three-thirty and met up with Kurt and Jenny. We didn't have much of a rescue plan, just that we were going to sneak onto the ranch in a roundabout way to help anyone who needed it. Around seven that evening, we had Jenny drive past the ranch, with Kurt and me in the back of the pickup truck like we were hitchhikers. She slowed down while we drove by the ranch gate where everything looked quiet. A half-mile up the road, I knocked on the window of the cab to indicate that we wanted to be let off. She pulled over. There was no traffic to be seen in either direction, so Kurt and I jumped out the back and high-tailed it into the woods, skirting the highway. We were near the southern boundary of the property and hiked carefully through the woods, stealthily moving from tree to tree. We spent several minutes at each hiding place listening for signs of activity. It took about thirty minutes to get close to the ranch house. We stayed in the creek below it, until we heard Cruiser and April talking. I gave a low whistle, trying to sound like an owl, and Cruiser whistled back.

"We're down here," I whispered as loudly as I dared. The two of them scrambled down the creek bank, and we had a solemn reunion.

I gave April a hug, and Kurt gave Cruiser sympathetic a pat on the back. When someone's patch goes down it's like a death in the family. There's nothing you can say, but the empathy runs deep.

"God, I'm sorry you guys got it." was about the best I could do. Perhaps because they had the afternoon to sit and think about it, they were surprisingly accepting.

April said, "We'll be OK." They looked at each other tenderly and I was sure they would. The two of them knew what really mattered.

"The first thing we need to do is get you guys out of here," I looked at my watch, "It's twenty 'til eight."

We explained that Jenny was going to drive by the ranch every hour on the hour, so we had twenty minutes to wait.

"Are the cops gone?"

"We think so," April said with a grimace, "A caravan left about an hour ago and we haven't heard anything else."

"There's nobody down here," Cruiser added, "We've been at the gate house for a while."

I sensed Cruiser and April were still on edge from the day's ordeal. "Then we have time for a toke." I packed my glass and we passed it around. "You guys can come with me to Honey Bear. I haven't hired a cook yet and I can always use another picker."

"Are you sure?" Cruiser asked seriously, "I don't want to jinx it."

In three years of growing, Cruiser had been busted twice and ripped off once. Sitting on a log in the creek bed at twilight, he felt as if a cloud was hanging over him.

"We'll just take you to the shaman to get a soul retrieval and a karma scrub first," I laughed.

Kurt stood up, "We better start moving, or we'll miss Jenny."

With that, we started down the creek for the short walk to the road. We reached the end of the driveway just in time to see Jenny driving slowly towards us. We flagged her down and quickly hopped into the truck. Cruiser and April climbed into the cab, while Kurt and I jumped in back. Kurt stuck his head through the slider and told Jenny we wanted to go to Honey Bear, a short distance.

I was opening the gate to Honey Bear when I got the first wind that something was up. I had hired a young guy to work around the farm doing odd jobs and help out at harvest. We called him "Emu." Emu was near the gate with a flashlight and a walkie-talkie. He hadn't recognized Kurt's truck in the fading light, but he was close enough to see me when I got out to work the lock.

"Goomba!" I heard my name called from the bushes, and then saw his flashlight signal. He scurried out from under the manzanita clump that was directly above the gate. "I'm so glad to see you." He was speaking with his customary flare for the dramatic, as he slid down the embankment to the driveway. "We had a chopper here for an hour before dark." As he talked, he drew map lines in the sky like a modern dancer. "They were all over around here and then they covered every inch of the hillside. They landed in the meadow by the old patch and went in on foot. I don't know if they checked the cabin or not, because we ran into the deep woods in back."

"Probably not," I said, "they would theoretically need a warrant for that," my voice betraying a hint of sarcasm. "Did they spot the new patch?"

Emu stroked his chin and furrowed his brow. "I don't think so. It's hard to tell, but they didn't crash the gate."

"What are you doing down here?" I asked.

"Big John thought it would be a good idea to have a gate look-out."

"Maybe in the morning, but they won't be back tonight. Get in the truck." Jenny pulled the truck through the gate and I locked it behind her. I jumped in back with Kurt and Emu and told Jen to step on it.

Emu called Big John on the walkie-talkie to tell him that friends were coming up the drive. The whole crew heard us coming and met us at the parking spot. Like everything else at Honey Bear, it was well hidden under the trees.

In addition to Big John and Emu, Zack the pickers were there. That year they were Mary Peckinham, who had worked for me at Serenity Park and introduced me to Alexandria, Purple Candy, who picked for me in the wilderness, and of course, Melody Austin. In all there were nine of us. It seemed like everybody had a story to tell, and we all talked at once. It's amazing how much information can be relayed through chaos.

After the first rush of jabber, some order returned and I explained what I thought was going down. It was too great a coincidence that Serenity Park would get busted, and then the raiding party would leave there and come straight to Honey Bear. "Somebody must have ratted us out."

That pronouncement set off another nervous round of jabber.

Jenny had to leave. She had dropped Casey off at a friend's that morning but didn't feel comfortable leaving him there overnight. Kurt stayed to help us clear out and I quickly organized work details.

"Who's eaten?" was my first practical question. Nobody had. "Candy, you and April stay here and get some dinner together, and Mary can help get the cabin clean." I picked up a small ice chest and handed it to Emu. "Get some ice and fill this with drinks."

Candy and April went into the kitchen. Mary didn't exactly know what I meant by "clean." I told her, "Just pick up all the pot-related stuff, the scale, the seal-a-meal, baggies, and anything else pot grower related." While she started piling things by the door, I told everybody else to come with me.

I had developed an early strain, and half of my crop was already picked and sealed. Most of the rest was dry and in body bags, but I also had a few later varieties that hadn't fully matured yet.

"Big John, how about taking Kurt, and get any plants that are still in the ground. What do we have left, maybe twenty?"

"At most," said Big John, "probably ten."

"OK, take some rope and a big camo tarp. Load the tarp with as many as will fit and take them as far into the woods as you can." I thought about leaving the plants hanging that far out. "String the rope as high as possible, so the deer can't get to 'em. Make sure you have cutters and some drinking water."

Big John started loading his day pack with beer.

"Cruiser, Emu, Zack, and Melody come with me to the drying shed. Let's meet back here in, what?" I shrugged looking at Candy who was starting to get busy in the kitchen, "What do you think Candy, an hour?"

"An hour and a half," she said without turning around.

Cruiser grabbed a bag of cookies. He hadn't eaten all day and needed something quick. I grabbed a couple of boxes of trash bags, and we started walking.

After my first bust, Honey Bear had lain fallow for several years. I figured it had cooled off a bit, but for harvest I decided to go "Guerilla" and had moved the drying operations off the property and onto an adjacent parcel owned by a lumber giant, Louisiana Pacific. It was about a twenty-minute hike from my property line.

Lost in our thoughts, we hiked in silence. An unseasonable rain had hammered the coast for nearly a week, and the forest floor was still soggy so we could walk through the leaves without making a sound. The forest smells different when it's wet. The aromas of plant life give way to the aroma of the various forms of decay. Only the sloshing sound of the ice chest announced our presence.

I formulated a plan while we walked and assigned chores as soon as we got to the drying shed. Cruiser and Zack would bag the processed pot, while Emu would work with me getting the branches into body bags.

That left Melody without a task. "Melody, gather up all the fan leaves and shake. I want you to scatter it all over; up and down the trails and into the bushes. If they bring dogs, I want them to smell pot everywhere, not just where it's hidden."

I thought for a minute then added. "When you're done, pick up anything that might have fingerprints; beer bottles, tools, and stack them by the dryer door."

We had fingerprint protocols in place, habits that I'd learned at Serenity, but you can never be too sure. Wiping off bottles, holding things between your knuckles instead of with your fingers, wearing gloves, and so forth. Things you talk about doing, but sometimes you don't.

We forgot about dinner and started to work. The walkie-talkie crackled at about ten-thirty.

"Hey you guys, dinner's getting cold." It was Candy. Big John and Kurt must have made it back because Big John had the other walkie. We had put a dent in the work, but I could tell we'd need to pull an all-nighter.

We got back to the cabin before eleven and wolfed down our dinner. Candy and April had put together a spaghetti feed with salad and garlic bread. I dragged out a couple bottles of Chianti Classico, and we had a few laughs while pretending to be wine snobs.

After dinner, I brewed a large pot of strong coffee. Big John said, "Too bad we don't have any marching powder." He didn't drink coffee, and with his eyes half-closed, was sinking deeply into the easy chair near the wood stove.

With a laugh I said, "OK Johnny, you got me. Let me grab the harvest party stash."

The marching powder put a smile on everyone's face, and I explained to the crew what still needed to be done.

"OK, Emu, get Big Blue, and back him up to the cabin. I want all the shit Mary collected loaded." I tossed him the keys. "And meet us at the dryer when you're done." With that, the rest of us headed back out to the drying shed.

We spent hours hauling bags of pot out into the woods and burying them in ravines under camo tarps and brush piles. The work was grueling, but we had enough people. By four-thirty am we had done as much as we could do for one night.

We put as much finished pot as we could into barrels. The rest we hid in small piles all over the hillside. The fresh plants had been cut and hung well away from the patch, and the shake had been scattered in all directions to confound the dogs. I had Melody bag some fan leaves and schwee buds. For one last subterfuge, I had her scatter some along the driveway on our way out. If the cops noticed the tailings, they might think we cut bait and split.

By the time we reached the cabin, Big Blue had been loaded with the processing equipment. At the last minute I decided to load the generators and some other valuables I was sure the cops would steal if they came in. By five-fifteen, Cruiser, April and Mary got into Big Blue while the rest of the crew and Kurt loaded into Emu's Subaru and made their way to Leggett. Kurt took a walkie-talkie and planned to meet up with Jenny to get his truck. I told Emu to leave the gate open since if the cops came, they would just bust it down anyway. Seeing it open, they might conclude that they were too late.

We had a rendezvous time and place picked out and if we needed to be rescued later, Kurt would be the one to pick us up.

Big John, Zack and I stayed behind to see what would happen. We loaded day packs with food, water, stash, and binoculars. Big

John loaded a small ice chest with beer and ice, and we started hiking to a hiding place we knew about, a rugged rock outcropping on the eastern edge of my property.

The pre-dawn hours were surreal, oddly serene considering everything that had just gone down. I twisted up a few hooters as the dawn goddess Eos did her thing. Looking out at the golden hills of California, it occurred to me how lucky I was. The pure autumn air carried hints of wildflowers and wild mountain herbs. Pockets of tule fog hung in the valley, softening the hard edges of reality, and the fall colors held my eye like an Impressionist masterpiece. As the sun god Sol showed his face, the radiant heat began to disperse the fog, and Monet's Garden quickly changed to Dali's Gateway to Paranoia.

Zack kept his binoculars trained on a small portion of the road that was visible from our vantage point. I was sure that if CAMP came back, helicopters would lead the way but there was no definite protocol.

"Here they come," Zack said and started counting, "four, five, six..."

They were speeding our way, and if they were gunning for Honey Bear, they'd be up our driveway in a few minutes.

"If you guys want to run, go now," I said to the boys.

"Fuck no," Big John said with a grin. "This is the shit, man."

"I counted at least seven rigs, mostly forest service Suburbans," said Zack as he climbed down from his perch. "Also saw a couple of four-wheel drive sheriff's cars and the stake-side truck."

The choppers came next. Flying in low, by the time we heard them they were only a mile or so away.

"Show time," I said lighting a joint.

Zack shook his head, "How can you think about smoking pot at a time like this?"

"Remember what Bobby Knight told Connie Chung?"

"Can't say as I do."

"If you're being raped, you might as well lay back and enjoy it." I handed him the joint. "Better take a toke, it might be the last one you get for a while."

The first chopper on the scene was another Bell 400, flying in from the north it started circling tightly over our camp. Widening its search, it flew over us a time or two, but we were able to stay hidden under some overhanging rocks.

We heard the convoy making its way up the rugged driveway, heading straight for the cabin.

"I guess they have a warrant. This is no open field search," I told the boys.

"How do you suppose they found us?" asked Big John. "Yesterday was the first time we got seriously flown all summer, and they never went near the patch."

"Fuck if I know," taking one last hit and putting the roach in my pocket. "Seems like somebody dropped a dime on Serenity Park and us."

"Yeah, but who?"

"I'm sure we'll find out, John, but right now it only matters that they did."

Chapter 19

Spider Webbing

The goons roared up the driveway with a big hard-on that quickly went limp, seeing that we'd cut bait and gotten the hell out of there. While they didn't make the big score they were hoping for, they had to know that they were shutting down a fairly sophisticated operation.

We figured they found our now empty patch and knew roughly the size of the outfit. We were a good-sized commercial plantation, but not one of those several thousand plant ops they busted every now and then. The chopper left the scene without ceremony. It had apparently gotten the message that the pot was gone, but some of the ground team stayed all day, leading us to believe that they were meticulously searching the woods. We pessimistically figured that they found most of our stash.

Kurt radioed in around two-thirty saying that he was in position, but cop cars were parked at the bottom of our driveway. Not knowing if the cops could intercept our radio transmission, we kept it short.

About ten minutes later a group of goons and one goonette emerged from the trees just below the cabin. Carrying automatic rifles, they paused for a moment, and then started walking across the meadow. It seemed as if they were heading directly to where we were hidden. They must have had some sort of tracking device, because the timing was too coincidental. We quickly gathered our shit and prepared to run, but the cops didn't seem interested in climbing the rocks. They veered off before they reached us and seemed content to circle the meadow looking for other trails. Not finding any, they walked back in the direction they had come. They passed close enough for us to hear their voices, but we couldn't make out what they were saying. It must have been their last look around because not long after that we could hear vehicles start up and begin their long descent to the county road.

When we finally ventured down from our hiding place and made our way back to the cabin, we found it a mess. The cabin was usually a mess but one of those "guy" messes. Cop messes are bull in a china shop messes. A mean mess. Crap thrown hard. A statement mess saying, "Don't like what we did here? Call a cop."

Assholes. No wonder no one likes them very much.

We tried not to touch anything and only stayed long enough to survey the damage. They had left some things behind; a packet of paper containing a warrant and a list of my things that they had confiscated. We also found a few empty film boxes, indicating that they had taken a photo record, several pairs of latex gloves, and fingerprint kits.

I had never heard of the cops going after growers like this and didn't like the looks of what I saw. After all these years, law enforcement was getting serious. Big John had left some clippings of himself from his days as a college basketball star and was frantic thinking that he'd lost his treasured mementos.

"Hey Goomba, look at this!" Zack was standing by the kitchen door holding a piece of paper.

"What is it?" I started down the stairs.

"Looks like cop notes. Fuck, what is this? Looks like a map of Serenity Park."

Turning back toward John I said, "C'mon, big guy, we gotta go."

Zack handed me the paper. Somebody had drawn a map of Serenity Park and the road leading to Honey Bear. The map of Honey Bear showed only the driveway, but Serenity Park had the cabins and tents with Cruiser and Nick written over their tent site, and MG and HC written over what would have been the cabin.

"Malcolm Gant and Harry Cook." Zack suddenly looked pale. "Nick was April's handle at Serenity. Somebody's dropped a dime on us."

Before I could ask who, we looked at each other and simultaneously said, "Angie."

Big John was climbing down from the loft with his scrapbook. The cops had either missed it or they didn't think it was important.

"Let me see."

I handed the paper to Big John and turned back to Zack. "If it was Angie, how did she know the way to Honey Bear?"

"Not from me," Zack declared, shaking his head.

Big John started to fidget. "Oh, shit."

"What?"

John looked away. He was crestfallen. Such a big kid. I could read him like a book.

"This is serious shit, let's have it."

"I'm sorry, Goomba." He handed the paper back to me. "Remember the day of the picnic, you were with that good looking brunette, what was her name?"

"Deirdre," I replied testily, "just cut to the chase."

"Yeah, Deirdre," he said, mispronouncing it Deedra. "Remember when you guys left for a while?"

"Yeah, what about it?"

"I needed a ride back here and they were going to town."

"They who?" I asked, but as slowly as Big John was getting the story out, I had already figured out what had happened. Standing at the scene so soon after the cops had gone already had me on edge. But when the puzzle's last pieces emerged and the flood of implications that accompanied them, I felt physically weak, almost nauseous.

"Malcolm and Angie," he said, as if he had to pry the words from his lips.

There would be time to yell and scream at each other later. Right now I didn't need Big John going into a funk. "It's a crap shoot Johnny, sooner or later you're gonna' roll snake eyes."

The cops had stolen our cold beer and there wasn't much more to do in the cabin, so I said, "Let's get out of here, this place is hot."

We slipped out the back door and disappeared into the woods. We stayed off the road on the way down the hill. There were several trails and we knew them all. We reached Kurt on the walkie-talkie and let him know we were on the way down, planning to skirt the driveway and arrive at the road near it. As we headed out, Kurt radioed back telling us to change our plan, there were still cops at the bottom of the driveway. They weren't giving up easily.

He had driven past the gate and was now east of the farm. We were worried that the cops had a scanner and might be listening to us over the radio.

"G calling K, You with us?"

"That's a big 10-4, what's up?" He must have been near the range limit because he was starting to break up.

"We're going swimming. Shootout Creek. Half an hour. Can you hear me? The radio's breaking up."

"Roger, good buddy."

I don't know what it is about radios, but you always end up talking like a trucker.

The last twenty-four hours had been hell, and I was losing steam. We headed east but between the road and us was a half a mile of nasty terrain covered with Bryce brush and ceanothus, nearly im-possible to hike across. By the time we busted through it, Big John had sprained his ankle and we nearly were out of gas but continued on, crossing the road and dragging our sorry asses along Shootout Creek, named after the shootout Garrett and I had with the rip-offs years ago. We found Kurt waiting for us with an ice chest full of cold ones.

I tossed my pack in the back of Kurt's truck and hopped in. Big John and Zack climbed in front. Kurt's parents' cabin was on the Avenue of the Giants, a section of old Highway 101 that passes through old growth redwoods a few miles south of Leggett. The crew was hiding out there and since it was over an hour away, I used the time to for some much-needed sleep.

I went out like a light and woke up when we arrived at Kurt's cabin and was surprised to see my ex-wife Carrie there. She had never been involved in my business while we were together, so it was a real shock to see her now. She may have even surprised herself, but when the chips were down, she came through like a champ. She had been home at the house we still owned together when the cops raided the place. They had held her for several hours while they trashed the place looking for evidence.

"They want you, Duncan." Tears were trying to well up in her eyes as she kissed me. "They were calling you the Pot Godfather."

"I like that," I laughed, trying to cheer her up. "It has a certain ring to it." In my mind I just thought, what a joke, I've never been anything but a small fry. Well, possibly a medium fry.

"I think it's serious," she said shaking her head. "It wasn't just the COMET team."

She had gotten the attention of the others with that statement and a circle of interest formed around her.

"The feds were there. DEA, FBI, BLM, you name it." She gazed at me intently. "Somebody talked."

"I know. It was Angie."

"Who?" The name didn't ring a bell.

"Angie, the stripper, I think I told you." Her face reflected that she remembered.

"Oh God, *her?*"

"Had to be, but I don't know why." I looked at Kurt. "Have you talked to Tex or Jefe?"

He shook his head, "No, I've been in the bushes all day waiting for you guys."

"My phone's in my day pack. Why don't you see what you can find out?" I turned back to Carrie. "Anything else?"

"They took your computer and I think they found some stash."

"It wasn't much."

We talked for a while, but I was fading. Carrie and I exchanged knowing looks. "What say we check out my sleeping bag?"

She laughed and shook her head, "Forget it."

The cabin was small and I opted to sleep outdoors that night. The forest floor yielded pleasantly to the weight of my body. Cradled under these magnificent trees, my mind revisited former lovers. Innocent Paula, Carrie, brave and steady. The comet Felicia. Statuesque Alexandria, and some others. Their faces, or how I remembered them, drifted through my mind like photos in a yearbook. Which one was the missing piece to the puzzle of my life?

The shade had been drawn on my conscious mind.

The redwood forest holds as much earthen magic as any place on Earth. Decay has gone on since the dawn of time resulting in soft pockets of humus, hidden in the caves of these giant trees' roots. Perhaps it's their size, perhaps their age, maybe it has to do with the chemical properties of the cellulose, or maybe it's the easy symbiosis that exists between wood, water, and banana slugs. Whatever, the magic seemed as thick as the shroud of morning fog.

I awoke at dawn. Comfortable in my sleeping bag, it was a crisp, cold autumn day but I couldn't lay there forever with so much at stake. So, I rolled out of my bag and walked back to the cabin. No one was awake. I got some coffee brewing and hopped into the shower. By the time I had dried off and dressed, the others were up or stirring.

Kurt came into the kitchen first, yawning and scratching his ass as he handed me the phone. "I talked to Tex last night. He's getting Jefe this morning and they're coming here. He asked if you know any good lawyers."

"No," I replied, "but I've got some catfish bait, I should be able to get one." Lawyer jokes are always good for a few laughs. Sadly, I'd come to understand that the legal profession viewed the drug war as a goldmine.

"What about that guy from Ukiah?"

"That pencil neck geek," I said, with a snort. "Don't mention that asshole! I wouldn't hire him to get the neighbor's stolen bicycle out of the impound yard." Approving nods.

"What if he represented you pro bono?" Cruiser asked.

"If I see him on the way to hell," I held a three-foot bong in the air, "I'll give him a pro bono in the ass." Much laughter.

April said in mock seriousness, "I don't think Duncan likes the guy."

My mobile rang. Tex needed directions to the cabin, so I handed the phone to Kurt. "It's Tex and Jefe, they're at Richardson Grove."

Thirty minutes later, Tex and Jefe rolled in driving a brand-new Land Cruiser and I was surprised to see Isa with them. The boys and I slapped some skin, and I gave Isa a big hug. We were all in it together, deep.

"CAMP has closed the roads to Serenity Park and Goomba's place," Tex informed the group. "They're using Serenity for a staging area and the word on the street is that all the CAMP teams in California are there. Looks like Nam."

As far as I knew, only Garrett had actually been to Viet Nam, but we all grew up with the nightly news reports. We nodded solemnly.

Jefe took up the story. "They rolled in with about 30 4X4 pickups with camper shells, dozens of ATVs, and a field kitchen."

Someone asked, "Choppers?"

"Fuck yes," Tex jumped in. "Choppers up the kazatz."

"How did you find all of this out?" I wanted to know.

"The Fat Man," Tex replied.

I asked, "Have you heard about any warrants?"

"Nothing yet. What about your crop?"

I shrugged, "I don't know. I gotta get back in somehow and get it out."

Jefe had an idea. "Talk to Fartin' Jack. He came by my place yesterday and wants to organize a commando raid to go back in. He met a rancher behind his place and thinks the guy might let you guys go across his land."

Carrie acted like she was shivering, "Sounds like walking into a spider's web." She put her face up to mine and pantomimed a kiss. "Walk away," she whispered as tears formed in her eyes.

"I can't," I said without thinking about it, not understanding that I could have and should have. I couldn't even believe Carrie was here but looking at her, I could tell she still loved me. Venus ruled part of me, an important part, but when the deepest part of me was exposed, I had warrior within. The conflict of the past two days had awakened him.

Carrie put her arms around my neck and asked, "Why not?" She shook me. "Why can't you just walk away?"

I sighed, and unable to find the words, put on my game face and stared at her.

"Mars in Scorpio," she stated. Then rolled her eyes and laughed, balling her hands up into fists and clubbing me on the chest. "Stay in outer space. See if I care."

Phone calls went out and by early afternoon volunteers for the commando raid started to arrive. Fartin' Jack came with Spaghetti Freddie and an old hippie friend of mine, Foster Wick, who I hadn't seen since our days living in Haight-Ashbury. We'd been tripping buddies back in the day, eventually going our separate ways knowing we'd meet up again someday. We did, but neither of us could foresee something like this.

"Hey everybody," I said loudly, "I want you to meet an old friend of mine."

The crew gathered around and I introduced Foster.

"How did you hook up with Jack?" I asked.

"Through Freddie," he said pointing at Spaghetti Freddie. "His half-sister is my girlfriend."

"Small world, huh?" I said, still a bit amazed to see him again. "I wish the circumstances were better."

Remembering some of our childhood exploits, Foster smiled and shrugged, "Seems like old times."

Garrett Nash had gotten wind of the predicament and called in to see if he could help. He couldn't make it until the next day but wouldn't dare miss the party. Having been to Nam, Garrett was the type of guy you wanted along in this kind of a situation.

We planned to hike in after dark that night, but only to re-con the area. First things first, we needed to be sure Old Harold would let us use the road across his farm. It was our best way in and a viable escape route if there was any pot left to save. Hidden in the same manner and vicinity, we figured if the goons found any of it, they probably found it all.

We spent hours in a makeshift situation room, complete with a forest service map covered with pushpins, going over options.

"Ok, here's the deal." I explained, "Any pot you guys bring back I'll split fifty-fifty with whoever carries it out. So, try to bring back an even number of pounds." I added to lighten the tone a bit.

The boys laughed and hi-fived, clearly happy with the terms.

I don't know if this exercise served any purpose other than making the time pass faster, but it was fun acting like little generals.

Jack's plan was to go in with his crew, grab anything left at his place, and carry it out to the woodpile. He hoped he still had plants in the ground. Since Old Harold had driven his truck to the wood-pile where they'd met, Jack figured he could load his truck there and head out.

My situation was quite different. I had barrels full of processed pot and some unprocessed bud still hanging in trees. We were looking at moving over 200 pounds of pot worth close to a million dollars out of Honey Bear and had a lot farther to go.

My property was behind the ranch, but nobody had ever tried to walk through the woods to get there. A mile or two doesn't sound like much, but over rough terrain and in the dark, it was going to be a real bitch. There was no way we'd be able to carry barrels full of stash back out of there, they were too heavy, and it was just too far. We were still without a solid plan but had an idea to take our goods out the back side of my property to a year-round stream called Silhouette Creek and float the barrels up to Highway 162 for pick up. Silhouette Creek was only about a quarter mile from the northeast corner of my land, luckily for us, all downhill.

The whole idea sounded hair-brained at first, but the more we thought about that option, the more we liked it. Not that the idea was all that great, but we just couldn't think of an alternative.

Emu had to be in court that day, so Cruiser and April were given quartermaster duties and sent to Garberville for food and a mountain of supplies from the hardware store. We needed flashlights, space blankets in case we got stuck out in the wilderness for a couple days, fire starters if the rain started up again, climbing rope, duct tape, and other odds and ends. I had an idea that we could link our barrels together and float the whole stash down the river. I asked Cruiser to pick up a dozen or so foot-long threaded eyebolts, nuts, flat washers, six carabineers, and some silicone glue. It sounded wacky, but just might work.

By four o'clock Cruiser and April were back from Garberville and we were ready to roll. Jack, Cruiser, Zack, and Freddie went in Jack's truck while Foster rode with Kurt and me in Big Blue so we could bullshit about the old days. Big John's ankle was still swollen and sore, so he stayed at the cabin with everyone else.

Old Harold wasn't at all surprised to see us. I think he expected it. He had to know what was going down on the other side of the hill from his place. It was big news in that part of the county.

Jack introduced us and we busted out some beer. Harold was nearly a hermit, so the trick was not to let the guy get talking too much. He seemed like the kind of guy who would go on for hours if you let him, and we didn't have that much time. But out of respect for him, and the favor he was doing us, we sat and chatted for over an hour.

We wanted to be well on our way by dark, so as the afternoon waned, we let Harold know we had to be going. He offered to show us the way to the woodpile on the hilltop, so I hopped into his 1950 Chevy pickup with him and headed up the hill. The others followed in Big Blue and Jack's truck.

We said good-bye to Harold at the woodpile and then followed Jack to the property line.

The mood turned serious as we donned our camo gear. The gods aided us by supplying moonlight. The moon after the harvest moon is called the hunter's moon. On a clear night it's bright enough to hunt by, and it was the hunter's moon that was coming full.

We walked in silence to a fork in the road that led to Jack's place. We were heading in different directions from that point, so we quietly wished each other well. I gave Foster a high five and told him we should get together soon and catch up on the lost years.

Kurt, Zack, Cruiser, and I walked the road to High Anxiety. A series of skidder trails went off the property past the Fat Man's farm and we were hoping one of them would end up near my property.

Past Fat Man's, the trails petered out pretty quickly as we descended into a deep ravine. The drainage was steep and involved some rock climbing but once we had scaled back up the other side, the terrain flattened out and the going was fairly easy. We walked side hill, veering to the south every chance we got. We knew if we went too far in that direction, we would run into the road.

Hours passed before we spied anything that was familiar but finally, around ten, we saw the backside of my hill. I knew my land and the property it abutted intimately, having walked just about every inch of it looking for growing spots, water sources, and hiding places. We skirted the northern border of the land until we found the trail to the drying shed. Earlier, we had made cardboard cones for the end of our flashlights that only allowed a pin of light to escape. That kept the lights more or less invisible from a distance, just in case the area was under surveillance. We reached the dryer in less than ten minutes and after another hour of poking around in the bushes, we concluded that the goons hadn't found anything. All of the bags and barrels were where we had hidden them. We should have jumped for joy but knew that we weren't out of the woods yet. I had been through so much strain, I think part of me wished the pot was gone. At least we wouldn't have to come on any more of these damn commando raids.

We decided to cram as many pounds as we could into our backpacks. Our two big packs held about nine pounds each, and the two little ones held four pounds. We got twenty-six pounds out the first night. At the time, the wholesale rate for that much pot was around $125,000 so it covered our expenses and left us with a little change jingling in our pockets, even if turned out that was all we could recover.

We headed back to Harold's around midnight, weighed down but with a definite bounce to our steps.

Jack's truck was gone by the time we reached Harold's place, but he had left us a note on the windshield. It read, "Goons on the hilltop, take care." I didn't know what that meant but it didn't sound good. It was after three am, so we decided to sleep for a few hours then drive out at dawn. I thought it would look too suspicious traveling in the dead of night.

I woke the boys at dawn and we were back at the cabin by breakfast. All things considered it had been a successful operation, providing the opportunity to cash in our chips and walk away with our winnings unscathed. But we never considered quitting—we got in once and could do it again.

Chapter 20

Night Moves

We were running on fumes. A debate evolved over the wisdom of trying to get back in. Letting the stash stay hidden was an option we all thought too risky. It just wasn't put away very well. Much of it was stored in plastic bags that animals could rip open and some of it was still wet and would soon start molding. Fifty plants were hanging in the trees and if it started raining again, they would be ruined. We had also heard a rumor that the cops were going to be hanging around for a while via a friend of ours who worked at the local deli where the cops had ordered fifty sack lunches a day for the next week.

We were going back in; it was just a matter of when. As a group we decided that the time was right away. We could nap that afternoon and head out around dinnertime. I wanted to find out exactly what Fartin' Jack had meant by his note but other than that, I was intent on going that night.

I called Jack's place but his wife didn't know where he was. We left a message for him to get in touch with us if he showed up.

April and Candy were doing the shopping in Garberville. We still needed a couple more barrels and some other provisions. They said they would keep an eye out for Jack or someone who might know where he was.

Kurt, Cruiser, and Zack tried to sleep, but I had trouble sleeping in the daytime so I made a pot of strong coffee and drank most of it.

An unfamiliar car rolled up the drive around four o'clock. I walked out onto the deck in time to see Foster getting out of a beat-up Peugeot.

"You can't get enough of this place huh? I thought last night's excitement would keep you satisfied for a while," I said. "Guess I was wrong."

He laughed. "It wasn't my idea. I bring news from afar, sahib."

"OK, but leave your goat outside."

He climbed the stairs to the deck and I gave him a hug. "Goddamn it's great to see you. I couldn't believe it when you showed up yesterday."

"Me neither! The boys just called you Goomba so I didn't have a clue who you were until I got here." He got a quizzical look on his face and asked, "How'd you end up being called Goomba"?

"I don't know why." Then I remembered why it stuck, "Big John started calling me that years ago and I told him if he called me that again I'd fire him. Within a week everybody I knew was calling me Goomba."

He laughed, "I guess that shows how much respect they had for you."

"Yeah, no shit. But I think it has more to do with the fact that you can't fire your help in this business." We walked inside. "How 'bout a beer?"

"Sure" he said, "And a bong rip if you can arrange it."

"I think we can come up with something," I checked my watch, it was 4:20.

The sound of our talking woke up the boys. They came into the kitchen as Foster was telling me what had gone down the night before; the genesis of Jack's note.

"Jack was lucky. The ones that he had in the ground were still there and he found all of what he had hidden." He finished his beer and I opened another for him. "I helped Jack and Freddie for a while, but the plan had been for me to go with Freddie and check out Bud Tatum's place, while Jack was hauling the first load out to his truck." He shook his head "Bud's place was trashed."

"What about the note?" Cruiser wanted to know.

"I'm getting to that," Foster assured him. "On our way back from Bud's, we heard cars driving on the ranch road. We climbed into some bushes above the road and watched as a convoy of cop cars passed."

Kurt moaned, "A convoy, how many is that?"

"Six or seven, I forgot to count. Anyway, when they'd driven past, we slipped down to the edge of the clearing to get a peek," he looked around, "how's it coming with that bong hit?"

In mock despair I begged, "Will somebody pack a bowl for this guy, I want to hear the end of this story."

Someone handed Foster the bong and after he took a rip, he continued the narrative. "They have an encampment in the big meadow at the road's end. Looks like a fuck'n Boy Scout jamboree."

"I know the spot you mean," I said, thinking back to the first summer. Ethan and I used to drive there and watch the sun go down. It was a beautiful spot and it pissed me off to think the goons were using it for their own encampment. They have a reputation for leaving trash everywhere. "They have room to park a few helicopters there. Did you see any?"

"We didn't get that close." Shaking his head he said, "We hauled ass back to Jack's, and got the fuck out of there."

The women pulled into the driveway with the last of our supplies, with Garrett arriving before their dust had settled. They headed up the walk with their arms full and I went to open the door for them. I turned back to Foster, "We're going back tonight, wanna come?"

"Going back," he nearly choked on his beer, "you guys are crazy." He stood there a minute lost in thought, then guzzled the rest of his beer and shrugged, "Sure."

Counting Carrie and April, there were nine of us going in and we must have looked like a camo-clad band of gypsies climbing out of two war-horse trucks.

"I hope you guys are having fun," Old Harold was leaning on the railing of his porch shaking his head. "Seems like a lot of trouble over some wacky-tobaccy."

"Someday I'll explain it to you Harold," I said with a laugh. "How's about a cold beer?"

"Sure, I'll drink a beer with you boys," he did a double take, "And girls." He hadn't noticed Carrie and April. "Sorry darlins', my eyesight ain't what it used to be, 'course these days you got to see more'n long hair."

"Harold, this one is my ex, so don't get any ideas. You can't afford her." Carrie had come along to drive Big Blue back to the cabin since we weren't planning on a return trip across Harold's farm. April would drive Kurt's truck back.

"Oh, I don't 'spose you got to worry 'bout that," he said with a grin as I handed him a beer. "I might steal all your beer though. Damn it's good!"

"Another mystery to one who's spent his life drinking Butt-wiper," I said with a snort, but I don't think Harold got what I was saying and I felt bad for a moment. This guy was saving our ass, I shouldn't be putting down the brand of beer he drank. "Next time I'll bring a case of Red-Tail."

We were on edge and it was going to be a long night, so I drank my beer quickly and gave Harold the last few we had. "We gotta go Harold, thanks for everything."

"Anytime! I enjoy the company," and tapping himself on the head he said, "You boys keep your heads down."

We drove up the hill but stopped short of the property line. If the goons were still camped out and we were sure they were, we didn't want them hearing Big Blue.

The raiding party consisted of Garrett, Kurt, Cruiser, Big John, limping but wasn't gonna miss out, Foster, Zack, and me. We all wore backpacks with provisions and supplies, and we took turns carrying the four new barrels. They had been modified with eyebolts and straps and that made carrying them easier. They were light but bulky. They also made a good deal of noise when they bumped into something, so we had to take care, especially going by Serenity Park.

I gave Carrie goodbye kiss on the cheek and we started out. Near the property line we were startled to hear a helicopter slowly whine and pop to life. We figured it would sit on the ground for a few minutes warming up and checking gauges. So, after we got over our initial fear, we realized we could make better time with the chopper covering our noise. We lit out on the double. By the time it finally rose into the air and departed, we were almost to High Anxiety, well past where we believed the goons were camped. Fifteen minutes later we were past The Fat Man's farm altogether and were beginning our long descent into the drainage. With the barrels and other weight on our backs, the going was much harder than the previous night. But if nothing else, spending the summer walking the hills as a pot grower gets you into great physical shape and once we were warmed up, we went up and down the canyons like billy goats.

I thought Foster would have a rough time, but he seemed to be in better shape than the rest of us.

I asked him, "How do you stay so buffed?"

"When I'm not helping out up here," he said grinning, "I'm a bicycle messenger in the city."

"No shit?" He reminded me of my bike. I hadn't thought about it since the trouble started, but I had an expensive mountain bike hidden at my farm. "I've got a Trek hidden up here somewhere if the cops haven't found it."

"What model Trek?"

"Oh God, I don't even know," I thought a moment but didn't recall. "I traded a Q.P. for the thing last year when Mac the Bear got busted. He's a friend of Freddie's, do you know him?"

"Yeah, I know Mac." His face lit up, "You got *his* bike? That sucker's ***Bad!***"

"I wouldn't have gotten such a flashy one," I added, "but I got a good deal and helped Mac out at the same time."

Foster knew bikes and was impressed. "You're kidding," he said shaking his head, "I can't believe you'd leave a bike like that in the woods."

"It's covered with plastic," but after I had a moment to think about it added, "I'd like to move it farther into the woods if we have time."

Foster said he'd love to check it out.

The moon rose higher in the sky as evening passed into night and brightened our trail. The closer we got to my property, the gentler the terrain became and we made better time. We arrived at the drying shed well before midnight and set our packs and barrels down. We rested for a minute, while Big John poked around in his pack for some food.

We had a quick snack and got to work. "Zack, get those last two barrels fixed up with the hardware." I said. The rest of us got to work filling barrels with as much pot as possible.

We now had six barrels and if the pot had all been processed, we could easily fit what we'd grown into them. Unfortunately, some of this pot was still on the stem. We decided to see how much the barrels would hold before we went and retrieved the wet plants. We had a quick snack and got to work. Cruiser and I worked at bringing the hidden bags to camp, while the others snipped the buds off the stems and filled sniff-proof "doggie bags." About twenty-five to thirty of them would fill a barrel.

"Don't pack the schwee buds. It's not worth the effort." I said at one point.

The processed pot filled four barrels, and we arranged the bags so that each barrel held about the same amount. The spot where the wet plants were hung was more or less in the direction we were heading, so we cleaned up our mess, grabbed everything and started walking to the east. The barrels each weighed a hefty thirty pounds, and the relatively short walk to the other side of my farm turned into some real work.

Big John and Kurt led us to where they had hung the wet plants. A few of them had fallen to the ground but other than that, things were as they were left.

I set my barrel down and unbuckled my pack's waist belt. Letting my pack fall to the ground, I gazed to the east. It was a quarter mile to the bottom of the hill. It was going to be a long hard walk into the drainage even though it was mostly grazing land. On the other side of the drainage was one of the biggest ranches in Northern California. I wondered aloud, "What would happen if we rolled the barrels down the mountain?"

"You'd either smash them or never see them again," Cruiser noted.

I didn't agree. They might get broken, but they would funnel into the drainage. "If we have everybody down the hill but the guy who pushes them over the edge, we can watch where they go."

Big John agreed with Cruiser. "These things will be going sixty miles an hour by the time they get to the bottom." Pounding his fist into his other palm he continued, "Does the word piñata mean anything to you?"

"You're probably right," I said, "It was just an idea."

Foster supplied the inspiration saying, "Too bad you don't have some padding you could tie on."

"We do! We have foam sleeping pads at the cabin, lots of them." It came to me in a flash when Foster said padding. The idea arrived fully formed. "We can tie the foam on with rope, wire, and duct tape. We have all that stuff at the camp."

Big John wasn't convinced. "I still think it's risky."

"Johnny," I said in mock solemnity, "Look around you, what isn't a risk?" Even John laughed, albeit nervously.

Speaking to the group I said, "You guys finish loading as much wet stuff as you can, and Foster and I will go get some foam," adding, "We can do a trial run and see if it works."

I suggested to Zack that he leave his pack since he was humping some buds, but he said he would rather keep his shit with him in case he had to run for it. My pack was lighter than his, and I had to agree he had a point. I put mine back on and we started off to the cabin.

When we were close, I told Foster to wait on the trail for a minute, while I climbed up to get my bike. I had decided to take it farther from camp and I knew Foster would like to see it. In fact, his eyes lit up like a Christmas tree when he saw it.

"Man, that's the hog's nuts." Foster had a way with words.

"I'll let you ride it when we're done hauling foam," I promised.

Foster and Zack followed me to the cabin where we collected mattresses from the bedroom and loft. I found a roll of tie wire and a hank of clothesline. We had carried a roll of duct tape in with us, but I found a few more partial rolls and we took them as well. Foam sleeping pads, like the empty barrels, are light but bulky. We made two stacks of four or five pads each and taped them together. I put a piece of rope around each one to use as a handle, and we set off.

The wet bud was in the barrels by the time we made it back with the foam. We experimented with a couple of methods but the one that seemed to work the best was sandwiching the barrel between two pads, cinching them up with a rolling timber hitch, and finishing the job with tie wire and duct tape. The eyebolts came in handy as anchors, and we were confident that the things would survive the trip down the mountain.

Big John still wanted to test one first. We had the walkie-talkies with us so it would be easy enough to send a man into the drainage for a trial run. I pointed to a grove of trees in the distance. "I'll aim 'em for those trees Johnny, so situate yourself at the tree line and keep your eyes open."

"What if it misses and goes straight into the canyon?" asked Zack.

"We'll find 'em." I was sure it would work. "Don't forget the radio."

He started walking, but it would take him a while to get to the bottom. "Let's finish wrapping these things while he walks," I said.

We quickly established a routine and had all but the last one padded by the time we got the "In place." call from John. We knew it was going to be fun to watch, so like kids at Disneyland, we rolled the first one to the edge of the clearing. I radioed John, "Heads up, you have a package on its way." We guided it to the first really steep spot and let it go. It gathered speed until it reached the escarpment and then disappeared over the edge.

When it reappeared a few moments later, it was really hauling ass. As far as we could see it was heading in the general area of the grove of trees but we didn't know if it made it for a couple of minutes.

Big John broke in over the air waves, "Goomba, you rolled a strike!"

We broke into wide smiles and did a little jig. I told the boys to send the rest of them down. We needed another foam pad, so I went back to grab it. Foster came along to get the bike.

When we reached the place where we'd left the bike, I told Foster to wait with it while I went to the cabin to grab two more mattresses. He hopped on the bike however, saying he wanted to ride it around a bit to get used to the shifting.

"You used Shimano's before?" Referring to the brand of gear changers my bike had.

"Oh hell yes." He hopped on the bike and made his way deftly down a steep part of the trail directly above the cabin.

I followed. But something was wrong and Foster was already too far ahead of me to stop him. From my vantage point I could see that the cabin door was open and I remembered closing it tight. Before I could say a word, a cop flew out of the cabin and ran straight for Foster. His years of dodging taxis in San Francisco had made his reflexes razor-sharp and I can only speculate on his calf muscles. He accelerated like he was shot from a cannon and leapt, bike and all, over a log that was in the trail. I don't know how he got the bike airborne the way he did and the cop was left grabbing air. Two or three other cops ran out of the cabin and joined the chase. While the hillside came alive with the sounds of shouting cops, crackling radios, and starting cars, I remained unnoticed in the shadows above the cabin.

The sounds of the chase receded into the distance, but about the time I started to hope that Foster was getting away, there came the petulant belching of gunfire. A volley of several shots, a pause, and one lone blast that echoed across the landscape. Oh my God, had they shot Foster? My mind went blank as I sank slowly to my knees.

I was at the confluence of hate, anger, and helplessness. My arms and legs were like rubber and I had to fight to stand. The sound of a car racing up the hill compelled me to get moving, but it was like trying to run in a dream. I struggled for a moment, but finally, the adrenaline caught up with me and I vanished into the shadows.

Garrett was the only one still at the rendezvous. The boys had heard the commotion and decided to get started without Foster or me. Garrett was going to wait a few minutes in case we showed up.

"Where's Foster"?

I said I wasn't sure. "He took off when we saw the cops. They chased him down the driveway and then I heard some shots."

"Those fucking assholes! Shooting a guy over green bud?"

"It all sucks Garrett," I said bitterly, grabbing the strap on the last barrel, "Let's get out of here if we can."

We could hear a chopper on its way, so we tossed the barrel over the edge and snaked down the escarpment behind it. The unpadded barrel made a whole lot more noise than the padded ones, but the chopper was over the cabin now and I was hoping its racket would drown out whatever noise the barrel was making.

I half expected the chopper to appear over us at any minute, but it never did. It came into view a few times, using a high-powered light to search the woods below the cabin. I hoped that meant Foster had gotten away but the more I thought about it, it was probably the most logical place to look for the rest of us. The property's ingress was from the direction of the road and that was the direction Foster chose to ride out. The cops could easily be thinking that was the direction we'd come from. We were going the other way, disappearing north into a wilderness area. Not exactly Hannibal crossing the Pyrenees, but by far the longest way out.

Silhouette Creek meandered aimlessly through the Emerald Triangle. It was a life-giving artery, supplying farmers and wildlife with the one substance they could not exist without—water. But for us it was an escape route. I had no idea how many other pot farms or cattle ranches were between the back of my property and the rendezvous spot, but at this point there was no alternative.

The boys had collected four of the six barrels. Big John said he was pretty sure one of them was farther down the creek, but he hadn't actually seen it. The good news was that we got well away from the property damn fast and none of the barrels broke, not even the last one that came down unpadded.

Cruiser and Kurt cut the foam off the barrels and Zack helped them hook the straps back on. Ever the environmentalist, Garrett pointed out the waste and mused over the fate of our jetsam. "Where do you think that foam is going to end up?"

"My motto is, worry about the foam when the foam starts to worry about you." I replied.

Garrett didn't like to joke about the environment and shot me one of those snotty zealot, "You don't understand" looks. I probably didn't, I just knew, environment or not, we had to get our butts in gear.

Everybody had a barrel to grab but me, so I took one end of the strap on Cruiser's barrel and the two of us carried it until we found the last barrel. It had bounced a quarter mile past the others. I was sorry I'd missed the show, the bounding barrels must have been something to see.

We didn't find the sixth barrel but by the time we reached the bottom of the drainage, there was more than sufficient water in the creek to try floating the five we found. The previous week of rain dumped a huge amount of water on Northern California, and the amount of run-off was amazing. Two weeks ago, this drainage would have been bone dry.

Cruiser fished carabiners and rope out of the bottom of his pack, and Big John and I helped him snap the barrels together. The five barrels ended up looking like the world's biggest sausage links.

In short order, the newly christened HMS Sausage was ready for its maiden voyage. With five of us on the rope in back, and one of us in front to steer, we let the line out and the sausage caught the current, which was much stronger than expected. The plan was working too well, as Zack chose to word it, "Slicker'n snot on a brass doorknob."

Silhouette Creek was raging and maintaining control of the HMS Sausage was no easy task. This became even more challenging when we reached the confluence of the Tomki River, running high and over its banks along rough terrain.

We stopped trying to manipulate the sausage from shore, and started floating behind it, hanging on to the barrels as floatation devices. We had to portage around two waterfalls, but hanging on for dear life we successfully navigated the sausage through some hairy whitewater rapids.

If the water had been warmer we could have floated the whole way to the rendezvous spot, but the frigid water got to us. Stopping to build a fire and rest, we noticed how much gentler the terrain had become and decided to make one last push for the rendezvous.

We had no idea where we were; our bones were numb and our minds weren't exactly running like Rolex watches. After the first quarter mile or so, the river entered a canyon and once again, floating with the barrels was our only option.

The first set of rapids proved too much for Big John and then Kurt. They fought their way to the riverbank and tried to keep up with us but the terrain was rocky and were soon out of sight. The four of us left in the water continued tumbling down river. Garrett finally let go and swam to shore with Zack following close behind. It was only Cruiser and myself now and we were on the brink of hypothermia. We needed to find an eddy soon.

The river raged on without let up and we quickly realized that if we didn't hit calm water soon, we'd lose our stash. But there was no calm water to find. Before we knew what was happening, the sausage shot over the edge of a fifteen-foot waterfall and we let go. It had bravely held together until then, but the barrels weren't designed for that much abuse. They got hung up in a snag; most of them busted to hell in pieces. We landed at the bottom of the falls in a churning tumult. With each gasp, my lungs took in as much water as they did air. I was alive but beginning to convulse. I lost sight of Cruiser. We'd been tossed ass over teacup, and I didn't know where he ended up.

A miraculously intact barrel surfaced near me. I grabbed it by the rope but wrangling it took more energy than it was worth, and it was worth about a hundred and fifty thousand bucks. My hands were too numb to hang on, and as I tumbled over another small waterfall the instinct for survival took over and I let go of the rope. Landing with a jolt, my chest took the full force of the fall onto a submerged rock.

Involuntary spasms punctuated my attempts at breathing and forced me to vomit water. The retching caused me to stiffen. It didn't matter what I tried to do; I was nearly paralyzed by now. I was breathing again, but my lungs must have been nearly full of water because I could only take in small amounts of air with each breath, and the pain in my chest was excruciating.

My only thought was to get out of the water. I headed toward the riverbank and was nearly to shore when I spotted Cruiser. He was tangled in a rope still tied to a barrel, looking like Captain Ahab on the back of Moby Dick. He wasn't struggling and I was afraid that he'd drowned. Swimming back into the currant, I nearly caught up with him before hitting another set of rapids. Propelled through the chute I crashed into him, managing to roll the barrel so Cruiser stayed on top. In tandem we shot the last bit of rapids. I'll never know how much more we could have taken, but numb and hardly breathing, I pulled Cruiser and the barrel to the edge of the river. To my relief he was breathing and we managed to crawl out of the water onto a spit of sand. Slowly we regained some lung capacity and instead of gasping frantically for air, we were able to breathe almost normally.

We took stock of our condition. It felt like I had broken a few ribs and along with the water, I was spitting up some blood. Cruiser was bleeding from cuts on his back and a large gash over his right eye. Considering what we'd been through, we emerged relatively unscathed.

We looked at each other and started to laugh. Not just a chuckle, but hysterical, uncontrolled laughter. We laughed about the water-logged barrel of pot. We laughed at the barrels that got away. We laughed at the blood. It didn't matter what we thought of or said, we just laughed.

One by one, we regrouped. Kurt, Garrett, Big John, and Zack each followed the sounds of our laughter and when they found us, we absolutely howled at the looks on their faces.

Big John was confused, limping, and more than a little pissed off. He'd reinjured his ankle and was doing the math on what got away, but Garrett knew the stark truth. Cruiser and I were in shock and near hypothermia. Hours to go until dawn, the six of us were soaked to the bone and Garrett correctly reasoned that if we didn't start a fire soon, one or more of us might not make it to morning.

A quick inventory of our packs yielded little that wasn't wet. We had a few soaked lighters and two candles, and Garrett had some napkins that had been in a plastic bag and managed to stay dry.

It took a good twenty minutes and a combination of blowing warm air and rubbing the lighter along his pant leg, but Garrett managed to get it working while Zack went about collecting kindling. The napkins helped, but it was the candle wax that finally got the fire going. Once Garrett had a small fire burning, he and Zack started hauling dead manzanita and we huddled around soaking up the heat.

Cruiser and I quickly sobered up. As our laughter diminished, our pain returned. We were both blue from cold and barely able to move. The warmth of the fire arrived like a god in a chariot.

Huddled around the fire, we all had time for reflection. It was only a few hours until dawn, but being wet and cold, the time passed slowly. Manzanita fires burn hot and fast, but die quickly so we were either too close, too far, too warm, or too cold to be comfortable. Garrett and Zack did the lion's share of the collecting firewood, while Cruiser and I stiffened with pain and Kurt and Big John sat shivering.

"Do you think we'll find the other barrels?" Big John asked no one in particular.

"I don't know and I don't care," was my answer. At that point I didn't.

Garrett remembered the barrel we didn't find at the drop zone. "There's one still in the gully in back of the ranch somewhere."

"Don't forget the nugs we got out two nights ago," I added, "Plus whatever's in this barrel," I said pointing to the barrel Cruiser had saved.

Forever the philosopher, John mused quietly, "I guess it could have been worse."

Cruiser and I exchanged knowing looks. "Yeah John, it could have been a whole lot worse," I spit out some more blood, "We could be out here without any green bud to smoke."

"Goomba," John intoned solemnly, "I always had a hunch you were crazy, but now I know for sure."

Epilogue

Dawn found me staring at the embers of the dying fire, reflecting on how I'd gotten to this place. I was turning forty in a few weeks and still hadn't answered the fundamental questions that I started out with—Who am I? Why am I here? I figured that my career as a pot grower was over. Now what?

I thought about Foster. Was he dead? I couldn't imagine the cops shooting an unarmed guy riding a bicycle, but the CAMP warriors seemed to be a different breed of law enforcement; closer to Storm Troopers than cops on the beat. When the emphasis shifted to seizing grower's assets, they became more like the rip-offs we were battling than peace officers sworn to protect us.

It was hard enough to think of Foster being dusted by the goons. To kill someone, or even just destroy someone's life, over green bud? That was a hard pill for this hippie to swallow. But I knew Foster was as agile as a ferret and bullets can't turn corners. Until I knew otherwise, I would let myself believe he had gotten away.

The world that I dropped out of all those years ago didn't exist anymore. The illegal marijuana business I was part of had become an enormous problem, so lucrative nobody wanted to fix it. Thanks to us, the local economy was awash in marijuana cash in more ways than folks realized.

Drop back in? I couldn't drop back in, feeling most at home living in the margins. I'm a student in what P.D. Ouspensky called The Fourth Way School, a polymorphous sect of philosophers who slip in and out of the cracks of the so-called "real world."

But events unfold the way they're meant to, and I remembered what the I Ching had warned about all those years ago—Chance of great success, but beware, when dealing with weeds they can grow quickly out of your control. It was eerie but sad, and I wondered whether the whole adventure was being guided by the muse of destiny.

Events of the last few days helped me realize that I was looking at a new world now, and I wondered if there was a place for me.

Times change; people change. Many of my ilk eventually cut their hair and traded in their respective gurus for financial security. They stopped talking about the moon in the first house and started talking about second mortgages and vacation homes. It's like life had become a paper version of the Oklahoma land rush—all about greed and acquisition.

Taking in the beauty around me, with only the sounds of flowing water and occasional snores from the boys I asked myself, Why am I out here? Have I gained insights into myself or have I just turned my back on the world? Am I what I hoped to be, a soldier in a war fighting for individual freedom, or am I only fooling myself?

But I know legalization will come eventually. The winds of change are forever blowing, and we can either catch the wind and sail to a place of new understanding or resist the wind and fight to stay where we are.

Am I healed of my psychic wound? The Fisher King's wound is also known as "The wound that never heals," so if that's what I have, why would mine be any different? I probably still have a scar but as far as I know, I'm not dripping blood all over the place anymore. The sword might still be in the stone but as far as I know, it's out of the Stoner.

Have I found the Love I was looking for, my personal "Holy Grail?" Let's just say I'm still working on it and leave it at that. The question's shrouded in mystery, and I don't want to fuck it up.

But enough of all that. Morning has broken and the boys are waking up, eager to get moving. Another day following the river. Will it bring us wealth or wisdom? With any luck we'll find a little of each and a whole lotta Love. If we're lucky, we'll do it all without getting busted.

We kicked wet sand over the last of the dying embers and started our long trek out of the wilderness. My body was aching and as we set out, I thought to myself—I gotta find a new line of work.

I know, I said that before.

Acknowledgments

Writing a novel is hard work. The list of people who inspired me to move this project forward is long, and I'm grateful to all of you.

A few people were vital to bringing these stories to life. Without Dr. Ellen Lev, Diane Conn Darling, or my sister, Sally Paton, there would be no book. Diane's help and encouragement got the project both started and finished, while Ellen was the angel sent to edit, revise, and give me confidence. My sister helped the project stay afloat and guided it to the finish line.

And special thanks to my beautiful and talented wife, Betsy, who saw the potential for "The Little Novel That Could" and was instrumental in bringing this book out of the shadows and into the light.

About the Author

A child of the Sixties, author Kevin Stewart is no stranger to the world of backcountry cannabis production and brings a unique insight into the complex challenges of the marijuana underground in the years before legalization.

Kevin lives in the Pacific Northwest with his wife and a menagerie of rescue animals.

www.ingramcontent.com/pod-product-compliance
Lightning Source LLC
Chambersburg PA
CBHW031336010826
48972CB00012B/497